All That Falls
A. N. Horton

Veil & Valor Books

Copyright © 2023 by A. N. Horton

All rights reserved.

No part of this publication may be reproduced, distributed, or transmitted in any form or by any means, including photocopying, recording, or other electronic or mechanical methods, without the prior written permission of the publisher, except as permitted by U.S. copyright law. For permission requests, contact Veil & Valor Books at veilandvalorbooks@gmail.com.

The story, all names, characters, and incidents portrayed in this production are fictitious. No identification with actual persons (living or deceased), places, buildings, and products is intended or should be inferred.

Book Cover by A. N. Horton

Third edition 2025

Dedicated to my husband for his unwavering support and unending love.

Contents

Part One - Rift	1
1. A Hole In The Sky	2
2. A Mortal Reminder	10
3. An Unwelcome Visit	18
4. A Shadowstep Forward	27
5. A Portal To Another Plane	33
6. A Deceptive Goodbye	43
Part Two - Refuge	51
7. A Captive Audience	52
8. A Family Affair	59
9. A Court of Light and Life	67
10. A Feast Fit For A Queen	75
11. A Morning Prayer	83
12. A Friend Indeed	90
13. A Breath of Fresh Air	96
14. A Brother's Keeper	104
15. A Fool's Bargain	113
16. Without A Trace	120

Part Three - Ruin	126
17. A Halfling and A Cursed King	127
18. A Fall From Grace	135
19. A Royal Mess	142
20. At Death's Door	151
21. A Different Kind of Fae	158
22. A Shot In The Dark	166
23. A Court of Conflict	172
24. An Evening Star	181
25. A Bitter Blade	189
Part Four - Redemption	194
26. A Confession From the Heart	195
27. A Wound That Heals	204
28. A Cave of Nightmares	211
29. A Warden of Hell	218
30. A Fire That Consumes	226
31. A True Gem	234
32. A Lesson in Combat	241
33. A Lack of Control	249
34. A Court of Chaos	256
35. A Daughter's Last Stand	263
36. A Mother's Welcome	268
37. A Vow Above A Bond	277
Epilogue	284

About the Author	289
Also by A. N. Horton	290

Part One
Rift

Chapter One
A Hole In The Sky

Rifts in the fabric of time and space were becoming a real nuisance.

I stared up at the swirling black hole and grimaced. It warped the surrounding air, shifting and contorting so that the starlight of the night sky shimmered. The lights of the Aurora Borealis weaved in and out of this world, dancing in a way that was entirely new and utterly terrifying.

I breathed out, watching as the tiny molecules of carbon dioxide exiting my body condensed into an icy mist before my very eyes. It was cold here; the climate bordering on inhospitable. Even my two thick coats, one of wool and one of fur, and thick, woolen socks weren't keeping the chill from reaching my bones. My teeth chattered as a familiar voice spoke from beside me, shouting to be heard over the cacophony of the fissure, the long, guttural wail it was making, like the world was crying out to us as it ripped itself apart.

"Professor Belling," Wyn Kendrick shrieked.

I turned toward a man who I could only describe as supremely average. Average build, average height, average light brown hair and dull gray eyes. Ridiculous wire-rimmed spectacles sat perched upon his nose, sliding ever downwards so that he had developed the habitual tick of pushing them back up again. The only difference in his appearance between here and the grim desk job he occupied in a nondescript government facility far away was the skepticism in his eyes and the little line of frost along his jaw.

"Every attempt we've made to close the rift has only resulted in ripping it open even further."

I frowned, turning my attention back to the breach, considering.

"If we could reverse the polarity—" I began, already knowing he would have a reason we could not. That was always the first attempt they made.

"It's too strong, too big," he told me. "Our machines can't generate enough power even in a more accommodating environment. But out here..."

"Right. Yes, I understand."

I narrowed my gaze, staring into the swirling mass as if it would reveal itself to me. As if it would gift me some epiphany, some solution to this celestial conundrum.

"It isn't behaving like a normal black hole," he said then. "Not that there is a normal black hole, to be certain. But what I mean is, it isn't exhibiting the sort of properties that one might expect from the astrophysical anomaly that you and I have spent our lives studying."

That he had spent his life studying. Men like Wyn studied the black holes, the celestial bodies, the stars and their alignments. I studied beyond those things. I studied past and present and future. I studied connectivity and meaning. I did not research black holes because I wanted to know how they formed or where they had come from. I studied them because I wanted to know where they would lead. And it was merely fortunate that my studies coincided with a point in history in which these anomalies had apparently decided to materialize in our own skies.

"You mean it isn't devouring every bit of matter surrounding it," I replied, raising a brow to remind Mr. Kendrick that I wasn't a fool.

If this were a true black hole, it would have created a field of gravitational pull so powerful that nothing could evade it. Not even light. Hence the name "black hole". And yet, soldiers milled about below it, glancing uncertainly upward from time to time as if waiting for a threat that they could actually shoot to present itself. Unanchored crates and equipment lay scattered around tents and snowdrifts. Scientists who were more concerned about marking themselves as intellectuals and distinguishing themselves from the common servicemen flitted from instrument to instrument in their flimsy lab coats.

"Precisely," Wyn answered with a nod, adjusting those accursed spectacles and ignoring my look of displeasure at being patronized, yet again, by a man in my field. "It's behaving just like the last three except even more erratically."

"How so?"

"The pattern of the swirls is different, more intense. Just like the last three, it seems to be moving quite a bit within itself but even more so. It's... tumultuous."

"Tumultuous," I repeated, turning back to the mass of inky black stained against the night sky. It was an apt word. Wyn and I had dispatched the last two of these ourselves without a problem but this one was different. I couldn't define how I knew. Just that I felt it. It wasn't just the sheer size of the anomaly. In fact, it almost seemed even larger than it was, like there was an even bigger aura surrounding it, a darkness we couldn't see, and it felt... angry.

"I should return to the university," I started, turning my attention away from the rift and back to Wyn. He was already nodding as I explained myself. "The Dean should be informed and I will reach out to my contacts in the world of academia. If they have any suggestions—"

"I don't have to remind you to keep this out of the press' hands this time, I assume," Wyn interrupted me, his tone changing from friendly scientific collaboration to authoritative warning. "We don't want a repeat of last time."

"The people had a right to know," I snapped, bristling at his insinuation.

"We cannot trust the people to regulate their emotional response to such news," he barked back at me. Sensing his own rising fury, as well as mine, he took a breath and sighed, trying to relieve some of the tension. But his eyes were still as cold as the frigid landscape around us when he added, "Not every anomaly is apocalyptic, Seren."

Perhaps it was the condescending insinuation that I couldn't tell the difference between a new avenue of scientific study and the end of the world, perhaps it was his assumption that he had any right to command me at all, or perhaps it was the use of my given name rather than the one he knew I preferred. But I saw red as the rage welled up within me and I prepared to set it loose on my disgruntled colleague.

Before I could tell Wyn Kendrick how I really felt about working with him, a booming roar of fury that shook the very mountains themselves interrupted us.

Wyn and I ducked, on instinct, and turned toward the only phenomena that could have made such an unnatural sound. We both stared up at the roiling black hole just as a full sized minotaur tumbled from the sky.

There was a moment of hesitation, of awe, as every person gathered in the camp stopped what they were doing to stare at the mythical beast that had just dropped down among them. My jaw slackened as my mind hurled itself into oblivion, trying desperately to understand the signals that my eyes were sending to my brain. A minotaur, exactly as described in ancient Greek legend, with the body of a giant, muscled man and the head and tail of a bull. It roared again and the sound filled my ears as I blinked away my shock. It was real.

The soldiers broke the spell first, shouting and running for their guns, taking up position all along the mountainside. They aimed the shaking barrels of their rifles at the fabled monster and waited for the command to shoot. The minotaur wasted no time either. It brandished the biggest axe I'd ever seen, raising it over its head and roaring so loud the mountain beneath our feet trembled. Wyn ducked but I remained standing, my eyes planted firmly on that axe.

Who was arming Minotaurs?

It lunged forward, swinging wildly at the gunmen on its left. Someone cried out and a hail of bullets rained down on the charging creature. The minotaur paused, raising gargantuan paws to shield itself, and then roared again, foaming saliva spattering the line of soldiers lined against the mountainside.

It charged, they ran. The minotaur scooped one of the soldiers up out of the snowdrift where he had fallen. I averted my eyes just in time to hear the clear crack of bone echo along the ridge.

"You have to get out of here Professor," Wyn gasped, grabbing my elbow and leading me backwards, away from the camp and toward the helicopter already preparing for flight, its blades rotating, creating a haze of dusty snow all around it. I squinted to see my things already being loaded on, soldiers shouting orders at one another to retrieve me. I yanked myself out of Wyn's grasp.

"I held my own in Belgium. Give me a gun."

Wyn stared at me for a moment, blinking incredulously through those frozen spectacles. Then he merely shook his head and headed for the helicopter with the rest of the fleeing scientists. I growled, turning and prowling through the camp until I found what I was looking for.

Muttering under my breath that this was what happened when you put the army in charge of astrophysics and natural phenomena, I jammed a magazine into the handgun I'd found, slung an ammunition belt over my shoulder, and strapped a pack of C4 to my thigh. Then I exited the abandoned tent to join the fray beyond.

The minotaur was lashing out blindly now. It was bleeding deeply from a cut in its left side, a long bloody gash that ran from its abdomen around its back. It reached out with its enormous hands and crushed anyone and anything it found beneath them. It roared, again and again, in agony, in pain, in brutal intimidation.

It was an animal, I reminded myself, just an animal. Like a boar or a bear. A carnivorous, ferocious beast that wants nothing more than to kill you.

But the truth was, I'd never had the stomach for killing. Not even when it saved my own life. Not even when it saved my uncle's. But I would do it, if I had to, and then I would turn my anger towards whoever had created the situation in which I had to. There were several to blame for this one. I'd get to them.

I took my chance when the beast was distracted by another line of gunmen shooting at him under precise directives. I rolled my eyes and darted quickly across the snow, staying low so as not to draw the creature's attention too soon.

I loaded the forgotten machine gun with the ammunition belt I'd brought along and then took aim.

The first round of my bullets struck home. The beast bellowed and reared back, dropping the man he had been holding fifteen feet in the air. The soldier screamed as his leg cracked against the cold, gray stone. I kept my focus and loosed another round.

The minotaur whirled around, predatory eyes narrowed as it sought me out, making me its new prime target. It saw me a moment later and, as it charged, I shouted for the men to get down and then let the machine gun do its thing. Bullets sprayed wildly without direction as I stepped away from the gun. The minotaur ducked and hurtled, snorting viciously as it lowered to all fours and rushed toward me. I waited patiently, fingers twitching over the handgun and the bomb.

When the creature was close enough, I ran for it myself, tucking and rolling at the last second so that I slid deftly between its legs. It growled in anger; the rumble causing the surrounding snow to shake loose, to slide down, down. It pivoted again to face me, prowling forward. I waited as it came closer.

Men were screaming again, surrounding us, but I didn't dare to look away from the beast as it reached me, sniffing once, twice.

It stilled.

The minotaur blinked at me, that enraged panic giving way to a strange calm. I could feel its uncertainty. It looked at me almost as if confused. My heart beat faster than it even had during the attack, faster than it had in a very long time. Because the way it was looking at me was something I recognized. Reverence. It had stopped attacking me because it thought it might serve me.

My hands were shaking. How had it known?

But then it became aware of something else as well. Cocking its head to the side, it glanced down to where I had attached the block of C4 on the underside of its upper thigh. It snarled and lunged.

I felt the heat on my face first, singing my skin just moments before the blast threw me off of my feet. I went careening into one of the nearby tents, arms splayed out in an effort to cushion my fall, reaching for nothing, for everything. My back hit something hard and a sharp pain shot up my spine. I winced as my legs twitched beneath me.

Blood rained down on the camp, on the soldiers, on the equipment, on me. My furry white coat turned red with it. The minotaur's guts landed on the wooden box beside me, the one labeled property of Hadley University.

More screams and the distinct sound of vomiting emanated from the camp but I hardly heard them. My eyes were already closing. As soot and ash filled the sky around us and the mountain below began to rumble, I fought to remain alert, conscious.

But it was a losing battle. And the last thing I heard, as I drifted into the world of dreams, was a lone, terrified voice, screaming one word.

"Avalanche!"

Chapter Two
A Mortal Reminder

I had been wrong before. There was no truer nuisance than an avalanche.

Soldiers lifted me, one and then two, the second of which was already limping himself. I was fading in and out of consciousness but I felt their hands holding me aloft, felt the sharp and frigid air beating against the cool skin of my face as we reached the helicopter, heard the tremendous roar of natural fury as a wave of white tumbled toward us.

"Just hang on!" one of them was screaming, inches from my face, over the whirring of the helicopter blades and the rumbling of the mountain.

"Hadley," I croaked, gripping him around the collar, my eyelids already fluttering closed again. "I need... to get back..."

But I was gone. Both mentally and physically as the helicopter lifted from the ground, the last of the soldiers still dangling from its sides, scrambling on.

We left it all behind. The rift, the equipment, the chunks of minotaur. Things we could have salvaged, things we could have studied. But I was already itching to return by the time my eyes opened again in a hospital room back in New York City.

No one was there to greet me. I wasn't surprised. I just stood, ripping the IV from my arm, and snatched up my briefcase that had made it back to the city long before I had and was in much better shape. I changed back into my clothes in the bathroom before making my way out onto the street. I had opted to forgo the bloody fur coat as I trudged through the streets of NYC but the stains on my trousers couldn't be helped.

So I ignored the horrified stares of everyday citizens as I made my way south.

"Is it true?" my uncle asked me the moment I stepped onto the Hadley University campus. "A real minotaur? Is it true?"

My gaze slid over him, as annoyed as I could ever be with my beloved uncle.

Xavier Belling was the head of the prestigious astrophysics program at Hadley University. He was to be blamed for my love of all things celestial and unexplained. And I could tell he was champing at the bit to gain some insight into this fascinating new discovery.

"I'm fine, thank you for asking," I remarked sarcastically. "Perhaps you heard of the avalanche as well? The one I was unconscious for as they flew me out on an emergency chopper?"

He just stared at me expectantly.

"It's true," I admitted and he beamed, bouncing on his toes as he followed me through the courtyard like a kid given permission to choose a candy at the confectionery.

"Remarkable," he breathed in awe. "You must tell me everything."

"Does this count as our faculty meeting for the month, then?"

I raised a brow. He laughed.

Faculty meetings for the astrophysics department only ever comprised my uncle and myself, since we were the only professors who taught the discipline. Hadley University had become the breeding ground for success in the venture of cosmic exploration. Our alumni had been directors of NASA, corporate pioneers, tech masterminds. And because of our achievement in the subject, the university had determined that it would be very selective about the students it deemed qualified enough to excel in the course of study. Therefore, my schedule was inundated with Intro to Astrophysics classes in which the Dean expected me to flunk over half of my students. So I deserved to be among the first scientists to interact with a minotaur since the dawn of recorded history. I had earned it.

"What did it look like?" He asked, drawing me out of my reverie, and I smiled as he opened the door to our wing of the sciences building and I stepped inside.

"It was enormous. At least fifteen feet tall. It was just like all the old stories describe it to be. Part man, part bull. All muscle and fur and rage."

"It attacked you?"

"It came with an axe."

My uncle paused. I turned to face him in the empty hall. High wooden beams arched above us, engraved with the Latin translation of one of my favorite quotes. Non est ad astra mollis e terris via. There is no easy way from the earth to the stars. And the unspoken challenge in the air of these hallowed halls that I had felt all throughout my youth. Prove him wrong.

My uncle's brows furrowed as he raised a hand to his head, scratching idly at the wild white hair that used to be honey blonde like my own.

"An axe," he repeated, his voice low, thinking. "What sort of axe?"

"A battle axe from the looks of it. I'm not exactly well-versed in ancient weaponry."

"It looked old then?"

"Extremely. It had writing around the blade, forged into the metal, something rune-ish."

"Intriguing. Most intriguing. Do you believe you could replicate it for translation if I should give you a slip of paper?"

"No," I replied, frowning. "I was a tad busy running for my life."

"Yes, of course, of course."

He waved me off and began walking back down the hall toward our offices as we had been before. I followed him, knowing better than to interrupt a brilliant man when he was so lost in thought. We passed through a polished hall adorned with portrait after portrait of various distinguished alumni and former professors, the Venetian tile clicking under our feet as we passed over it.

"They said you... blew it up," my uncle said with a frown as we reached his classroom and pushed through the door. His tone was not chiding but I could hear the disappointment in it all the same.

"I didn't have a choice," I told him. "It was raging, wild. The guns weren't having any effect on it and it was killing our men."

My uncle nodded in understanding but his frown remained as we passed through one of the smallest lecture halls on campus and one of the oldest. Rows of pristine wooden chairs lined against thick, polished mahogany desks sat facing a single lectern at which my uncle stood most mornings, waving his hands about like a lunatic as he posited on the speed of light and dared his students not to trust their own eyes. Behind that lectern sat a door and beyond that door was my uncle's office.

Professor Xavier Belling's office was always a horrible mess. Books and letters were open and strewn about. Jars of some unidentifiable scrounged up body parts suspended in strange liquids on every shelf. Fossilized bones and a row of neatly polished fangs of various shapes and sizes. One might never know that he was an Astrophysicist at all if it weren't for the telescope in the corner, pointed out the window, and the spectrometer growing dusty on a top shelf. But I knew that Professor Xavier Belling's interests were as vast as they were limitless. At first, I'd gotten the chills every time I entered this place. Now, I simply ignored it all and focused on him.

"Something strange happened," I told him then, lowering my voice out of habit as I broached this particular subject of conversation. "Before I killed it, when it had finally reached me, it stopped."

My uncle's eyes met mine. I had captured his interest.

"Stopped?" he inquired, curiously. "What do you mean it stopped?"

"It sniffed me, smelled my scent, and froze. It looked just as confused as I was, like it wasn't certain anymore if it should make a meal out of me or not."

"Interesting," my uncle agreed, tapping his chin.

"Do you think it knew?" I asked, unable to breathe as I did. "That it... sensed me?"

My uncle's gaze flicked to me again, brushing over the angular features of my face, the high cheekbones, violet eyes, and honey blonde hair.

"I think it's entirely possible," he answered after a moment and I loosed a breath, closing my eyes. "I don't know how much time the Fae spend with their monstrous prisoners but I imagine it may be enough for the creatures to recognize their scent."

I flushed scarlet. I hated talking about this subject, hating being reminded of that half of me, the part of me that no one could ever know about, that my uncle and the few others we had trusted with my secret had taken great pains to keep hidden.

"Especially if they are arming them with battle axes and shoving them into the mortal plane," I snapped, nostrils flaring.

I didn't want to believe it, that the people I shared half of my heritage with could be so evil as to send an ancient beast plunging into the world of the mortal once again. But I couldn't deny that it was a possibility.

After all, what did I know of my immortal kin other than what the stranger who had delivered me to my uncle when I was just a baby had told him? That there was a plane of existence somewhere above our own and that Fae and other mythical humanoids had brought there all creatures of lore and legend when it had become clear that humanity simply could not handle the existence of magic in our world. So they had separated it from us. As simple as that, my name, and a sympathetic admission that my father, my uncle's brother, had died and that was why I'd been brought to him.

"Now, now, let's not be hasty," my uncle warned, holding his hands up in surrender. "I know you're inclined to blame the Fae for these unfortunate circumstances but we do not know how that monster escaped, nor how he gained a weapon in the process."

I opened my mouth to argue but he held up a hand.

"Still," he continued with a tone designed to placate me, "I will ensure that the Dean is made aware of these... fresh discoveries. If the DAA wishes to look into it—"

I cut him off with a scoff. They had commissioned the Department of Astrological Anomalies just after the first rift had opened over five years ago. They had summoned my uncle then, among the other highly respected scholars the government called upon when it lacked the expertise to investigate a natural phenomena itself, and they had dispatched it with the use of their now patented polarity reversing machine. Since then, the equipment had been used to close two more rifts.

Because they had to be closed.

"How are we going to close it?" I asked then, changing the course of the conversation from the minotaur and reverting to the reason they sent me north in the first place.

My uncle frowned.

"I've been thinking about that," he confessed. "If it's as big as they're saying it is and now monsters are dropping through it unprovoked, Seren, you know we've encountered nothing like that before."

I flinched at the use of my birth name. He noticed and offered a slight apologetic smile.

I understood what he wasn't saying, what we never said. These weren't black holes because they weren't a natural phenomenon, an inexplicable occurrence of nature itself. They were something else. A portal of some sort, being opened into the only place where monsters such as the minotaur could exist, the place that only my uncle and I knew was real.

"Are you saying there's no way to close it?" I asked, terror snaking like ice through my veins.

"I will never say there isn't a way. But there isn't one I'm currently aware of."

My shoulders fell. I sighed.

"The Dean and I have been working on some potential solutions," he told me. "I've written to Mr. Kendrick and—"

"Mr. Kendrick," I scoffed, crossing my arms. "The man who ran from the field like a coward? The man who fled from a discovery that any researcher worth their salt would practically kill to examine?"

"Ren," my uncle started, correcting himself, calling me by my preferred name, "I know you don't care for the man. Frankly, I'm not fond of him myself. But the DAA has access to broader knowledge and governmental resources that we might need to face what's coming."

What's coming... I hesitated.

"I will not be around forever, you know," my uncle said then, his voice soft, almost a whisper. "I can't always be mending bridges you're content to burn."

I uncrossed my arms, letting them slump at my sides. I didn't want to have this conversation, not now, but I had avoided it enough times already.

My uncle had been trying to speak with me about this for months now. I didn't want to know why. I didn't want to think too closely about what he might know, about what might be precipitating this dialogue.

"You should make amends with Wyn Kendrick," he told me. "You don't want to live the rest of your considerably long life regretting how much you could have achieved if only you'd accepted a little more help."

I frowned, taking in the white hair, the wrinkled face, the squinting, nearly blind eyes. I could remember my uncle in his youth as though it were yesterday. It had taken little for me to love Professor Xavier Belling. The man had the best stories and the most exciting way of telling them. His passion for his work was a living, breathing thing and he passed it on to me in those years that it was just the two of us living in his moderately appointed faculty apartment, staring up at the stars and calling them by name, musing about what might be out there and never voicing the fact that we might be the only two people in the world who actually knew.

But because of what I was, because I was only half related to Professor Xavier Belling, I had to watch as his honey blonde hair turned white, as his vision left him so greatly that I had to read him his own lecture notes, as his skin sagged and wrinkled. Meanwhile, I remained physically young. I wasn't. I was nearing sixty now. But I still looked like a woman in her early twenties, or perhaps late teens. A byproduct of being half immortal. No one knew how long I would live. It wouldn't be forever. I was already aging quicker than a full immortal. But the length of lifespan for a hybrid seemed to vary based on the power of their immortal parent. And since I had never met my mother...

"Whenever Wyn Kendrick deigns to visit again, I promise you, most favorite uncle, that I won't be completely vicious."

Xavier frowned and shook his head. He sighed, exasperated, as I turned for the door. I would feel guilty about so severely disappointing my elders at a later date. Right now, I needed to prepare for my classes.

Chapter Three
An Unwelcome Visit

There was nothing that Dean Keegan Clarke despised more than American business interrupting his afternoon tea. And there was nothing I loved more than disrupting his colonial heritage.

"Ah, Miss Belling," Dean Clarke spoke in greeting as I stormed into his office uninvited, his poor secretary Margery running after me in a huff, her ludicrous perm bouncing atop her head.

"I—I couldn't stop her, sir," Margery panted, bending over to catch her breath as I came to a stop a few feet from where the Dean was inspecting his afternoon pastries, a bored expression on his face, thin lips pursed, shrewd eyes focused.

"You never can."

Margery blinked, straightening up and looking from the Dean to me as if she were going to disagree. But I raised a brow in challenge and she backed down. She stomped her foot like a petulant child and stormed back to her desk, slamming the door behind her harder than was strictly necessary.

"I'll remind you," the Dean began then, still not looking at me though his tone had taken on that measured wariness of his. The vaguely threatening, confusingly mild taunt he reserved just for me. "Your status here is in a very precarious position at the moment. What with that outburst at the DAA a few months ago and now this business with a minotaur."

"The minotaur which I single handedly saved a regiment of DAA special ops from, you mean?" I asked, raising a brow as I crossed my arms, baiting him.

"The very one."

He finally selected a pastry and, placing it daintily on a small platter, allowed his eyes to flick up briefly to me before he turned and made his way back to his desk.

"Xavier says you were unable to close it."

I froze, biting my tongue so severely I thought it might bleed. *You failed.* I could almost hear his voice sneering at me though he had never, would never, say it in such a way. Still, I felt it there, hanging between us, the words unsaid, the words he meant. *You failed and, not only have you disappointed this academic institution which raised you but you've put the mortal plane in peril.*

"Did he tell you about the minotaur as well?" I asked, treading lightly, trying to discern just how much my uncle had disclosed to the Dean.

"No," he replied with a shrug and I relaxed for only a moment until he continued. "Wyn Kendrick did."

My blood boiled in an instant, jaw tensing as I remembered the coward that ran when confronted with something he didn't understand and the last conversation we'd had on that mountain.

"DAA bastard," I swore.

"Bastard he may be but he's lived another day, moved on to another rift, another assignment. You, however, might have died."

"I didn't."

"Sheer luck."

"Cunning is the word you're looking for, I believe."

He narrowed his gaze.

"What you did put yourself in jeopardy. Not to mention this institution," he snapped and I understood. "I've been fielding calls from Congress and the press all morning, wanting to know about the rift, about you. Do you understand how hard it is for me to hide you, to hide what you are, when you've allowed yourself to become the girl who slew the minotaur overnight?"

The girl who slew the minotaur.

I gulped.

"I'm sorry, Dean Clarke," I said and I meant it. Truly.

Dean Keegan Clarke was the only other person besides my uncle that knew what I was. Outside of the university, outside of the people I had grown up with who knew me and protected me, there were scientists who would want to study me, extremists who would want to kill me, and leaders who would want to use me. I tasted bile as my gut roiled with what I had almost exposed.

"You will get your things in order and you will return to close this rift," he commanded and I stood up straighter, like a soldier receiving her orders. "I will have your classes covered. Xavier and I will help you in any way you can but Ren, we must close this rift."

"Yes, Sir."

"If they are growing, if monsters of ancient times are returning, it's going to become more and more difficult for me to continue convincing the director of the DAA that these are mere astrophysical anomalies. Soon, we will lose access, you will lose access, and therefore, the person who has the greatest insight into what these are beginning to seem like they are will be barred from investigation. Do you understand what I'm saying?"

"We're running out of time."

"Precisely. Whatever you find out, Professor Belling, and I mean no matter the source, you come directly to me. Have I made myself clear? Ignorance can not divide us. Not with the weight of the DAA bearing down on us."

"I understand, Dean Clarke. And I assure you, I will report to you the moment I've returned from the rift."

The Dean opened his mouth as if he intended to lecture me even more but then merely waved me away instead and I assumed that I was dismissed. My required debriefing with the Dean after every journey completed, I strode from his office, already pulling out my phone.

The DAA couldn't be trusted. But they already knew about the rift, had gotten there even before I had. Given their significant advantage of resources, I had to move fast. I began typing out an email to another female professor I had met a few years ago at a conference about, of all things, telescopic technology. She didn't work at Hadley. She was located on the other side of the country. But if anyone had any ideas on how to properly amplify a polarity machine, I thought it might be her.

So engrossed was I in my email that I hardly realized how far I'd walked until I reached my classroom. Pushing inside and grabbing the briefcase I had left just inside the door, I headed for the room on the other end, my office, still tapping away on my phone. My mind was such a jumble of bewilderment that I failed to realize I wasn't alone.

I had reached my desk, set my briefcase down, and sent my email before I looked up to see a devilishly handsome man sitting in the seat across from mine.

His dark hair had a bit of length to it but flowed upward from the crown of his head in a soft wave, undoubtedly the work of some gravity-defying product. His eyes were dark as well and set below his arched brow. He possessed smooth, perfect bronzed skin, a chiseled jawline, and lips that spread slowly into a smirk the more I examined him. I refrained from rolling my eyes. As attractive as he was, his pretty face wasn't what had me staring. He was emitting a soft purple glow.

From experience, I knew what that meant. So I let my eyes slide over him to the other half-formed shape on his right side before taking my seat and folding my hands in front of me, trying to appear unguarded.

"My office hours are from one to four," I said impatiently, fiddling with the cuffs of my sleeves to appear distracted as I regarded him. "I'm afraid you're early."

"Make an exception," he drawled, that vexatious smirk still drawn upon his lips.

I raised a brow, leaning back.

"Why should I?" I asked. "For a Fae."

His smile snapped right off of his face. That arrogant expression turned to vague mistrust and expertly hidden surprise. I could feel his unease as he leaned, ever so slightly, toward me. He fidgeted, one finger rapping silently against his thigh, the only indication that I had made him uncomfortable.

"How—" he began but I answered before he could finish.

"Whatever glamour you're trying to impose doesn't work on me. Nor are the invisibility efforts of your friend seeing any success."

In a blink, another man materialized behind my visitor. I made a concerted effort not to jump at his sudden appearance. Though I was unused to seeing magic wielded so casually, so easily, I would not give them the satisfaction of knowing how very on edge their use of it made me. This new male sported dark hair so long it hung past his shoulders and had to be gathered, half up, into a band at the back of his head that held it out of his face while leaving the rest of it free and flowing. His eyes were brighter, almost golden, and he had the remnants of a thin and jagged scar, now raised and white, running across his face diagonally from right chin to left temple.

"You're a hybrid," my visitor spoke, sitting back in his chair, propping up a knee, and rubbing his chin in wonder. "Incredible."

"Don't call me that," I hissed, turning my attention away from his companion.

He held up his hands in mock surrender.

"Forgive me," he said but I knew better than to believe it was a genuine apology. "Usually, those living in the mortal realm, even with Fae blood, can't see through my glamours or that of my men."

"What do you want?" I snapped, having lost all patience with them.

"We might have gotten off on the wrong foot."

"When? The moment you waltzed into my office uninvited, made yourself at home, and set your friend up to ambush me? Or thousands of years ago when your ancestors—"

"First of all," he drawled, leaning forward so that his face was hovering over my desk, just inches from my own, "my friend was not set up for an ambush. I simply thought that having two Fae males standing around your office when you entered might scare you off. It seemed less... intrusive for it to be only me. Second, I'm not here to hash out literal ancient history. What I have to offer you is far more current."

I leaned away from him, eyeing him skeptically. Fae were notoriously tricky and this man looked like the swindler to swindle all swindlers. I frowned, tapping my finger against the desk as I examined them both. Their clothes were finely made. All of deepest black with little intricate designs embroidered in thread at the sleeves, the hems, the collars. They looked young but that could be deceiving. No one knew that better than me. All in all, there was little to go off of from their physical appearance. They were presenting themselves well. They possessed the immortal beauty known to inhabit all Fae. But that glow... it wasn't from their flawless skin.

Fae were supremely powerful beings, vessels for the most potent magic. It was why they were the self-appointed guardians of the Immortal Realm. Because they were the only beings powerful enough to keep all the others in check. Most of the time, when they traveled to the mortal plane, their powers dimmed significantly. Someone like me could hardly detect it. But this man before me, he was glowing with it. It was flowing from him in gently pulsing waves, like a caress against the air. His companion's aura was not so strong but it was still there, more so than most others. Which only meant one thing. These men were not your average Fae.

"What offer?" I finally asked, unable to stop myself.

He bared his teeth at me in a glittering grin.

"My name is Canis but my friends call me Lark. And you are Seren Belling."

I tensed. He noticed but he made no mention of it, simply raising a brow as he continued, leaning back in his chair.

"You see, Seren—"

"Ren."

His eyes flicked to mine.

"Ren," he corrected slowly, letting his tongue roll over the word as if savoring the syllables. I took a breath. "I'm looking for a way back into the Immortal Plane and I'm told you're the one to talk to."

"Back in?" I asked, blinking as I tried to catch up. "What do you mean you're looking for a way back in? Are you... stuck here?"

"In a manner of speaking."

He waved his hand in the air as if the matter wasn't of any importance. But his companion snorted, and Lark's gaze snapped to him. The man cleared his throat and fell silent at that penetrating glare. Even I shifted uncomfortably in my seat at that hint of simmering, silent rage.

"Fine," he said with a sigh. "I've been... banished here. For a little over half a century."

"Banished?" I balked. "Half a century?"

"A little over."

My nails were digging into my palms now. Only the sting of them alerted me that I was clenching my fists as hard as I was. I had paled. I knew it from the way they were looking at me, watching me. They didn't speak, didn't move, as if afraid I would scurry away if they did. Maybe I would. What did a Fae have to do to be banished from their plane for half a century? And how much more was a little?

"You've been here the whole time?" I asked, stunned.

"Well, not here," he gestured around at my office, at the university itself, "but yes. My father and I had a... disagreement. It got heated and he's a powerful man so here I am. But a man can only be content to live on the wrong side of The Divide for so long."

"You want to go back," I repeated, still disbelieving. "And you think I can help you?"

"I hope you can. I heard about you from another professor. One in Oregon. A fine woman. I'm sure you're familiar with who I speak of."

I was. I had been emailing her on my way into this conversation. We had spoken of astral planes, long ago, all in theoretical terms. At least, I had pretended it was a hypothetical, asking her if she believed, as one of the best astrophysicists of our time, that other planes existed and, if so, if she thought we could travel to them. She said we would be fools to think we knew of everything our universe had to offer.

"She informed me you had become aware of a door of sorts," he spoke of these matters as if they were casual though we both knew they were anything but.

My heart raced and I fought to maintain my outward composure as I considered how best to answer. I hadn't thought about the door in years, hadn't let myself. I had allowed myself to get too close, to look too hard, and I had vowed never to do so again.

"Perhaps I have," I answered slowly, narrowing my eyes in a new examination. I would have to tread even more lightly here. "And what do I get?"

His gaze turned feral as his eyes dipped from my face, downward. He raised a brow as his attention snapped back to my face. More specifically, my lips.

"What do you want?" he queried, his voice thick, husky.

I rolled my eyes.

"Pig," I snapped and his friend chuckled behind him.

"Well?" he asked, spreading his hands wide, raising his brow once more in challenge.

"Help me heal the rift."

He frowned.

"A rift," he repeated. "Don't you mortals patch those up all the time?"

"This one isn't patching," I answered, snarling at the last word and the condescension of it. "In fact, it's dropping full sized minotaurs from the sky occasionally."

"Is it?"

His eyes widened a fraction in genuine surprise. He turned back to his companion, the two of them exchanging some silent communication I couldn't understand for a moment that seemed drenched in an unmistakable sense of doom before turning back to face me.

"Very well, Ren Belling, take us to your rift."

Chapter Four
A Shadowstep Forward

It wasn't my rift. But pointing that out to Lark and his companion, whom I still did not know the name of, seemed futile.

I told them of the travel plans that the Dean had forwarded to me. Written upon a government form letter from the DAA was my flight plan, my accommodations at the local mountainside inn, a complete itinerary regarding my expectations of performance for the following week, and a list of contacts both within the DAA and outside of it. Wyn's name was at the top of the list. I tried not to show my disgust as I read the email aloud to the Fae who were busy exchanging looks of pure confusion.

"Can I see that?" Lark asked once I'd reached the section of my itinerary dedicated to potential research opportunities in the area. He leaned forward, holding out his hand, palm up.

"Sure," I muttered, flipping my phone and holding it out to him.

But he grabbed my wrist instead.

Suddenly, it felt like my chest was caving in on itself. I opened my eyes and wondered if I even had. Nothing but swirling blackness, warped darkness, surrounded us. I gasped but found no air. That's when I panicked. My lungs contracted, my vision swam and then spotted as blinding white light filled the world and I fell to the ground, wheezing.

"First time is always hard," Lark's companion spoke for the first time. His tone was sympathetic as he reached down a hand to help me up.

I would have taken it, grateful for the kindness, but I realized in that moment how cold my hands were and I looked down to find them buried in a thick blanket of snow. I lifted one, letting the flakes cascade through my fingers, the bitter cold already numbing my fingertips. I scrambled to my feet and whirled, eyes darting around in dazed fascination.

We were here. On the same snow-blasted mountainside I had traveled to before. The rift loomed high above us, churning and whirring as always. It seemed to contain something similar to lightning now. It sparked occasionally, a crack of white light streaking across it before disappearing within its own inky black.

The DAA was back in full force. Scientists were scrambling to retrieve their equipment from the snowbanks. Those were significantly higher now than they had been before courtesy of the avalanche which I had narrowly escaped with my life. They dusted off the gauges and blew the powdery snow from the smaller instruments, casting glances toward the top of the mountain from time to time, fearful of another snow slide. Soldiers patrolled the area in which the minotaur had fallen, keeping their eyes on the skies and their guns at the ready. The sight gave me pause, a bolt of terror shooting through me at the thought of another mythical beast falling from that open hole in the sky. This time, it might be even worse than a minotaur.

"I would say it gets easier," the friend spoke again as he came up beside me and looked out at the camp as well, "but I still hate it myself."

I looked his way then, examining him truly for the first time. He was smiling broadly, clearly amused by my struggle.

"What was that?" I snapped, whirling around and pointing sharply at Lark who stood a few feet away, examining the surrounding scene. "What did he do?"

"Shadowstep," Lark replied simply.

I just blinked, wanting further explanation, but not wanting to admit that I needed it.

"How am I supposed to explain to my colleagues why I wasn't on the plane, how I got here before them, and why I am accompanied by two arrogant pricks that look more like bodyguards than scientists, one of which I don't even know the name of?"

"Rook," the man at my side told me. "My name is Rook."

I stared at them in stunned disbelief and then threw my hands up in irritation, pacing away from them, my steps uneven in the snow.

"And we aren't all pricks," he added, calling out to me as I strode away. "One of us didn't sweep you away against your will."

"Thank you, Rook," Lark grumbled and I turned on him.

"You can't just use your magic whenever you wish," I snapped. "Not here. Not unless you want to expose your entire plane to mine. These are intelligent people, some of the world's most foremost scholars. They won't be deterred by some half-assed excuses. So we had better think of a story and quick."

"We hold a private interest. We flew you here on our private helicopter. America isn't the only one investigating this phenomenon. Take your pick."

I bristled, jutting out my chin in preparation for a fight but then I shivered involuntarily. Until that moment, I had failed to notice that I was on the side of an arctic mountain in a blazer and jeans.

"Cold?" Lark asked, raising a brow.

I clenched my jaw and glared at him. He smirked with amusement and waved a hand. Suddenly, I was much warmer and far more uncomfortable. I glanced down at the incredibly tight black pants and low cut black coat. Shifting a bit, I could tell I wasn't wearing a shirt under said coat. Or a bra.

"Black suits you," he told me, his gaze narrowing in appreciation as he took a step back to admire his work. Rook chuckled from behind us.

"You forgot a few pieces," I growled.

"Did I?" he asked, feigning innocence with a shrug. "My apologies. Fashion isn't my forte."

"It wouldn't have to be if you had given me time to pack."

"We won't be here that long."

I let out an exaggerated sigh, crossing my arms and clenching my jaw.

"You're so confident in your abilities?" I asked, shaking my head.

"I'm quite confident in many of my abilities," he mused, letting his gaze rake over me once more. My cheeks burned as I whirled around to the man standing silently behind us.

"Aren't you going to do anything at all about him?" I snapped.

Rook tilted his head in thought for a moment before waving a hand in my direction. Suddenly, my underwear was back and even a thick black turtleneck to boot. I stared down at the change, mouth open. Rook just smiled slightly and shrugged.

"This is worse than I thought," Lark said then, interrupting our conversation. Rook fell silent as I stepped forward to Lark, looking from him to the rift where his attention had drifted.

"What do you mean?" I asked, forgetting his impropriety for a moment. "You can help us, can't you?"

I had just watched this Fae transport us halfway across the world with a simple touch. If he couldn't mend this rift and our machines weren't capable of reversing the polarity, I was out of options. The entire mortal plane was out of options. I would fail us. I would fail all of us.

Lark just stared up at the rift, lost in thought. In my desperation, I turned to his friend once again.

"He can do this, can't he? Can't you both? I mean, surely two of you—"

"Take us closer."

My mouth snapped shut. I bristled at being commanded in such a way, whirling back to face Lark who was still watching the rift intently as if he couldn't pull his gaze away from that swirling black mass.

"Follow me," I barked, annoyed. "And don't say a word."

I turned away from them and stomped forward, up the slight incline of the mountain toward the camp. Wyn saw me coming before I arrived and set the box he had been hauling aside, placing his hands on his hips as he caught his breath and looked me over.

"Professor Belling," he said in greeting. He watched me warily, as if afraid I would brandish a gun and shoot him where he stood if he took his eyes off of me for even a second. "It's good to see you've made it back in one piece. The president has been demanding more information on how you took down the minotaur. If we could speak privately for a moment..."

He gave a pointed look over my shoulder to where the two hulking Fae males stood out against the snowy backdrop of the mountain.

"Are you still in charge of this camp?" I asked, doing my best to sound friendly but I could do nothing to hide the implication of my words. Asking if he was still in charge but leaving the rest unsaid. *After you abandoned it, after you left your men to die, after you failed your mission.*

"I am," he replied, puffing out his chest in that way that insecure men always did to assert their authority.

I gave my own pointed glance over my shoulder at the Fae. That purple glow was brighter around them now, shimmering. Glamour. I wondered briefly what they looked like to Wyn Kendrick as I turned back to the man.

"These are some of my contacts I spoke to you about just before everything happened," I said. "They seem to think they have some ideas about how to solve our problem."

"That's wonderful," he replied and I could feel the relief behind his words as he spoke them. "Tell me."

He waited, expectantly.

"They're Russian," I blurted.

Lark turned slowly toward me.

"I know you don't want to cause an international incident, Wyn," I continued, lowering my voice so as not to be overheard. "These men and their government have just as much interest in closing the rift as we do but they will not use their equipment where they can be spied upon by the American military."

I gave a pointed glance at the soldiers patrolling the rift on the other side of the encampment. Wyn's gaze flicked from me to the men behind me, eyes widening as he realized what I was implying.

"I can order them away for a time," Wyn told me. "I'll open an account at the tavern in town, tell them to drink for the fallen, take the night off. I'll make up some story about how we've been monitoring the wavelengths of sound from the rift and don't see any immediate danger. But you won't have long. An hour at most. And it won't be until this evening."

I nodded, reaching out and giving his arm a squeeze of gratitude.

"Thank you, Wyn," I said with a smile. "We'll be here."

Chapter Five
A Portal To Another Plane

We spent our time waiting for nightfall at the tavern in the town a little further down the mountain. Rook shadowstepped to the town, preferring to avoid the embarrassing mortal labor of walking down the mountain on his own two feet. Lark offered to take me again but I refused. My gut was still roiling from the last time and I would rather trudge down that steep incline than puke all over the cobblestones in front of my colleagues. So Lark merely shrugged and fell into step beside me as I began the trek down.

"You said that man was in charge," Lark spoke suddenly once we were halfway to the town. I glanced his way before turning my attention back to where I was stepping so I wouldn't trip over a fallen rock.

"Wyn?" I asked. "He is. Of the camp, at least. This entire mission is his responsibility. Closing the rift is his responsibility. He's a field agent for the DAA. That's the Department of A—"

"I know what the DAA is," he grumbled.

"Right," I bit back through gritted teeth. "Well, whenever a rift opens up, the DAA assigns one of their field agents the task of closing it. Whenever the rift is proving harder to mend than others, Wyn requests help from Hadley and the university sends either my uncle or I to assist. Lately, I've been the lucky one."

"And when the minotaur came?"

"He ran."

Lark's lip curled in open disgust.

"Not an outstanding leader," he remarked.

"No," I agreed with a snort. "He's not."

"Why aren't you in charge?"

I glanced his way again.

"Why would I be?" I asked. "I'm just a professor and not even the head of my department. I'm here in a consulting capacity only and because the Dean of Hadley has some very useful connections."

"Connections that a DAA agent believes capable of calling upon another foreign power to help heal a monster-dropping rift?" Lark asked, raising a brow in my direction.

"I thought it better than telling him you're a supremely powerful magical being."

"Supremely?" he smirked.

I rolled my eyes, ignoring him, and forged on.

"If he ever got over the shock of it, he would turn you into our government for experimentation straight away. And that's not to mention the fact that you're from a separate plane of existence which you've been banished from for a little over half a century now. Some people might ask about why that is, you know."

"You didn't."

"No, I didn't."

"Why not?"

I could practically feel his gaze boring into me and so I looked over my shoulder as I answered.

"Everyone has the right to keep their own secrets," I told him with a shrug. "If you wanted to tell me, you would. Regardless, our deal still stands."

Then, because I was no longer watching where I was going, my foot slipped on a loose rock and I fell backwards. With a yelp, I braced myself for the sharp sting of hard ground on my frozen arse. But the hit never came. And I opened my eyes to find myself in the enigmatic Fae's arms.

"Our deal still stands," he drawled, the warmth of his breath heating my face as his eyes gazed down into mine in a way that should have made my skin crawl. I hadn't met many Fae but if any of them had ever looked at me the way he was looking at me now, I would have done everything I could to shrink out of my own skin. But somehow, with him, it wasn't menacing. I was as much a curiosity to him as he was to me. Perhaps that was naive of me. But I didn't care. Not now. Not if he could heal the rift.

That gaze dipped to my lips and a hot flush crept up my cheeks. I should have moved, should have pushed him away and stormed down the rest of that mountain, but I didn't. And I wasn't even sure why. Anyone else, I would have pummelled for daring to look at me like that, to touch me like he was. But I stayed in his arms for a heartbeat too long as the realization dawned upon me that I wasn't moving because I didn't want to.

Panic rose within me and I blurted the only thing I could think of to end this dangerous silence.

"Why do you want to go back?" I asked, my voice barely above a whisper.

Something about the question seemed to break the spell and he helped me back to my feet before stepping away and waiting for me to take the lead again.

"I just mean, if your father was angry enough with you to banish you," I clarified, continuing along in our walk mostly so that I could watch my feet and not have to make eye contact with him again. "You said he was a powerful man. He must be powerful indeed to have the right to banish anyone."

Lark did not answer me for a moment. I could practically feel his trepidation. He was considering my question and the best way to answer it. He was playing for time.

"I did something that my father believes is unforgivable," he finally answered.

My steps faltered again and he reached out to steady me but I held up a hand to show him I was alright.

"How long did he banish you for?" I asked.

"One hundred years," he replied.

"Then it must be forgivable. I mean, he plans to forgive you in a hundred years, right?"

I looked over my shoulder to find his lips stretching into a grin.

"I suppose you're right," he told me, that dark gaze warming to something almost friendly. Somehow, that was the most unsettling expression of all.

The land beneath our feet flattened and we stepped off the rough stone path onto the beaten snow road of the town. I sighed and turned to face him.

"Lark—" I said his name and those dark eyes flared with something I didn't dare attempt to identify.

"There you two are," someone spoke then, interrupting my attempt at reconciliation and Lark's examination of me.

I turned to see Rook strolling toward us. He appeared to be at ease, lazy smile plastered on his lips. But I saw the way his eyes scanned the town while he walked as if expecting some form of danger from the harmless mountain folk going about their business.

"I was starting to think another minotaur had gotten to you," he joked, eyes sparkling with mischief as if he almost wanted the challenge of a minotaur. Or maybe he didn't consider it a challenge at all if he was joking about it.

I frowned. It hadn't been a joke when it had picked up the DAA soldiers I had shared many meals and sleepless nights with, tossing them about as if they were dolls, cracking their bodies against the stone, blindly swinging that axe at the rest of them as they tried to shoot it down.

"I need a drink," I muttered and pushed past the two of them, heading for the tavern.

The ale was terrible; I remembered that from last time, but in this frigid climate the alcohol was the only thing that kept these people warm at night. When the temperature dropped below zero, nobody cared what the ale tasted like. I was already a pint deep before the Fae entered, the faint purple sparks of their glamours shining around them. I wasn't sure what had kept them for so long. Perhaps they were creating a plan for taking on the rift, maybe they were making fun of Wyn, maybe they were questioning this deal they'd made with me, or maybe they had gotten sidetracked by their own vanity as they shifted their appearances to become something these mountain dwellers would deem ordinary. It hardly mattered.

I took another sip as they crossed the room and separated. Lark walked toward me while Rook went to order ales at the bar. I waited for him to sit before I spoke, in a much fouler mood than I'd been before.

"What do they see?" I asked, nodding my head toward the people sitting at the tables scattered around us.

Lark just leaned back in his seat, watching two men playing cards near us.

"What do you mean?" he asked.

I rolled my eyes.

"I can see the glamour," I told him. "I can see you're using one but I can't see what it is. I just see you, your face, and the glamour. I see when you drop it and when you put it back on but I don't see what it is. So, what do you look like to them?"

"I look like them," he replied. "So does Rook. All beards and potbellies. If they looked too closely at our group, you would be the odd one out here, Ren."

As if for emphasis, he dropped his eyes and allowed them to sweep over me again, but I was thinking about what he'd said. I would be the odd one out. Me, a professor, in this ridiculous black as night ensemble they had crafted for me. Me and not these two glowing Fae in even more elaborate finery unfit for this mountain, faces that looked to be chiseled from marble, piercing gazes that followed me wherever I went. Not them. Me.

"And before?" I asked. "With Wyn?"

"Same as them," he repeated. "We blend in with the people that surround us. Lab coats and glasses, all lanky and scrawny."

He wrinkled his nose, eyes drifting to the people drinking at the bar.

"We keep our faces, mostly," Rook explained, joining the conversation as though he had been part of it all along. I narrowed my gaze at him, wondering just how good that Fae hearing was, as he settled in next to Lark, sliding his friend his mug before taking a pull from his own. "It's easier when you don't have to change your face and we aren't as good at glamouring as—"

Lark's sharp glare cut him off. The newfound certainty that they were definitely not telling me everything had me shifting uncomfortably as Lark leaned across the table, lowering his voice and pinning me to my seat with a narrowed gaze.

"I answered a question for you," he drawled slowly, his voice like velvet in the quiet of the mundane tavern. "Answer one for me."

I watched him cautiously as if I could derive his intentions with just a look. I couldn't, though, so I gave a curt nod.

"How does a consulting professor, not even the head of her department, know about a door to the Immortal Plane?"

I tensed. He was using my own words against me. Not the head of my department, a mere consultant, that's what I had told him I was. And it was true. All of it. But perhaps I shouldn't have disclosed so much to these strangers. Perhaps I shouldn't have let them so completely into my life. They certainly weren't taking such liberties with me. So I frowned and sat back in my seat, glaring back at Lark. Rook looked between us but kept silent, as if knowing better than to speak. He was obviously accustomed to allowing Lark to take the lead.

"Your people come and go from our plane as they please," I spat, not without venom in my tone. "Although it's technically against the rules. That's what they erected The Divide for in the first place, was it not?"

Lark did not answer so I answered for him.

"I may not know the history as well as you, I may not have lived through as many things as you must have seen, but I can reason out the rules of a place that exists for the sole intention of separation well enough on my own. Your people are not supposed to come here. But they don't seem to care. Some of them come as if they're on vacation. As if they can just traipse about our cities unbeknownst to us. But I see them. I always have."

"What do you mean you see them?" he pressed. "How do you identify us?"

"You glow."

He blinked at me, dumbstruck. Rook snorted.

"We... glow" he repeated, uncertain.

Perhaps he was beginning to wonder if I was actually insane. He wouldn't be the first.

"You glow," I repeated, crossing my arms as I sat back further in my seat. "All of you. Some more so than others. And if I get too close, I can feel you. I can feel that you don't belong and you know it. How do you shadowstep?"

Lark's jaw tensed and I felt Rook's scrutiny burning into me from his side. But I kept my composure and held Lark's gaze as he spoke.

"This is what we're doing?" he asked, feigning a tone of amusement but I could tell he was on his guard. "Trading question for question?"

I just quirked a brow and waited.

"It's a rare ability," he confessed after a moment. "Not common within my realm by any means, available to a select few."

"So not all of your kind are capable of it. Especially those here as mere tourists. Therefore, it stands to reason that there's another way between planes, a door of sorts, an easy method of travel your kind created, undetected by us. I'd even wager you know where to enter it on the other side."

"The Court of Wanderers," he told me with a nod and Rook's gaze snapped to him, lips curving downward in a frown. I flicked my eyes to him quickly, uncertain. It was clear that he wasn't happy with Lark for whatever he had just disclosed to me but Lark didn't seem to care. He just kept nodding, encouraging me to continue.

"But you don't know where it leads to here, do you?" I asked. "Because you can shadowstep. So even before you were banished, you never took the common route to visit our plane, did you?"

His lips quirked up into a smirk and I could tell he was pleased with my deductive prowess. Pride leaked into my voice as I continued. It wasn't that I wanted to impress him. Maybe I did. But this was the culmination of my life's work, the answer I'd been seeking since I was old enough to know the question, and now I had two Fae sitting in front of me who knew of the door, at least the other side of it. They had presented me with the opportunity to confirm what I knew, at least a part of it, and my heart was racing with exhilaration at all I'd already discovered. A Court of Wanderers? What could that mean? Where could that be?

"That professor in Oregon, she had heard whispers of a town up north where people trudged in and out of the wilderness. Not hunters; they carried no weapons. Not hikers; they didn't wear the proper clothes or bear the equipment. She thought they were aliens but I knew what they really were. So we went to check it out. It was there. It wasn't even guarded. She couldn't see it. But I could."

I didn't want to tell them the rest. My throat bobbed as I swallowed, my mouth suddenly feeling quite dry. I took a sip of ale and looked past them to the dusk beyond the windows. Nightfall wouldn't be far now.

Lark narrowed his gaze but didn't ask me to continue. Rook looked as though he was on the edge of his seat, waiting. But I couldn't. Because I hadn't even allowed myself to think about it. Not for ten years now. Not since it happened. And I had never told Professor Chelsea Woodward that I had seen it, that I had let her search that unassuming little cottage, turning it inside out while muttering about wormholes and multiple dimensions, and find nothing. Because I had wanted to know that such a thing existed. I had wanted to confirm my own suspicions of the Fae having created such a door between planes. But I hadn't wanted to go through it. I hadn't wanted to travel to the other side. Not because I was afraid of what was waiting for me on the other side but because I was afraid of what wasn't. Even as a woman pushing sixty, despite looking nineteen, I couldn't bear the possibility of being abandoned by my mother twice.

So I'd lied. I'd lied and told Professor Woodward that I had found nothing, I'd consoled her when she fell apart in the woods beyond, bemoaning a lifetime spent in search of a portal to another plane, the confirmation that multiple dimensions not only existed but were reachable from our own.

But I didn't look back. Not even once. And I wouldn't be doing so now if I didn't need the help of these Fae so desperately.

"It's time," Lark said so suddenly that I jumped, having been lost in my own thoughts.

But he wasn't looking at me anymore. His head was turned and he was gazing outside at the early evening. He twisted in his seat slightly and those dark eyes met mine.

"We should go."

Chapter Six

A Deceptive Goodbye

It was cold and dark and the two Fae I'd come here with had lost their patience for my fear of shadowstepping. So before I was even finished arguing for the path up the mountain, Lark grabbed my hand and the world squeezed in around me. Reeling and choking, I collapsed into the snow at the top, hands splayed out before me as I fought to catch my breath.

"Bastard," I spat, which only earned me a chuckle from Rook.

I rose to my feet again, knees wobbling, and brushed the snow from my coat, my legs, grateful for the thick turtleneck that Rook had supplied when some of the powdery substance stuck to my neck where it melted against the warm skin there and dripped down onto my high collar.

"We're alone," Lark said, keen eyes searching the deserted camp.

I looked up from my task and did the same.

"I told you I could do it," I muttered.

I lifted a boot and set it down in the deep snow, then another. It was much harder to walk now with the freshly fallen snow but I was too stubborn to ask for help so I took my time reaching the camp itself instead. Then I moved to the machinery and instruments that Wyn had left on for our use should we need them. I checked the gauges, walking among them in examination.

"Whatever those are," Lark began, "we don't need them."

I opened my mouth to argue, but snapped it shut a moment later as I watched him peel off his coat. Beneath that elegantly embroidered black tunic, he wore a black button-up shirt, the top button undone, the skin of his chiseled chest peeking through. He took his time, methodically rolling up his sleeves so that his muscled arms were on display as he gazed up at the rift, face contorted into an expression of purpose.

"It's not polite to stare," a voice muttered beside my right ear.

I jumped and turned to find Rook standing beside me. Scowling at him, I whirled around to check another instrument but found it had been unplugged when the hulking Fae brute at my side had trodden over the cord. I sighed, placing my hands on my hips, and turned back around to face him.

"Don't you have better things to do?" I snapped. "Like maybe help him?"

"He doesn't need my help," Rook replied with a shrug. "And besides, he told me to look after you instead."

"Look after me? Why would you need to—"

But a horrible groaning sound interrupted me. At first, it sounded mechanical, like an engine grinding to a screeching halt. But there was something deeper to it, something more sinister, more alive. I felt a chill in my very bones at that sound but watched, frozen in my tracks, as Lark raised both hands, and then pulled them together as though it took everything in him to do so.

The rift above came careening to a halt, crying out its dissent as it did. Then it reversed directions. For a moment, the surrounding air seemed to be sucked in. Then it froze again and there was no movement at all, just a huge blot of inky blackness pigmented against a brilliant night sky. Lark dropped his hands, letting them hang at his sides. He tossed his head back, his eyelids fluttering shut. And that darkness, it leeched from the sky, slithering downward in wispy tendrils of smoke, first toward Lark and then into him.

Gasping, I stepped forward but was stopped from going any further by Rook's warning hand on my shoulder.

"Don't," he said.

I glanced at him once to find his lips set in a firm, grim line. It wasn't a suggestion. It was a warning and one that he intended to enforce should I decide to disobey him. He took his orders to look after me quite seriously indeed.

I turned back to Lark. He was shaking now, his arms and legs twitching as if his body was fighting the rift, the darkness he was absorbing. His jaw clenched, his throat bobbed, but his eyes remained closed. He did not cry out even when it pulled him from his feet, lifting him a few inches off of the ground, levitating him above the powdery drifts of snow. That inky black clung to him, enveloping him, suffocating him. But underneath it all a purple glow emerged and began pulsating brighter and brighter until it shot from him in a blinding beam of light. I gasped, raising an arm to shield my eyes, as Lark dropped back to the ground, steadying himself. I blinked away the silhouette of that light and opened my eyes to find that the rift was simply... gone.

I ran forward before I could stop myself and, this time, Rook made no move to stop me. I reached Lark a moment later and, thanks to my snow-induced clumsiness, barreled into him much harder than I had intended. But he didn't fall. He merely caught me by the shoulders and helped me to my feet.

"You did it," I gasped, gaping up at him in awe. "I can't believe you did it."

"Your confidence in me knows no bounds," he drawled sarcastically.

But I couldn't stop smiling. This was it. This was the solution. He was the solution. For all of our equipment, all of our studies, we had never closed a rift as efficiently as this single Fae male had. I knew I had promised to take him home, to get him back to his plane, but maybe I could convince him to stay a little longer. Maybe I could convince him to shadowstep to the other rifts, to heal them all. Maybe...

A slow clapping sound from somewhere nearby interrupted my thoughts. I whirled around to find Wyn emerging from the brush, a smug grin on his lips, surrounded by a dozen soldiers who all emerged at the same time, their guns trained on us, though I noticed the barrels were shaking even worse than they had been when facing the minotaur.

"Wyn?" I asked, stunned. "What are you doing?"

Rook was by our side in an instant. Lark stepped protectively in front of me, shielding me.

"I have to hand it to you, Ren. I didn't think you could actually do it," Wyn spoke differently now. His voice was not the same stuttering, uncertain whimper. Now, it was oozing arrogance and that grin, I wanted to slap it right off of his face. "My superiors were right. Never trust a Half-Fae."

My world came crashing to a screeching halt. Half-Fae. He knew. He knew what I was. He knew what existed out there beyond the bounds of our reality. And if what he was saying was true, so did his superiors. I stopped breathing. For how long had the leaders of our country, the elite of the world, known about the existence of magic, of these supremely powerful beings, and kept it from the masses? And how long had they suspected I was one?

"They knew you'd have friends on the other side," he boasted now, his former tone of academic congeniality entirely gone, replaced by something unflinchingly wicked. "They merely waited for a situation desperate enough for you to call them. And now that they're here, they won't be leaving anytime soon."

My face burned with anger and shame as a feeling of foolish stupidity washed over me.

Sixty years. I had lived at Hadley University for sixty years and I still looked like a student. I taught classes, I interacted with pupils, I attended faculty meetings and required training. I hid when the more distinguished visitors came, of course. And I lied about who I really was from time to time, donned disguises when someone I had met before came back decades later.

I should have left. I should have started a new life somewhere far away, created a new identity for myself. But I hadn't. Because I was weak. Because I had people in my life that I cared about, connections and relationships that I didn't want to leave behind. And because I knew my uncle would never live as long as me and I didn't want to miss even a moment of his fleeting mortal life.

"I hate the DAA," I muttered.

"Men," Wyn barked and the soldiers strode forward, guns still trained on the two Fae.

Slowly, tentatively, they raised their hands. Gawking, I did the same.

They had to have a plan. They had to. Lark could summon whatever he wished into existence, could swallow up enormous rifts in the fabric of space and time. Rook could turn invisible. They could shadowstep and whatever else I wasn't even aware of. Surely, they wouldn't allow themselves to be taken by DAA soldiers, by the man who couldn't even defeat a minotaur without the help of a hapless professor and a cache of C4.

"How did you know?" I called out because keeping Wyn talking felt better than doing nothing and, if they had a plan, they might need time to make it work. I could give them that, at least.

"You trust too easily, Professor Belling. I always warned you about that."

My heart dropped into my stomach. Someone had told him. Someone had told the people above them. Someone I trusted. Someone I knew.

"Who?" I growled.

"Where's the fun in that? How about you convince your little friends to surrender to us and I'll tell you everything you want to know."

I had no intention of doing that but I had to keep Wyn talking. I had to stall him for as long as I could.

"Where would you take them?" I asked, pretending not to notice the way Rook glanced my way, the way Lark's fist clenched at my side.

Wyn grinned as if he had won. I wasn't so sure he hadn't. The Fae behind me had barely moved. Any hope I held that they were formulating a plan was fading fast.

"Back to headquarters," Wyn answered as if it was the stupidest question in the world. Perhaps it was. But, if he would not tell me anything about who ratted me out, I was running out of subjects to broach with this traitor. "So that they can tell us more about these rifts they seem to have no trouble getting rid of."

"More? What more do you need to know? They're rifts, natural phenomena."

"Please don't insult my intelligence, Professor."

I blinked at him. He couldn't be insinuating that these rifts, these holes in the barrier between our worlds, were being created on purpose. It was a wild enough theory when my uncle had proposed it but my uncle was a dreamy academic. This was the DAA.

"What we are certain of," Wyn continued, "is that they know more than they're saying."

My lips parted slightly.

"Men," Wyn barked again and the soldiers lurched forward and then suddenly, so suddenly, fell to the ground, their throats all split open, gurgling and choking on their own blood.

I let out a scream as my eyes darted from the dying men to the bloody knife in Rook's hand, his hair gently flowing in the breeze he must have created with how fast he had moved. My eyes bulged from my head as I stared at him.

But then something else drew my attention. A familiar sound that caused dread to pool in the pit of my stomach. A low groan, a sinister whirring. I turned to find Lark standing nearby, his hand outstretched. From it poured the darkness.

Wyn screamed something and his men backed away. He backed away, running again.

"Lark," I screamed over the groaning. "Please, don't do this. Don't bring it back."

But it was already forming. Not in the sky, but in front of us. A flat plane of black swirling and contorting into a familiar shape. Realization hit me hard, like a punch in the gut, as I stared at the dark shape. A door.

Oh.

I understood just a moment before Rook was stepping through and I hadn't gotten the chance to say goodbye. I scrambled forward, stumbling in the snow, as Wyn commanded his men to aim, to stop the Fae. I hardly heard him as I reached Lark, gripping him by the sleeve and staring up into those dark, churning eyes.

"Thank you," I whispered, a tear freezing on my cheek.

He raised his hand in a caress against my face, running the warm, calloused pad of his thumb across the tear. It melted away. He cocked his head to the side, that penetrating gaze still firmly on my face.

"Goodbye," I told him softly.

He didn't say a word, just turned and stepped toward the darkness.

I turned away from him, not wanting to see the moment he disappeared, already preparing myself to be captured and questioned by the DAA. I would tell them everything now. It couldn't hurt for them to know about Lark's banishment or that he and his friend hadn't told me anything at all about their plane, about the deal I'd made with them to ensure the safety of the mortal realm. They couldn't fault me for that. They would question me about my parentage, about the other half of my ancestry, but they would find that I knew even less than they did.

Perhaps capture was my fate. Perhaps this was always how it was going to end for me. I had been a fool for believing that I could live in the mortal realm forever, could work with the government and the academic institutions without the longevity of my life ever being discovered, ever being questioned. So if this was my fate, I would meet it with my chin held high, knowing that I had closed at least a few of these rifts, had helped my people significantly, before they caught me.

But before I could say anything, before I could call out to Wyn and tell him not to shoot, someone grabbed me by the elbow and jerked me forcefully backwards.

I only had time to gasp before I fell into that swirling vortex and darkness swallowed me whole.

Part Two
Refuge

Chapter Seven

A Captive Audience

My scream followed me into the next world, a realm of brightest orange.

"Get her out of here," Lark hissed before my body even hit the cobblestones.

Rook obeyed, pulling me upward, bodily, and dragging me away from the crowd.

Crowd.

I blinked once, twice. There was, in fact, a crowd of onlookers surrounding the swirling black mass that Lark was now closing with far more ease than he had before, simply snapping it up and walking away, his black coat trailing behind him despite the uncommon heat.

Heat.

I blinked again. I was sweating, I realized, under my turtleneck. It was hot here, so hot that it was nearly suffocating. The people who had stopped to watch had moved on now, merging back onto the busy streets in their clothes of varying shades of orange, made mostly of sheer gauze and light linens so that all the parts of their bodies that weren't considered private were exposed. Men's bare chests glistened beneath orange mesh shirts or bare legs poked out from beneath linen shorts. Women wore pants of gauze, billowing around their bare legs, thickening at the top so that nothing above their upper thighs could be seen. They wore no shirts at all. Just bright orange brassieres or bandeaus.

They rushed in and out of buildings, also painted varying shades of orange and garnished at the top with amber and fire opal. The streets were an orange clay brick, stacked meticulously and worn down to smoothness over the years. Everyone was walking. Everyone was moving, going somewhere. No one was paying attention to the mortal being dragged away by two Fae in deep black tunics.

"Let me go," I yelped, lashing out at my captor, landing a kick to Rook's calf.

He hissed in a breath but kept me firmly in his grip.

I looked back at Lark who was following us, his dark eyes scanning street after street as we passed. They were becoming less and less busy, I realized. He was taking me out of this city. He was taking me somewhere we couldn't be seen.

"What have you done?" I barked at him over my shoulder. "You weren't supposed to bring me here. I'm not supposed to be here."

"That makes three of us," Rook muttered.

My gaze snapped back to him.

"Let me go," I begged him in a whisper. "Please, Rook."

His jaw twitched, the only indication that I might have actually gotten to him.

"Even if we did," he murmured, his voice low, "where would you go? What would you do?"

I went limp in his arms. I stopped kicking, stopped fighting. I just paled. Because he was right. Even if I broke free of my comrades turned captors, I was still stuck in the Immortal Plane, surrounded by ethereal beings of ferocious volatility. Any of them could shred me to pieces with a single thought. I was a rabbit and I had just walked into a wolf's den. Well, I hadn't walked in myself, had I?

I glared over my shoulder.

"I thought we were friends," I snapped, putting all the venom and vitriol in my voice that I could. "I thought I could trust you."

"Unwise," Lark said simply.

My lip curled, my fists clenched, and I got a little bit of that fight back. I wrenched hard and whirled on him. Rook reined me in, my having gone as far as I had only because I had caught him off guard, but not before I could gnash my teeth at Lark, my face only inches from his.

"I'll kill you," I spat. "I swear it."

"Before you go making promises you can't possibly hope to keep," he drawled easily, unfazed entirely by my empty threat, "you may want to hear what I have to say first."

I blinked and Rook was pulling me through a doorway. It was dark here. We were in an alley off one of the major streets. Inside the door was a set of copper stairs, the closest metal to orange they could find, I supposed. They pulled me up those stairs and through a door at the top into a modest apartment. Lark snapped his fingers and little bulbs of floating light flared to life all throughout it.

Rook deposited me onto an orange leather couch and strode to stand beside it, arms crossed in front of him, chin up, eyes straight ahead. Like a soldier would stand, I realized, like a man awaiting his leader's command. I pulled my glare from Rook to Lark, putting all of my hate and anger into that stare as I met his dark eyes.

"They were going to kill you," he said after a moment.

"You don't know that," I snapped.

"Yes, I do. And, more importantly, you do too."

I did not respond. I just glared at him, gritting my teeth. I could feel the anger radiating off of him as well, the indignation that I would dare to risk my life in such a way.

"Why did you stay there?" he asked. "You're only half mortal. You found the door and yet you left it untouched. You chose to stay there with them. Why?"

I said nothing so he sat slowly onto an armchair across from me, also orange. Everything was orange. The rug, the wallpaper, the cabinets and shelves. Everything. Different patterns and shades but still, it was practically nauseating, this city's commitment to the theme.

"Why would I want to return to the people who abandoned me?" I asked and couldn't help but notice how Rook tensed at that. Still, I maintained my glare on Lark.

"You never wondered why they did?" Lark asked, genuine curiosity in his tone, a curiosity that I did not have the patience for. "Why no one came searching for you in the mortal realm? Why they left you behind with that crackpot uncle—"

"Don't you dare speak of him that way."

Lark paused, watching me closely.

"In all this time you've been running around closing up the rifts, did you ever stop to think about why they were appearing in the first place?" he asked.

"Of course I did," I spat, insulted. "I'm an academic. It's an intriguing situation. But I examined it based on what I knew. They didn't follow the patterns typical of black holes. They did not exhibit any of the signs of other astrological—"

"You did not assess the rifts with the entirety of your knowledge, Ren. If you had, you would have considered an alternate explanation outside of the realm of science. Your colleague did."

I bristled, reeling back as if he had struck me.

"Are you saying that Wyn Kendrick did a better job at evaluating the rifts than I did?" I asked, stunned.

"Yes," Lark answered, growing irate with my affront. "And he started out with far less information than you."

I went completely still, my mind utterly emptied as though my brain itself had ceased functioning. There was a ringing in my ears as I came to terms with what this powerful Fae was suggesting. I had prided myself, my entire life, on my relentless search for knowledge, on my scholastic achievements and academic research, while actively ignoring the single most significant discovery in all of human history. I'd been given this information at birth and I had hidden it because I had been asked to but I had not tried to investigate on my own either, to examine myself and that half of me which I had spent nearly sixty nears pretending did not exist.

"They would have killed you," he repeated. "Your chosen people."

I saw red. Roaring in frustration, I lunged for him. He was there, sitting primly on that armchair, one leg crossed lazily over the other, and then he wasn't and my nails were tearing into upholstery rather than his smug face. I whirled to find him standing beside Rook, brow raised in warning.

"Now, now, now," he chided with the click of his tongue, "we weren't finished talking."

"I am," I snapped and stormed toward the door.

He didn't stop me, though we both knew he could. He let me walk away, let me take those steps back down to the street and stomp down that alley.

"You won't be welcome here," he called out from the door through which I had just exited.

I balled my hands into fists and clenched them so tight that my nails cut bloody half moon shapes into my palms. But I hesitated in the shadows, not yet ready to step into the street beyond, because I knew he was right. Like it or not, I was a mortal in the immortal plane. They wouldn't want me here. They would chase me out. Or worse.

I blinked out at that passing sea of orange, people hastening somewhere, not even looking my way. Not yet.

I looked down at my outfit. Black coat over a black turtleneck, tight black pants, thick black boots. They had dressed me like them, in their color. No orange. Not a drop.

"I never wanted to force you," Lark spoke again and his voice was a whisper against my ear, his warm breath on my neck sending shivers through me. "But we ran out of time and, I'll be the first to admit, I'm not the most patient man."

I turned my head slightly to the side, looked up into those dark eyes only inches from mine, chest heaving.

"I won't drag you back to that apartment," he promised and my shoulders relaxed slightly, knowing that I wasn't in immediate danger, not from him. "I won't capture you like some wild beast. It's your choice. It will always be your choice."

My breathing hitched, my expression softened.

"You never had a choice before," he said. "You were placed in the mortal realm and that's where you lived for sixty years. Give this place a chance. Give us a chance. And then decide. I'll take you back the moment you say you want to go."

"You said it yourself," I muttered, staring out at the Fae passing in the streets beyond. "I'm not welcome here."

"You will be with us. They won't dare to touch you if you're with us."

I turned to him, tilting my head to the side.

"Why not?" I asked. "Who are you?"

Lark set his jaw, frowning as he turned out to the masses passing us by without a second glance.

"I'm going to go back and Rook and I are going to have a nice dinner while we await our visitor," he told me, ignoring my question. "You're welcome to join us. You're welcome to stay with us for as long as you wish. I will answer your questions. But for now, have dinner with us."

He held out an arm and I stared at it with trepidation.

"I am your friend, Ren," he said then, his voice soft now too as he leaned closed to me, eyes firmly on mine. "But don't trust me yet. Let me earn it."

I stared at him for a moment, considering, but in the end I took him by the arm and walked back to the apartment where Rook was waiting, even allowing a small smile of relief when I returned.

Chapter Eight
A Family Affair

I expected the two Fae males to wave their hands and dinner would appear on the table, laid out like a fabulous banquet fit for a king. But they actually cooked with their own hands. I couldn't tear my eyes away as I watched them move seamlessly around each other in the apartment's small kitchen, tossing each other herbs and spices, bickering about how much lemon juice was enough and how much was too much. It was so utterly normal.

I was so distracted, however, that I didn't hear our visitor enter until she spoke.

"You two have spent far too long in the mortal realm."

I turned at the sound of the melodic feminine voice to see the most beautiful woman I had ever laid eyes on. She was tall and slim, her frame looming even higher in the black stilettos she wore on her feet, open-toed, nails painted a deep purple. Her legs were smooth and toned and went all the way up to her short black skirt and sparkling, drooping top. Her lips were painted plum and her eyes were like starlight as she turned her megawatt smile on me, tossing her dark, wavy locks over a shoulder.

"Is this her?" she asked. Her voice was like honey, sweet and genuine.

I just blinked at her, understanding for the first time why my ancestors might have believed themselves standing before a goddess so long ago. Maybe that had even been this woman herself.

"Cass, this is Professor Seren Belling. She prefers to be called Ren," Lark introduced, tossing a dishtowel over his shoulder as he strode across the kitchen and leaned against the counter I was sitting at to make the introductions. "Ren, this is my sister, Casseiopia."

"Cass," she corrected, sticking out a hand.

I shook it and she grinned from cheek to cheek.

"You're half Fae," she blurted.

"Cass," Lark muttered a low warning.

"I'm sorry," she said to me. "It's just, these two haven't told me hardly anything at all about you. Tell me what you do. Something with the rifts?"

She was moving quickly, already settling onto the bar stool beside mine as she leaned forward, interested. She placed a hand on my knee and Lark's gaze shot to the contact.

"Oh, yes," I answered, caught off guard by her overwhelming friendliness.

Something about Casseiopia put me at ease. She was bright eyed and friendly, teeth gleaming white in her radiant smile that seemed permanently affixed to her face. She came across as someone I could actually talk to. Someone who might tell me something about her world instead of keeping me in the dark until it was convenient for her, instead of grumbling or growling at me any time I asked a question, instead of commanding me all the time.

"I work for Hadley University," I told her. "It's a prestigious university in the mortal plane. Well, in my country at least. My uncle and I make up the entire astrophysics department. Anyway, when the rifts started popping up around the globe, the DAA, that's the Department of Astrophysical Anomalies, hired us as consultants to help their agents close them."

She just listened intently, nodding from time to time and showing genuine interest. She didn't snap at me to inform me she already knew what the DAA was. She didn't interrupt me with an observation or a question that she deemed more important. Was she entirely certain that she and her brother were genetically related?

"Fascinating," she breathed and it didn't feel condescending. It almost seemed like she truly found it fascinating. "How do they treat you there? Mortals. Do they know what you are?"

I frowned. What I was.

"Most don't," I confessed. "It only… causes trouble to tell people."

She nodded, giving my knee a squeeze where she still held it. Lark cleared his throat and she released me.

"Well, welcome to the Court of Wanderers," she said jovially, raising both hands before dropping them to her sides.

"Is that where we are?" I asked, raising a brow as I glanced over at the Fae males who were suddenly very interested in their plating. "No one bothered to tell me."

"Oh yes, the Court of Wanderers is the only one you can travel into from the mortal realm. All the other courts have wards and protections to keep travelers from the other side out."

"So none of you are from here."

Lark tensed. Rook frowned. Casseiopia looked away from me for the first time, glancing to her brother for guidance.

"What makes you say that?" Lark asked in challenge, turning toward us. He stepped forward and braced his powerful arms on the counter in front of us in a way that flexed the muscles in his forearms and waited.

"The distinct lack of orange in your wardrobe," I said. "And the overwhelming use of black."

Cass snorted at that. Rook couldn't contain his grin.

"I'm assuming color is a strong indicator of where you're from here, which, what did you call it? Court?"

"Yes," Cass answered, nodding. "They are called Courts. And they are all color coded, as weird as that is."

"It's the only reason for the repulsive amount of orange in this city," I replied, wrinkling my nose and she laughed.

"Not every Court is as... proud of their color as this one."

"What are they?" I asked. "The courts?"

Cass' smile faltered. Her gaze flicked quickly to her brother who interrupted before she could speak.

"The geography lesson can wait," he drawled. "Dinner's ready."

Though the Fae used no magic to make the food, they made it disappear and reappear on the table in the dining room. I flinched at the casual use of magic, wondering if I would ever get used to it, as I followed Cass over to the table. We arranged ourselves around the average wooden dining table. Rook took one side, Cass and I took the other. Lark sat at the head, the side I was closest to. Rook dug into the meal before anyone could say a word.

"I see your table manners have been utterly vacated," Cass quipped. She gave a dramatic wave of her hand and Rook's food disappeared from his plate and back onto the serving tray in the middle. Cass raised a brow in challenge. "Try again."

"I didn't miss you," Rook groaned, pointing at her with his fork.

"Yes, you did," she remarked with a grin.

He smiled back. I looked between them.

"How's father?" Lark asked then and both of their smiles vanished.

Rook's fork clattered to his plate as he gaped openly at Lark who hadn't even looked up from his food. Cass glanced uneasily toward her brother.

"He, um, he's the same as always, I suppose," Cass answered after a long moment of silence.

"Hm. I would have thought Ursa would have killed him by now."

"Lark—"

"Given that she tried to kill me."

Cass' cheeks burned. She stared down at her napkin.

"I know you've seen her," he said then, that intense gaze aimed directly at his sister. Even Rook had stopped eating. "He is an immortal king. She's fighting for a succession that may never occur. She tried to kill me, her own brother, to claim a throne that may always be his."

"Lark, I didn't—"

"Why?" he snapped, his dark gaze gone icy cold.

Cass closed her eyes.

"What has happened, Cass?" he asked, his voice oddly strained. "Be honest with me."

"There was an attempt on father's life," she answered, her voice barely a whisper.

Lark's jaw tensed. Rook gaped.

"When?" Lark growled a moment later and I jumped in my seat at the raw power behind it.

"Last year. When she came for you. It was poison. We thought he was... we thought he would die."

"And where was Taurus?"

"He was—she went after him too."

Casseiopia was suddenly very interested in her purple nails.

"Cass," Lark started, carefully. "What happened?"

"He nearly killed her, Lark. You know how powerful he is. Almost as powerful as—" her eyes flicked to me and she hesitated. "He tried. He tried to kill her and he might have if I hadn't found her. I took her to the Court of Blessings and they healed her but she was unconscious for six months after that. Every day was touch and go. I tried to tell you, I did, but I couldn't find you."

"Where is he now?" Lark asked, his jaw clenched in pure rage.

"The Sanguine Throne."

"That figures."

It wasn't the time to ask so I remained quiet even as I filed the small nuggets of information away to bring up later. Court of Blessings, Sanguine Throne. Court of Blessings, Sanguine Throne.

"Once they know you're here..." Cass trailed off, looking from her brother to Rook and back again.

"We have no intention of staying in this orange monstrosity of a city," Lark said then and my gaze slipped to him. We didn't? He met my eyes and gave me a small nod of almost apologetic understanding. "I've been meaning to pay Sophierial a visit."

Rook's lips parted again in surprise at that.

"The Court of Light and Life," Cass muttered, nodding in understanding. She turned to me as if to explain. "It is forbidden to kill on their lands."

I nodded slowly, appreciating the explanation though I was several steps behind it.

"This Ursa woman is still trying to kill you?" I asked, showing how far behind I was as I glanced at Lark.

Rook became suddenly very interested in his food again. Cass huffed out a breath and waited for her brother to respond. Lark just watched me, fork dangling from his hand, and swallowed slowly.

"Ursa is my sister," he told me and the color drained from my face. "Taurus is our brother. We are all siblings, all four of us."

I just blinked at him, lost. He set his fork aside so that it clinked gently against his glass and cleared his throat, tenting his arms in front of him so that his hands folded together near his chin.

"It is a tradition in our court, the Court of Blood and Bone," he began slowly, holding my gaze as he explained, "that succession is not determined by birth order or even by preordained choice of the former monarch. Our father is the king. The four of us are his heirs. If he should die, we will fight to the death to win his throne."

My jaw dropped in shock. Both at the revelation that Lark was a prince and at the atrociousness of the custom he had just informed me of. It was one of the most barbaric things I'd ever heard and I had spent a good deal of my adolescence studying witch trials.

"You can't yield?" I asked, stunned.

"You can," Cass chimed in then, her expression one of sorrowful compassion. "I already have. My siblings know I don't intend to fight them for the crown. They know I will yield to whoever wins."

"And you?" I inquired, turning back to Lark, in awe that he could even consider taking part in such a brutal ritual.

He frowned deeply, crumpling up his napkin and throwing it hard on the table before him.

"I would yield," he spoke. "I have no desire to kill my own blood. But I can't. If Taurus or Ursa took the throne, things would get even worse than they have under my father. I can't let that happen."

Rook was nodding his agreement. Cass was frowning, that bright smile of hers having faded at last, but she wasn't arguing either. I just gaped at all of them.

"You all agree with this?" I asked, astounded. "You think he has to do it?"

"It's the only way," Rook muttered.

"You can't at least help him?"

So that he doesn't have to kill his own brother, his own sister. So that particular evil doesn't stain his soul for all eternity.

"If we interfered in any way, we would be executed," Rook grumbled, having clearly considered it as an option before.

"No one can kill the royal family except, of course, the royal family," Cass mused, as if the idea itself might have been funny if it were happening to anyone other than her family.

I turned to Lark, watching him swirl the contents of his glass around in brooding silence. It was hard to believe the man who had sealed my rift, the arrogant bastard who had waltzed into my office as if he owned the place and knew exactly how to get under my skin, was destined for such a fate. Before I could think about it, I reached up and grabbed his hand, pulling it into the warmth of my own. His skin was cold but, when that dark, penetrating gaze met mine, I did not look away.

"She told me what happened when she came for you," Cass said then, so quietly that I almost missed it. "She told me what you did."

Rook looked up at Lark and it seemed, for the first time, that I was not the only one unaware of something.

"I need a stronger drink," Lark said simply and then rose and strode toward the kitchen, leaving us all in his wake.

We spent the rest of dinner eating silently and avoiding eye contact with one another.

Chapter Nine
A Court of Light and Life

Apparently, magic was traceable. Lark's magic was like his fingerprint, which meant it could be recognized, it could be tracked. And, since he was supposed to have been banished for another forty or so years or whenever his father forgave him, whichever came first, it was indisputable that his father had a trace on him. I was told that meant that if Lark used even a moderate amount of magic while in the immortal plane, anything more than a household chore or a simple glamour, his father would know. And that, apparently, would be a terrible thing.

Since Rook had been banished alongside him as well, for reasons that I still didn't know, that meant Cass was the only Fae among us capable of using the full capacity of her magic. Therefore, she had to shadowstep all of us to the Court of Light and Life one at a time.

"Let's get this over with," she declared the next morning, clapping her hands together and heading straight for Rook. "One shadowstep to the Ivory Throne at your service."

"Not the throne," Lark interrupted, his tone warning. "Outside."

Cass nodded.

"Are you alright?" Lark asked as I shuffled on the balls of my feet.

I turned to find him watching me warily, intense gaze fixed on my face.

"I'm fine," I lied. "Court of Light and Life sounds better than any alternative. Particularly, Blood and Bone."

Rook snorted at that. Even Lark's lips stretched up into a quick smirk.

"Ready?" Cass asked, reaching toward Rook.

"Don't rumple my tunic," he grumbled so Cass slapped him hard on the chest and they both vanished into thin air.

"When you meet them, it's going to seem like they are the embodiment of all things good," Lark spoke quickly. "Just remember, they aren't all that different from us."

"What do you—"

But Cass was back.

"Ready, Ren?" she asked, reaching out a hand, far more gentle with me than she had been with Rook.

I held Lark's gaze for a beat longer before reaching out to Cass. The moment her warm hand enveloped mine, the world squeezed away. I kept my eyes closed this time, hoping that I wouldn't feel so sick on the other end if I didn't watch the world spin around me. No such luck.

I landed roughly, as always, but remained on my feet, even if I did take a few stumbling steps forward and nearly tumbled off a cliff. I probably would have if Rook hadn't reached out to grab me at the last second, pulling me back against his chest.

"Ashes, Cass!" Rook cursed. "You didn't have to take the novice to the edge of a cliff!"

"Oh, Ren, I'm so sorry!" Cass was shouting from where she had landed gracefully a few feet away. "I'm not used to shadowstepping someone that doesn't know how."

Rook held me a moment longer until I caught my breath and stepped aside. Then he released me.

"It—it's okay," I stuttered, still in shock as I peered down at the jagged rocks below.

We were in a desert above a canyon. Sand so white it almost looked like snow surrounded us. I could already feel it in the practical hiking boots Cass had summoned for me that morning, the coarse grains grating against my socks. And those jagged rocks below, they weren't rocks at all. They were the towering spires of a city. A city built into the smooth rock around it. Gold glistened from rooftops, beautiful sandstone buildings glimmered beneath, and people walked between them but not like they had in the Court of Wanderers.

The pace was slower here, almost lazy. No one hurried about, rushing from one place to another. There were no gaudy orange jewels or varying shades offensive to the eye. It was all natural sandstone and gold and the people who strode about wore white gossamer gowns, long for the women, short for the men, so similar to the togas of Ancient Greece that I wondered absentmindedly if these Fae weren't who the Greek gods had been modeled after. What lucky mortal had been given the opportunity to see this place of wonders all those centuries ago? Who wrote them down first? A Mycenaean singer, Homer, Hesiod?

Lark appeared then with Cass, straightening his sleeves as though the shadowstep hadn't affected him at all. I shook my head to clear the thoughts of ancient Greek philosophers and artists long dead and wondered how many times he had done it now, if it had become as second nature to him as walking.

"When we get inside, find somewhere to hide, Rook," Lark commanded and his companion nodded stiffly in response as we started walking around the cliff, making our way towards a set of steps carved into the side nearby.

I glanced at Cass, confused.

"Technically, Rook is forbidden from entering the city," she said simply.

I gaped at her. Banished to the mortal plane? Forbidden from entering the Court of Light and Life? Who exactly was this quiet, stoic friend of Lark's who had saved me from falling off a cliff just moments ago? I chanced a glance back at him but he wasn't looking my way. He was staring out at the city below with something akin to sorrow in his expression.

The climb was torturous for a mortal such as myself. I didn't have the stamina of the Fae and I was breathing harder and sweating worse than any of them by the time we made it halfway down. I stopped then, pulling my sweater up and over my head so that I was only in my tight gray racer back tank that matched my thin gray leggings.

Cass had chosen the ensemble herself, warning me that athletic attire, something that could breathe and withstand the heat, would be the most appropriate clothing for the journey and deciding upon gray to show that I belonged to no court. When I had bristled at that, she had taken my hand gently and explained that, while there was nothing she wanted more than to see me in black, I should take my time with the decision. Declaring yourself to be part of a court, wearing their colors, particularly when spending so much time with the royal family of said court, was no small decision. I decided not to tell her that her brother had already dressed me head to toe in the color of their court himself while we were in the mortal plane. It seemed like something that might start a fight and, though I was curious to see the results of that fight, it felt an unwise thing to start a fight between two siblings while the other two were trying to kill them. Or, at least, trying to kill Lark.

"Are you coming?" Rook asked, peeking his head back around the stone which they had all already passed ahead of me.

I took a deep breath and tied my sweater around my waist and nodded. He took one look at my exposed shoulders and grinned.

"Don't," I warned, and he just burst into a fit of laughter, reaching out a hand.

I took it, grateful for the assistance as the steps closer to the bottom had grown more and more rickety. Still, I couldn't help but trail my fingers along the smooth sandstone as we passed it. The beautiful beige and ivory natural striped pattern was intoxicating, as it seemed to envelop the entire city within a sort of vortex motif.

When we finally reached the city below, we stepped onto a street that looked paved with sand itself, compacted and hardened but just as white and pristine as the loose sand blowing in the breeze on the cliffs above. Lark's penetrating gaze passed over me once we were within eyesight of one another again, lingering on the part of my appearance that had changed. I didn't dare tell him to stop. I wasn't sure that I wanted to.

It had been a long time since any man looked at me how Lark always seemed to. And I didn't mean the brief flares of desire. I meant the way he always examined me as if I had a puzzle etched on my face and he was forever missing one of the pieces. Like he was always curious about what I might do next and always surprised about what I chose. But he still didn't trust me. I knew that because I didn't trust him either. Not entirely. There were things that both of us weren't telling each other but maybe we didn't need to.

Rook pointed and Lark tore his gaze away from me and then we were moving and I could breathe again. I strode beside Cass on our way through the city. At first, she pointed out a thing or two, muttering a historical fact or cultural tidbit. *This is the most famous jewelers in the whole plane. They have the absolute best olives here. There's a woman who plays the harp at* the top of the Tower of the Sun on the same day every year, some mournful lament, and no one knows why. But her commentary became less and less the deeper into the city we walked and then broke off entirely.

No one looked at us. No one stopped and stared as we passed, the Fae in their pure black that stood out in sharp contrast in this city of white, and me wearing clothes that so obviously did not belong in this place, sweating from the climb and huffing my way up the sand streets. I couldn't have appeared more mortal if I'd tattooed the word across my forehead.

I guessed, from the direction we were walking and the surrounding buildings, that the Ivory Throne was the palatial estate just ahead of us, embellished with more gold than any of the others, huge golden gates cutting off the street just ahead.

"Bone Court," a high, feminine voice cooed from nearby. I glanced ahead to find an ethereal-looking woman with long brown hair falling below her breasts, little pink flowers woven within it, standing on the other side of the gate.

"We are here to see Sophierial," Lark said simply, his tone clipped compared to the girl's melodic cooing.

"I am not permitted—"

"We seek refuge at the Court of Light and Life."

Her jaw snapped shut. Her eyes widened just a fraction as she took us in then, all of us, those immortal eyes sliding over my companions and then landing on me. She gave a soft gasp of surprise.

"If you could fetch Sophierial—"

"Canis," someone called out then, a soft and delicate voice.

I looked past the girl with the brown hair to see another striding up behind her, arms outstretched so that the long sleeves of her gossamer gown trailed behind her along with the train of her skirts. She wore a crown of ivy in her long auburn waves. Freckles dotted her nose and cheeks, leading up to her brown eyes. She looked young, even younger than us, but something in her eyes told me she was the oldest one here. Or, at least, close.

"Sophierial," Lark replied, jaw clenched at the sound of his true name.

I looked between them, considering. She had called him Canis, not Lark, a name that he had claimed his friends called him. His words from before we shadowstepped away from the Court of Wanderers hit me then, a reminder, a warning.

When you meet them, it's going to seem like they are the embodiment of all things good. Just remember they aren't all that different from us.

"What trouble have you brought to my door?" Sophierial asked, her eyes sweeping over us in the same way her sentry's had, lingering on me.

"We seek refuge," Lark repeated and then added, narrowing his gaze to a point, "and hospitality."

"Which you shall have."

She clapped her hands and the sentry jumped to attention, standing straight and awaiting her orders.

"Canis, you may follow me to the dining hall. It's nearing lunch and you must be starving from the climb. Semyaza, take the girls to the dressing room. Let them freshen up and find the mortal something... immortal to wear."

With a sashay of her hips, Sophierial led Lark away. He glanced back at me once, lips pressed together and gaze hard, before following her into the estate. When they had gone, Cass and I turned to Semyaza who kept her distance from the Bone Court princess as she led us toward the opposite side of the manor. I realized then that I hadn't the slightest clue when Rook had vanished. I looked back at the city behind us once more, wondering where he had gone.

The estate itself was nothing short of sheer elegance. The main halls, which Cass and I traipsed through warily, were arranged in a square surrounding a beautiful central courtyard which overflowed with crawling vines, porcelain statues, and marble fountains. Little offshoots from the hall opened up into larger concourses or separate rooms, all of which were light and airy, open and breezy.

The palace containing the Ivory Throne seemed to prefer not to use walls or windows when it didn't have to. Most of the rooms were open on one side, furniture continuing into the outdoor area as though the atmosphere hadn't changed at all. And truly, it hadn't. Some magic kept the heat of the desert at bay, keeping the whole place at a consistently cool and comfortable temperature. But it brought the desert inside as well, in other ways. Carved from sandstone, this palace was not competing with nature, nor was it a refuge from it. It was one with its environment, capitalizing on the harsh vastness of the desert to bring out the beauty within the biome itself. It was an architectural wonder, a palace fit for the living gods within it.

I could have wandered the halls for hours, brushing my fingers over that smooth sandstone, eyeing every vine and bloom which boasted the Fae's ability to create life where it did not thrive naturally, appreciating the sculptures and art adorning the walls and archways. But Semyaza was impatient with her role as attendant and hustled us into a room while muttering something about not keeping the Queen waiting. So I left the beauty of the estate behind and trudged forward into whatever the Queen of the Ivory Throne had waiting.

Chapter Ten
A Feast Fit For A Queen

Less than half an hour later, I stood in front of an enormous, gold-plated mirror wearing an exact replica of the white gossamer gowns that Sophierial and Semyaza had been wearing. Semyaza had scrubbed me clean before magicking my blonde strands into some lifted style of the court and smacking my face with a pouf of white powder until I looked like an innocent cherub. Pleased with herself, she had left Cass and I alone in the dressing room and gone to inform Sophierial we were ready.

She hadn't so much as touched Cass. Whether that was out of respect for the Bone Court or because she was terrified of the darker Fae, I wasn't certain. Now Cass was walking up behind me with a grimace.

"You look just like them," she said.

To a mortal, it might have been a compliment. Did I look like Aphrodite, the sexual goddess of love and beauty? Maybe Artemis, the innocent virgin goddess of the moon? But to me, I simply looked ridiculous. Like a bride still clinging to the mast of her chastity on a ship that had sailed long ago. I frowned.

"I thought you said I shouldn't wear a court's color until I had decided to be a part of it," I recalled, wrinkling my nose at the fabric as I lifted it with a finger.

"Good listener," Cass said, sucking her teeth.

"So why would she dress me in white?"

"To claim you," Cass muttered and then added, with a shrug, "and to piss Lark off."

My head swiveled so that my eyes snapped to hers.

"I can fix it," Cass whispered conspiratorially, her eyes twinkling with mischief, "if you want. Unless you prefer to look every bit the chaste virgin."

"How?" I asked.

She snapped a finger and the dress changed. I changed. My lips, now a deep cherry red, parted in surprise. Kohl lined my eyes, making them intoxicatingly dark. The pale powder was gone from my skin, replaced with a thin glittery shimmer over my natural skin tone. And the dress. It was now a shimmering gray, still light so as not to offend our host but most definitively not white, and the billowing sleeves were gone. Instead, it hung over my shoulders in two thick straps that dipped low to expose my cleavage and disappeared entirely in the back. The skirt was mostly the same. Only now, there was a long slit in the left side all the way up to my thigh. I knew without testing the theory that it would expose my entire leg when I walked. And my shoes. The simple satin ballerina flats were gone, replaced with shimmering silver stilettos. My eyes widened in shock.

"Too much?" Cass asked, biting a nail. "The shoes can take some getting used to."

"I've been a working woman for forty years," I told her. "I can walk in heels."

Cass grinned.

"You look delicious," she purred, gripping me by the shoulders and looking into my reflection with me. "You look... like us."

Something stirred in my chest at that and I pushed it aside immediately. I shouldn't feel a little flutter of pride in looking like them. I shouldn't even be standing among them. I shouldn't even be here.

"Lark told me you could take me back," I said then, my smile having vanished. "If I want."

Cass' smile faltered as well. But she held my gaze.

"I could," she told me then. "Any time you want."

She waited. For me to give the command, for me to beg her to take me home. Maybe I should have. Maybe I should want to return to the university, to my uncle, more than I did. Maybe I would drown in guilt if I stayed here any longer. But this court and these people. I'd been here for less than forty-eight hours and I'd already learned more about the Fae than I ever could have hoped to back in the mortal plane. I owed it to myself, to academia, and in fact, to my uncle, to learn everything they could teach me before I returned. And not only that but I suspected that a certain DAA agent would await my return with questions I didn't want to answer. Not yet.

"I'm starving," I told Cass instead and her smile was back, spreading across her lips as she stuck out an arm and I wrapped mine around it.

Semyaza was not pleased when we finally emerged. That graceful smile of hers disappeared the moment she laid eyes on me. But I kept my head held high as I walked arm in arm with Cass all the way across the manor to the dining hall.

Sophierial was already inside. She and Lark were speaking too quietly for us to hear from outside so Cass and I stepped into the dining hall.

I turned to Sophierial and Lark. Partly because I could feel the goddess' disapproving glare on me from the moment I entered. But also because I was being burned from the inside out by the penetrating gaze of the Fae beside her. He took his time, starting with my face, the darkened eyes, the red lips, then sliding down to my exposed shoulders, my generous cleavage, the cinched waist of the gown, and down my thigh to my stiletto heels. His jaw clenched, his dark eyes flaring silver for the briefest second. I blinked at him, chest heaving.

"Sit, sit," Sophierial was instructing us, having gathered enough grace to look past my rebellious appearance. "Before it all grows too cold, now."

Lark crossed the room in a few long strides, pulling out my chair for me. I nodded graciously and gathered my dress to sit myself. When I bent forward, Lark's gaze found my open back and I heard the intake of breath as he stiffened beside me. Heart hammering in my chest, I kept my eyes away from his, worried I might melt to the core if I looked at him one more time.

But then he moved away to pull Cass' chair out for her and I could breathe again. Cass muttered a thanks to her brother as he stepped away.

"Refuge," Sophierial began speaking as Lark took the seat between myself and our esteemed hostess, "is not a status given to just anyone."

Her gaze drifted to me before returning to Lark.

"We are aware that the rules of our city hold certain advantages for those who would wish to do us, or any on the Immortal Plane, harm," she continued, her tone firm, formal. "Those who wish to pursue Refuge within our gates must prove that they are fleeing imminent danger, that they cannot resolve their issues peacefully without our interference, and that they will abide by our rules while they remain within the city walls."

Her gaze flicked to me again and I bristled.

"Furthermore," she continued, "you must convince our council to approve such Refuge."

"Or the Queen," Lark corrected her as he reached for his wine. "You can supersede your council's decision when the decision is one concerning a royal member of another court."

"For you and your sister, yes. But your friend—"

"There is nothing you can say that will convince me that a mortal is not always in imminent danger simply for their presence in our realm."

"Even so."

"My father told me centuries ago that you sought an alliance between our people."

The Queen's elegant smile faltered then. I tried not to gape at the word centuries.

"Is that something you still seek?" Lark asked, swirling the deep mahogany liquid in his glass, sniffing it, as if he were discussing something no more important than the weather or the latest fashions.

"I have been advised," Sophierial replied, slowly, choosing her words carefully, "that an alliance with your people would be unwise."

"Because we are evil. Because we delight in spirits and shadows and carnal pleasures of the flesh, yes?"

I froze at the last, lowering my head so that I might not blush myself to death right here in front of a Fae Queen.

"Because you cannot be trusted," she argued, narrowing her gaze, offended.

"Oh, I agree," Lark replied, finally raising his gaze to her. "But neither can you."

The air felt more charged somehow. Cass was eating politely, staring down at her plate and hardly moving. Sophierial and Lark were locked in a silent staring contest. Nobody moved, hardly at all, and yet I felt it, the shift. Magic readying to be loosed if necessary. The skin of my arms prickled with goosebumps and I took a deep breath in preparation.

"Which one is it?" Sophierial asked then, breaking the silence and the tension. "Your brother or sister?"

Lark's jaw tensed but he answered, "Both."

Sophierial nodded absentmindedly, turning her attention to the food on the table, lost in thought.

"And would this be considered interfering?"

"I came to you myself. This course is my action. You will not be held accountable."

"The last time you came to me, Canis, you were banished for half a century," she reminded him and I looked up at him but he seemed unfazed by the remark.

"So how much worse could it get?" he asked.

Sophierial stared at him for a minute and then burst into melodious laughter. She cackled for so long that Cass joined in, although uncomfortably. Tears sprung from the Queen's eyes and she wiped them away with a pale finger, still smiling as she turned back to him.

"I've always liked you, Canis," she said then, regaining control of herself as she waved her arms and a second course sprung from beyond the walls, drifting through the air and settling over the nearly empty plates of cheese and grapes. "Your heart is not so dark as your father's. And you've always had a good sense of humor."

Cass grinned at that, far more relieved now that the mood of this dinner had seemed to take a considerable turn for the better. I couldn't help but smile myself.

"And the mortal," Sophierial called out suddenly. "What's the story with her?"

"The mortal," Lark drawled, his voice a low growl, "has a voice and can speak for herself."

I blinked at him and then cleared my throat, dabbing my lips with my napkin and setting it aside.

"I'm not completely mortal," I confessed. "Lark and I met healing a rift in my realm."

Lark's eyes were on me again but I made a concerted effort not to notice as I stared straight back at Sophierial who was examining me over the rim of her wineglass.

"Not completely mortal?" she asked, eyebrow quirked in curiosity.

"Ren is half Fae," Cass explained, somehow sensing that I couldn't bring myself to say the words.

I gave her a soft smile of gratitude and looked back down at my plate. It was foolish, I knew that, and weak. Sophierial could sense that as well. I knew she could. But I had spent a lifetime denying half of my existence and the last forty-eight hours being hated because of the other half. I would always be "the mortal" here just as I would always be something other, something unnatural there. It was just easier to hate what you didn't understand, what you feared or despised. And I was at least half of that for someone no matter where I went. I should have been used to it by now. I would never belong here or there. I would never belong anywhere.

"Half Fae," Sophierial muttered a moment later, her eyes narrowing in her examination of me. "Fascinating."

"As delightful as this evening has been," Lark remarked, setting his glass down with a tad more force than was strictly necessary, drawing our hostess' attention back to him, "the three of us have had a very trying journey and it would be much appreciated if you would allow us to retire for the evening."

"Of course," Sophierial replied, sitting back in her chair and blinking as if stunned that she had momentarily forgotten her hospitable manners. "Semyaza! Barachiel!"

She clapped and two of her sentries appeared. One male and one female.

"As you know," Sophierial began, her tone taking on a matronly lilt, "our court has rules we expect all guests to abide by. Therefore, men and women will stay in opposite halls. Any fraternizing and our agreement is void. Semyaza and Barachiel will show you to your rooms when you are ready. I thank you all for a lovely meal and such entertaining company. Canis, a pleasure as always."

With that, the Queen of the Court of Light and Life swept from the room, her sentries standing at attention as her long white train floated past them and disappeared down the hall. Then they followed her out, likely waiting in the hallway beyond for us to emerge and request our rooms.

"What about Rook?" I asked since no one else seemed concerned enough to voice the question.

"Rook," Lark began, looking from Cass to me, "will be fine. He knows the city better than any of us. He knows how to stay hidden for now. Cass can shadowstep out to him whenever she needs to."

"It doesn't seem right for us to be staying here, like this," I said, gesturing at the enormous feast before us, "while he's out there on the streets."

Lark cocked his head to the side but Cass smiled.

"That's sweet of you to worry about him," Cass said kindly, "but I assure you, Rook will do just fine for himself. For now, we need to worry about staying alive in the Court of Life."

Lark nodded his agreement.

"I thought you said it was forbidden to kill here," I said.

"What I should have said," Lark began, leaning forward, "was that it was forbidden to get caught."

Chapter Eleven
A Morning Prayer

Cass didn't seem to mind sharing a room with me. It was made easier by the fact that the enormous room had two sets of everything contained within it. Two Queen-sized beds stood side by side with about three feet of space between them, two full sized armoires, two dressers, two closets, and a conversation pit of cushions and fluffy pillows in the center. Our washroom was just off to Cass' side, complete with a porcelain claw foot tub and every modern luxury a palace could afford. On my side, the wall was gone completely, open to the vast expanse of empty sand leading right up to the cliff wall. It was all white, of course, right on brand.

"I'm starting to doubt what you said before about not all the courts taking their color so seriously," I told Cass that night as I emerged from the washroom after having taken a proper, unrushed bath and sliding into a set of silk pajamas that were exactly my size. After a long day, that felt like the best bit of magic I'd seen.

Cass snorted at my joke, setting aside the bottle of purple nail polish she had been using to touch up her toes. A moment later, the bottle disappeared entirely with a snap of her fingers.

"The Wanderers aren't the worst. I'd say it's tied between these guys and the Rivals," she told me.

"The Rivals?" I asked, cocking a brow as I slid under the warmest comforter I'd ever felt.

"Red," she told me.

"You aren't including your court among the obsessors?"

She looked up at me, raising a brow in question. I rolled my eyes.

"Oh, come on," I teased. "The constant black, all of you. It's like you don't possess another color in your wardrobe at all."

"We don't," she said with a shrug. "Besides, black is slimming."

I chuckled.

"Lark and I," she continued after a moment, "we have to wear it. It and nothing else because of who we are. For Rook, it's a choice but whether he does it because of his black soul or because of his loyalty to Lark, I don't know."

"What did he do?"

Cass hesitated. My eyelids were already drooping but I waited to see if she would answer, anyway.

"Rook is... from here, originally," she answered after a moment. "He was born in this court. Let's just say that the good folk of the Light Court don't take it very well when someone leaves."

"So why did he?"

Cass' eyes were on me then. I felt them burning against my skin almost as badly as her brother's always seemed to. I was prying, I knew, but I was desperate to know more about the people I seemed to have allied myself with.

"Something you should remember," she said then, her voice turning serious. "People who claim to be the most good are also usually the most hypocritical."

I didn't have time to process that in my exhausted state before I fell asleep in the most comfortable bed I'd ever laid in.

The morning came without warning and I woke up feeling as though I'd never slept. After the most grueling forty-eight hours of my life, it turned out I would need more than five of sleep. But we didn't have the time because Semyaza strode in at seven in the morning, flinging our curtains wide and letting in the morning sun. Cass grumbled and buried herself in her sheets. I echoed the sentiment, trying to throw an arm over my eyes to shield them. But Semyaza wasn't having it.

"You'll miss your morning prayers," she chided, pulling back my covers and grabbing my arms to help me upright. I just watched her, confused and half asleep.

Prayers? Who did gods pray to?

I half expected Cass to laugh and throw a pillow at our meddling sentry but instead she rose from her bed reluctantly and shuffled off to the washroom. After a moment of poking and prodding from Semyaza, I followed.

I didn't dare ask for an explanation the whole time we freshened up and dressed. It seemed like requesting such a thing might be offensive, to Semyaza at least. So I just brushed my hair and dabbed on a bit of makeup, turning just in time to see Semyaza entering the washroom again, another white gossamer monstrosity draped over her arm. This one was true to toga fashion, with a strap over one arm, leaving the other exposed, and cascading down the legs to trail on the floor below.

She raised a brow but Cass snapped her fingers and another gown of shimmering gray appeared on my body. It was loose and flowy, much like the toga, but with embellishments that I had a feeling the sentries of the Life Court might consider vain.

Semyaza's face screwed up into an expression of rage and she tossed the white gown on the floor, ballerina slippers sliding out from beneath it and skittering across the marble, before storming from the room in a dignified huff.

"She just keeps trying, doesn't she?" I asked with a sigh.

"She will," Cass replied in warning, striding up to me where I stood in front of the mirror. "Hold your ground. You don't have to be anyone you don't wish to be here, Ren."

Cass wore a dress as well, this one black and sparkling but covering all the sensitive areas and trailing to the floor like mine.

"Is that why Rook left?" I asked, prying further, again, than I should.

Cass stiffened again, so much so that I almost felt bad for asking. She was only trying to help me, after all.

"Hypocrites are hypocrites. No matter how much white they wrap themselves in or how many rules they bind to their court. It's not so different here from the mortal realm, Ren. Remember that. People lie everywhere."

I decided not to point out the fact that she hadn't answered my question about Rook at all as she took my arm and led me from the washroom.

"Prayers?" I asked in a whisper as we paused in our room for Cass to collect her shoes.

"To the sun and the moon and whatever else these people decide to worship," Cass told me with a roll of her eyes as she slid into her black stilettos, using my shoulder to keep herself upright as she did and I wondered why she didn't just use her magic to transport them onto her feet. "We aren't active participants in the religion but the Queen's guests not attending morning prayers would be a slap in the face of the Court."

I nodded in understanding and followed Cass out of our room into the hallway beyond.

"Besides, it will be a good chance to catch up with Lark," she told me. "If my brother has a plan, he's been entirely too close-lipped about it. I intend to loosen them."

I couldn't help my smirk at the determined look on Cass' face as we made our way down the hall, joining the others flowing in from all areas of the palace, all with long flowing hair, all dressed in wispy white.

We made our way, like a herd of cattle, to the courtyard in the center of the palace, open to the elements above and teeming with all manner of flora and fauna that I knew for a fact rarely thrived in the desert. Magic was at work here.

It was easy to see why something like this might be considered holy. Scattered amongst the fertile beds of soil and potted plants were porcelain statues of male and female Fae that must have lived millennia ago. Or still were, I reminded myself, shivering at the thought. Immortality was not a concept that I was quite comfortable with yet. But it was a wonder. What these people must have seen, what they knew.

Maybe worshipping the sun wasn't so crazy after all.

Cass followed a line of people as it branched off and circled around the back. When the man in front of us stopped walking, turned toward the nearest statue, and knelt to his knees, we did the same. I had a brief moment of disappointment that I would get my pristine dress dirty in the mud beneath me but it faded when I remembered this wasn't my dress. And these weren't my people.

"It took you long enough," Cass snapped below her breath and I turned to see that Lark had followed us down our line.

He was kneeling next to me, so close that our elbows were touching as well as our thighs. My face burned and I lowered my head, pretending to be lost in reverent prayer, to hide it.

"I need you to go to Rook after breakfast," Lark whispered back to his sister without looking at her. From afar, it would look as though he were simply bowing his head in prayer. I readjusted myself to look the same and bumped into him with my hip.

"Why?" Cass hissed back.

"It isn't safe for him to stay here. Sophierial has her suspicions. And I need him to go to the Court of Rivals, anyway."

"Rivals?" Cass asked, her gaze snapping toward her brother briefly before she remembered her prayers.

"Taurus never came for me," Lark explained. "He could have but he didn't. If I can reason with him—"

"He'll tear Rook apart."

"Rook can hold his own."

"He nearly killed Ursa."

"Ursa's intentions were murderous herself."

"Lark—"

"I just need to know, Cass. If the time comes, I need to know how many of my siblings I actually have to kill."

She fell silent at that. We all did. I shuffled back and forth on my knees, trying to ease some of the pressure on my joints, quite certain a rock was lodged somewhere in the sand beneath me. No one else was fidgeting, though, so I grit my teeth and fell still. Did these people not have knee joints either? Perhaps I should have attended more mass with my uncle. At least then I would be used to this infernal kneeling.

"I'll go to Rook," she promised after a moment. "But you need to tell me how long you intend to stay here."

"As long as it takes."

"As long as what takes, Lark?"

"The Queen is open to a partnership with the Court of Blood and Bone. I just have to... woo her."

"So now we are fraternizing?" Cass asked with a sigh, rolling her eyes at Sophierial's chosen term. Lark grimaced.

"We're doing what we've always done, sister," he replied, his voice low, dangerous. "We're doing what's best for our people."

Neither of them spoke again through the duration of the morning prayers and, as hard as I tried to focus on the rituals taking place in front of me for academic purposes, I couldn't help but think about what had been said amongst my companions. Fraternizing with the Queen. And Lark hadn't denied it.

It shouldn't have mattered. He was free to fraternize with whomever he wished. But for some reason, I couldn't help but be miserably irritable for the rest of the day.

Cass left after breakfast, as instructed, and didn't return until lunch. I spent the time in between pacing my room, bored but afraid to emerge and face Semyaza. I tried not to think about Rook, alone in a city he seemed to have a shaky past with, or Cass shadowstepping in and out of the palace in a way that was likely against the rules, or Lark doing God knew what with God knew who. I just sat and waited. And then waited some more.

Chapter Twelve
A Friend Indeed

Two Weeks Later

"There are three major courts in the immortal plane," Cass was telling me two weeks after our hushed discussion at my first morning prayer ritual.

She had taken on the job of educating me about her people and their customs after Lark had apparently told her, in some conversation I had not been privy to, that it might be important for me to know this information if I was going to take part in morning prayers and holy feasts as I already had in the short weeks I had been here.

Lark had all but disappeared entirely. I hadn't seen him once since the day he proclaimed he was doing what was best for his people, not even at the morning prayers. Whatever he had managed to say to the Queen seemed to exclude him from all the mundane rituals and rites that the rest of us had to abide by.

"The Court of Blood and Bone, their color is black, that's us. The Court of Light and Life, that's this court and white, obviously. And the Court of Peace and Pride, their color is brown. Our court is at the southernmost tip of our realm. This court is at the north. All the minor courts fall in line between us and the Court of Peace and Pride encompasses us all, wrapping around us on every side except the south."

"What's in the south?" I interrupted, looking up from the notepad I had sitting on my legs where they were crossed beneath me in the conversation pit of our room.

"Hellscape," she answered.

I hesitated, my pen hovering over the page as my mouth fell open.

"Hellscape?" I repeated, stunned.

Cass nodded slowly from across from me where she was reclining, lazing on a mountain of cushions she had compiled for this very purpose.

"Yes," she told me. "It's a dark and desolate strip of land far to the south, even farther south than the Bone Court, where no Fae dwell. It has one entrance, the key to which is held by the appointed Warden, but no one ever comes or goes except to check up on things."

"Things?"

"Cerberus, Hydra, Minotaurs, Dragons," she listed and my eyes bulged more and more with every word she spoke. "All the nasty little beasts we banished from your world thousands of years ago and brought here with us to protect you from. They stay locked up in Hellscape and the Warden checks from time to time just to make sure they're still there."

"Who has dominion over Hellscape?"

"We do. The Bone Court always appoints the Warden and they always appoint one of their heirs. That's why everyone else thinks we're monsters, because we're in charge of literal monsters," she told me and then, a moment later, her head popped up and she looked at me. "Well, that's not the only reason."

I frowned. Right. Killing your own blood to take the throne might also have something to do with that perception.

"There are six minor courts between the Court of Light and Life and the Court of Blood and Bone," she continued her lesson, dropping her head back down as she spoke. "They are a rainbow. Red, Orange, Yellow, Green, Blue, and Purple. You know that orange is the Court of Wanderers. They are the travelers, the ones tasked with holding the portal to the mortal realm. As such, they're also a big location for trade, specifically luxury goods like jewels and textiles. Above them is red. That is the Court of Rivals. You may have heard us talking about that being where Taurus is now. It's directly below the Court of Light and Life because the Ivory Throne is always trying to keep a handle on what goes on there. If you think the Court of Bone is a place of debauchery..."

Cass trailed off, snorting.

"They fight to the death for fun there," she said. "Just throw two Fae in the ring and let them tear each other apart. It's barbaric. Though the pleasure houses can be fun if you know where to look."

My cheeks colored and she grinned before turning back to stare at the ceiling and continue.

"The yellow court," she muttered, as if reminding herself of where she had stopped. "That's the Court of Blessings. They are known for their healing prowess. A lot of aura balancing and meditation in the yellow court. Very zen. The green. They are the Court of Friends. Quite the wholesome bunch, that one. And very bohemian. They're all about nature and love and prioritizing relationships. You'll never meet a nicer Fae than the ones in the Court of Friends. Below that is blue. That'll be the Court of Scholars."

I perked up at that.

"The Grand Library is there and a university of sorts though no Fae considers themselves a student. Anyone with something to research ends up there. They have knowledge gathered spanning millennia. They have the skulls of the very first Cerberus there."

My lips parted in surprise.

"Then purple," Cass said, moving on. "The Court of Dreamers. Those are the artists. The musicians and performers, painters and sculptors, and that's where the Dream Weaver lives."

"The Dream Weaver?" I asked.

"She's this old crone who can interpret dreams. Puts you to sleep and walks right into your subconscious. I've heard she can be very effective but I've never gone to her myself. I'd like to keep my thoughts mine and mine alone."

I smiled at that.

"So Rook," I said then and Cass' smile faltered as she glanced my way. "He was born here but he left and joined the Court of Blood and Bone. Is that common? Leaving the court one is originally born in?"

"It's not uncommon," she answered thoughtfully, sitting up to give me her full intention. "But his was. Giving up the light for the dark, that's not a choice one typically makes willingly. It's more common in the minor courts. Maybe a dreamer is born amongst the scholars. Maybe a healer is born among the Wanderers. Better to let them move than be miserable their whole lives. Better for them to find a place where they can be who they truly are, to use their fates-given gifts to their highest potential."

"Did Rook find that place?"

"Rook should tell his own story."

Cass stood up, readjusting her short skirt, and I took the hint.

"What's your story?" I asked then, changing the subject from Rook.

"I'm a Princess of Darkness," she replied with a shrug. "My story isn't much more than that."

"You have three siblings all trying to kill each other."

"Allegedly."

"Cass, there's more to your story."

She crossed her arms and narrowed her gaze.

"Is it my story you're after or Lark's?" She asked me after a moment.

My cheeks blazed red.

"Yours," I informed her though I couldn't deny that the realization that her story would likely be entangled with his, as his sister, had crossed my mind and she seemed to have sensed that.

"I'm the youngest," she told me anyway. "And all I've ever wanted, ever, my whole life, was for my older siblings to get along. And for my father to be not so much of an ass."

I snorted. She smiled too but then the light in her eyes dimmed and that smile turned into a frown.

"I've known, since the moment I was capable of understanding the words, that eventually my family was all going to kill each other. It's our birthright. And I hate it. I hate it almost as much as I hate the stupid politics and the way we let everyone believe we're so evil, so wicked. We aren't," she said and I waited for her to continue because it seemed like she had more to say. Not for me, but for herself. "Rook came to us, not because of what we represented, but because we allowed him to. The minor courts, they were afraid of making the Court of Life angry. The Court of Peace and Pride is overpopulated enough already. But my brothers welcomed him with open arms and fought my dad tooth and nail to let him stay. Even Ursa defended him when some emissary tried to put a hit out on him. Because that's what we do in my family. We protect each other. Until we don't. But now, because he came to us, because we made him a part of our family, now every Fae from every other court is going to look at him as though he's got some secret withering away his soul. I just—I don't want the same thing to happen to you. If you decide to stay, I mean."

Stay.

There it was. The question she wasn't asking me. The one I hadn't even allowed myself to ask me. Was I going to stay with them? Was I even welcome to stay with them? For Cass, it seemed that I was. But for Lark? I might have said yes two weeks ago. But this new distance between us had me wondering and I wouldn't stay where I wasn't wanted. But even if I was, even if they all welcomed me with open arms as they had Rook...

"Could you get a letter to the mortal plane?" I asked her then. "If I wrote one."

Her brow furrowed in confusion but she nodded.

Then I walked to the desk on the opposite side of the room, pulled out some stationary, and wrote a three sentence note to my uncle.

I'm safe. I'm in the immortal realm. I'll write again when I'm able.

Then I wrote his name on the front and crossed the room and handed it to Cass. She took one look at the name and the note vanished into thin air. I jumped. I would never get used to how easy these things were for them. But then I met her eyes and reached out to grip her arm.

"You aren't wicked, Cass," I told her. "You've been kinder to me than most mortals I've met in my lifetime. You've welcomed me as if I was one of your own. You've taken the time to teach me about your people, your world, and you've made me feel comfortable in a place I never even thought I could survive. I look at you and I see nothing but good. No matter what the others say about you, about your court and your family, you're my friend and, frankly, you might be the best one I've ever had."

She watched me for a moment, eyes widening a fraction at my honesty.

"Was that too much?" I asked, tensing and suddenly feeling awkward. "Humans have a tendency to be more forthcoming with their emotions. Short lives and all that. I didn't—"

Before I could finish, she gripped me by the shoulders and pulled me in for a tight hug.

"Thank you," she whispered into my hair as she held me close, "friend."

Chapter Thirteen
A Breath of Fresh Air

It took another week before Cass was satisfied that I could be trusted wandering about the grounds of the palace myself without being snatched up by some sadistic Fae. It helped that the Queen had formally introduced us all as her honored guests at a holy feast just three nights prior. That had been the last time I'd seen Lark and the first time in weeks before. He had looked resplendent in his deepest black as always, looking bored at his place beside the Queen as he swirled the wine around his glass and spoke to her in low tones.

I had tried not to watch them and failed.

But now I was going on a walk through their sacred garden, needing to get out of the room for some fresh air and to escape the tedious loneliness of our room now that Cass was off on some errand that Lark had tasked her with.

So I was in a particularly foul mood that afternoon as I stared up at a statue of one of their saints, arms crossed, glaring at her and the way she reached out as if to save all lost souls.

"I was wondering where you'd gotten to."

His voice froze me to the spot. I dug my nails into my arms where they were and bit my lip hard to keep from saying something I might regret, trying to remind myself that I had no reason to be angry with him, not really.

"I went to your room but you weren't there," Lark added when I didn't respond.

I kept my gaze firmly on the statue as I replied.

"Isn't that against the rules?" I asked.

"Princes can afford to break a few rules from time to time."

He had meant it as a joke, a lighthearted mention of his status here and how ridiculous these hypocritical rules were. But I just huffed, shaking my head so that the soft waves of my honey blonde hair bounced around my shoulders. He walked around until he could see my face and took a moment to observe me, taking in my obvious irritation, my closed off body language. His eyes flicked down to where my nails were digging into the skin of my arm and back to my eyes. I tried to ignore the intensity of his observation but it only heightened my irritation until I was gritting my teeth at the audacity of it.

"You're angry with me," he said simply.

"No," I replied, shaking my head and turning away. "No, I'm not."

I strode off, needing to put some space between us, needing some distance to cool my temper. Why was I even so upset with him? Because I hadn't seen him in three weeks? As if he owed me constant attention or even an explanation for his absence? I sighed.

"You are," he persisted, watching me warily. "Why?"

It was a fair question but one I did not have a satisfactory answer for. Anything my mind brought up as a potential response sounded pathetic or desperate or both. Because why was I angry? Because he left me. Because he brought me all the way here, all the way to the Immortal Plane and then to this strange, beautiful court, only to abandon me entirely. Because he was infuriatingly difficult to puzzle out. Because one moment he would stare deeply into my eyes as if there was no one else in the world and the next he was off to some scheming and planning that didn't involve me or even an acknowledgement of my existence. Because he hadn't denied it when Cass had accused him of fraternizing with the enemy. Because that simple comment had made me lay awake for hours every night, wondering if he was somewhere off down these very halls, lying next to her in her bed, stroking her smooth, pale skin and whispering things in her ear that would make me blush to hear from his lips. All of that. All of that and more because, even though I had just met this man, this prince of darkness, this supremely powerful Fae, I was completely, utterly captivated. And I hated that. So I hated him for making me feel it.

But I couldn't tell him that. Because we barely knew each other and I would run away myself if someone I hardly knew expressed such fascination with me after such a short time spent in one another's company. So I settled with another issue, the one that had nothing to do with him. Or, at least, that's what I told myself.

"I don't know why I'm here," I said then, sitting down on a marble bench nearby, staring down at a bed of tulips so that I didn't have to look at him. "You and Cass have so much on your plate, what with your family... situation. And Rook is dealing with his history here and you both have your banishment to contend with and it's all so big and I'm so... small. And I'm a burden. And I shouldn't—"

"No," he interrupted me, his tone low and firm. He strode forward and sat beside me. Before I could react, he reached out with one finger and tipped my chin up so that I was looking into his eyes. "You are not a burden. You are not small. You are not insignificant in any way. Your life, your problems, are no less important than ours."

The whole time he spoke, he kept his fingers under my chin, his gaze burning hot upon my face. My skin heated, a faint flush creeping up my cheeks. His thumb moved lazily, almost absentmindedly, stroking my chin close to my lips. His gaze drew down to them. My breath hitched and I waited, expectant. Then he blinked and dropped his hand and the moment fizzled out between us, though I could still feel the desire coursing through him, emanating from him.

"Cass says I'm welcome here," I breathed, hardly able to summon much more than a whisper as we maintained eye contact across the narrow bench. "She says that I'm one of you now. But I'm not. Not really. I'm not one of you and I'm not one of them."

Them. He knew what I meant. Mortals. The mortal plane. My home. If I ever even really had one.

"So, where am I supposed to go?" I asked. "What am I supposed to do?"

"I don't know if you've noticed," he started and his lips spread into that mischievous smirk of his, "but none of us are welcome here. Rook and I were literally banished. Cass has forsaken everything her family stands for. As far as my father is concerned, she's dead to him."

I frowned, my heart going out to Cass, a girl the whole world thought was wicked, shunned by her own father for refusing to take part in the brutal murder of her own family.

"So if you're looking for somewhere you can belong, you might find that here, in our merry band of unwanted outcasts," he said. "If you're looking for answers to your questions, you might find those here as well. If you ever want to meet your mother, she's here."

I tensed.

"Not now," he whispered, soothing me. "But when you're ready. If you're ever ready."

I just watched him then, those dark eyes boring into my own with something like genuine concern. He didn't touch me again. But his hand twitched as though he wanted to. This dark and beautiful Fae, this Prince of the Court of Blood and Bone, this troubled brother and exiled son. He was fighting for his life and he had somehow found the time to throw me a life preserver as well.

"I'm supposed to hate you," I told him, narrowing my gaze as if in suspicion.

He chuckled, standing from the bench.

"Likewise," he said.

I cocked my head to the side, looking up at him as he glanced around the courtyard.

"Where have you been?" I asked, more out of curiosity now than anger. "I haven't seen you in weeks."

"I apologize for that," he answered with a frown and I thought he might actually mean it. "Sophierial is keeping me busier than I expected."

It was a worse punch to the gut than I expected.

"Fraternizing?" I asked, trying for a light tone, trying to make it seem like a joke.

He met my eyes with a sordid grin and I knew I'd failed. My uncle always said I got vicious when I was angry. I supposed I was about to prove his point.

"Jealous?" he asked.

I rolled my eyes.

"Not so much," I answered. "I just take my cues from you, princeling. So if you're going to break the rules, that means I can, too."

I shrugged, delighting in the way he clenched his fists when I called him princeling.

"And you have an interest in breaking that particular rule, do you?" he asked, raising a brow in challenge. But I wasn't one to back down. He would learn that eventually. Might as well be now.

"Maybe," I answered with a shrug, acting aloof. "Who knows how long I'll be staying here. It gets quite boring when Cass is away. That attendant of Sophierial's, Barachiel, was it? He's always trying to entertain me, bringing books to my room or offering to take me to the library. Perhaps I should mention I've thought of an activity more stimulating than reading."

He tried to hide it but I saw. The brief flash of annoyance, the tick of his jaw. I felt his fury, white hot and burning like a roaring fire. I grinned wide, triumphant.

"Give it a try," he shot back, turning and striding from the garden, off to do whatever he'd been doing for weeks. "Perhaps then I won't have to listen to him gripe about his duties so much."

I snorted as Lark left me sitting on a bench among the tulips.

I'd taunted him and he hadn't backed down. I could give him credit for that. Still, I couldn't help but notice, over the next few weeks, that Cass was abandoning me to my boredom far less than she had been before. And Barachiel never came to my room again. I couldn't help but experience a thrill at having gotten to the Bone Court Prince so grandly.

It was another three weeks before Cass received a note during our morning lessons and vanished without warning. She didn't return until after lunch and, when she burst into the common room where I was settled into an over sized armchair reading a book of theological theory that Semyaza had been more than thrilled to fetch for me, she wasn't alone. Lark was with her.

"What—" I started but Cass interrupted before I could finish.

"Rook's back."

I was on my feet in an instant. Six weeks. We had been here six weeks without Rook, knowing he was off somewhere trying to talk some sense into a very dangerous and volatile Fae. I couldn't hide the relief that flooded through me at Cass' words. If he was back, he was alive. Maybe the rest wouldn't be such good news. But he was alive.

"And?" I asked.

"Taurus wants to talk," Lark replied.

My eyes widened. Cass just frowned.

"And Rook?" I asked, looking between them. "How is he?"

They glanced at one another, as if stunned I would think to ask such a thing. I was equally stunned that they hadn't.

"Rook's fine," Lark answered after a moment. "I told you, Ren, he can take care of himself."

"When it comes to hiding out here," I corrected him. "But you sent him to your powerful, volatile brother alone."

"Taurus has always liked Rook more than he liked me. It was safer to send him than either of us."

"Besides, Rook can be very persuasive when he wants to be," Cass added, voice lowered.

I gaped at her tone, wondering what experience she might have with Rook's persuasiveness.

"He wants us to go to him," Lark said then and some of the hopefulness from a moment before went out of the room. "He won't set foot here. Not as long as Sophierial lives."

Cass nodded as if that was something she had expected.

"For what it's worth, he's promised not to murder me the moment I set foot in the Court of Rivals," Lark said and I just stared at him, wondering if he was joking, but his expression was entirely serious.

"And we should just take his word for it?" Cass finally snapped.

Lark took a deep breath and turned away, pacing. I got the sense that this was not the first time they'd had this argument.

"He almost killed Ursa, Lark," Cass reminded him.

"Ursa went there to kill him, Cass," Lark argued. "Rook has arranged for a peaceful meeting somewhere private. There's no honor in killing me quietly. He wouldn't do it without a crowd."

I cringed. Was that really his best argument? His brother wouldn't kill him unless it could be verified by hundreds of spectators? Suddenly, I felt ill.

"Lark—" Cass pleaded.

"Father is still alive," Lark reminded her instead, bolstering his argument with an even stronger claim. "No one should be trying to kill anyone. Not yet."

Cass looked like she wanted to say more but thought better of it and fell silent. I said nothing as well, know that there was nothing that either of us could say that would convince Lark not to give his brother this one final chance at peace, this last opportunity to do the right thing. Even though neither of them seemed particularly convinced that there was any chance he might take it.

"When do we leave?" I asked simply.

"Tomorrow."

Chapter Fourteen
A Brother's Keeper

No one seemed all that concerned about the fact that we had begged for refuge just six weeks ago and now were already leaving together to visit one of the most powerful Fae in the realm who, coincidentally, was half of the reason we had needed refuge in the first place. In fact, I wasn't certain the Queen of the Court of Light and Life had been informed of the reason for our swift departure at all. Which was why I kept my mouth firmly shut as Cass and I left our room that morning and strode, not toward the common room, but toward the gates.

Lark was already awaiting us there, milling about impatiently.

"What took you so long?" he asked through gritted teeth, on edge, when we reached him.

"Semyaza wouldn't stop fussing over her gown," Cass said with a roll of her eyes and a jerk of her head in my direction.

It was true. Semyaza had been particularly irritable this morning, spending over an hour brushing through my hair and selecting my attire for the day. She had finally given into the idea of gray and had brought me a gown of gray chiffon so fluffy that I could barely put my arms down. But I hadn't dared to complain, not when she was finally coming around to the realization that I would not be wearing white while staying within their walls and not while she was muttering under her breath the whole time about all the work it had taken to find a gown that wasn't white, how she had needed to trade for some dye in the market and oh, how she hated going to the market.

"She shouldn't be wearing a gown at all," Lark growled, annoyed.

Cass just raised a manicured brow and he shook his head, frowning.

"Fine. I'll whip something up," she muttered, turning toward me and cocking her head to the side, thoughtful. A moment later, she cast a glance over her shoulder at her brother. "Unless you'd like to strip it off her yourself."

His jaw tensed. His gaze flicked to me once for the briefest of moments in which I thought perhaps he might actually be considering it. But then he loosed a breath in an exaggerated sigh.

"You always get so crude when you're nervous, Cass," he accused.

"I do not get crude," she argued, waving a hand so that my muted gray gown transformed into a glittering cascade of silver, tight tunic and tight pants beneath with shining silver combat boots laced halfway up my calf. "I am always crude."

I snorted but Lark just pointed, exasperated.

"Go," he barked.

Cass rolled her eyes but reached for me. I tried my best to pretend I wasn't gritting my teeth so hard they might shatter. The jaunt confirmed my suspicions that I still wasn't used to this whole shadowstepping business but at least I didn't go reeling off a cliff on the other side this time. Though Rook, who had apparently been waiting for us on the other side, did grip me firmly by the elbow to keep me from falling as Cass disappeared again.

"It's not getting better," I said through gritted teeth.

"It won't," he said simply, negating everything he had told me before.

"I'm glad you're alright."

His gaze snapped to mine, apparently shocked by the admission. I just turned away and finally chanced a glance up at the city before me. My lips parted in stunned surprise.

Where the Court of Light and Life had been hidden in the depths of a valley, its shining gold spires not daring to peek over the cliff's edge in perfect, defensible position, the Court of Rivals was in open desert. The sand was not so white here but more of a burnt orange color and grittier, hot to the touch. But it turned to rough stone the closer you got to the city.

The city itself was not red at all, as I had been expecting it to be. And not everyone wore red. Some did, favoring a crimson shade mostly, but some wore gray or beige, more neutral, earthy tones to cool in the warm climate. The buildings were all in the style of a Spanish Villa, clay walls and tile roofs, all neutral, earth-tones as well. The city itself was massive and sprawling so far that I couldn't see the end of it on any side. Lights flashed from the streets, illuminating the sky above, and I could hear raucous sounds of music and laughter even from this far away.

I pulled my gaze from the enormous iron gates and looked back to Rook who still hovered at my side.

"Rivals," I said, lost in thought. "What does that mean? What does this Court stand for?"

"All manners of debauchery," Rook answered me, pumping his brows suggestively as a wicked grin split his lips.

I rolled my eyes.

"It's named for the fighting pits," Lark drawled as he and Cass appeared behind us.

I looked back to where he was striding toward us before turning to face the city with a frown.

"Fighting pits?" I asked.

"They're centuries old. From the days of colosseums and battles of blood feuds. Men volunteer to fight to the death, to gain the status of warrior."

My eyes widened as I thought the word I was beginning to realize I thought of often in this realm. Barbaric.

"They've been banned everywhere else," Lark continued to explain. "But the Court of Rivals is..."

He trailed off.

"Debauchery," Cass intoned, using Rook's word for emphasis.

"Yes," Lark agreed.

And then we were walking toward the city in a way that made it feel like I might be walking to my doom. I couldn't stop thinking of that word as we walked. Debauchery. Fighting pits where men voluntarily risked their lives just to be considered some mighty warrior. I remembered Cass telling me about that now, in our lessons, and was embarrassed that I hadn't put it together sooner. With that memory came another. She had mentioned pleasure houses as well. I thought I might understand Rook's choice of terms even better than before.

"If anyone asks you if you have the time, don't answer," Cass muttered under her breath as we passed through the massive iron gates.

Ahead, Rook howled with laughter. My face was heating, despite having no idea what she was talking about, as I turned to her.

"Why?" I asked out of curiosity.

"It's code," she said. "It's how they ask you if you're... available for payment."

My eyes widened and I clamped my mouth shut as if terrified of what other code I might unwittingly agree to if I dared to speak in this court.

"If anyone asks you the time," Lark growled from behind us, "you come straight to me."

I felt that pulsating power radiating from him once again and fought the urge to shiver at the sheer rigidness of it. Cass chanced a look back at her brother, her lips drawn down into a frown for some reason that I couldn't fathom. I was too focused on my steps, walking through this city of sin while keeping my eyes out for anyone who might have seedier intentions than I. That pulsing power kept at my back though, urging me onward through the cracking streets and stumbling masses.

I could see and feel the others' power as well, of course, but each of them were different and none were like Lark's. His was a force. Dark and unyielding, pulsing and pressing against the confines of his very being as if every moment he were fighting to contain it, as if he simply released it rather than having to summon it when needed.

Cass' power was more of a steady thrum hovering just beneath her skin, glowing outward in a constant shine that made her appear even more radiant than she already was. Rook's power wasn't so immediately obvious, so overpowering. I suspected it was because he wasn't Fae royalty like Lark and Cass. But it was there and had its own unique signature. It was sharp around the edges and jutted outward from him in moments of stress or anger. It was fascinating, watching them, seeing their powers surge and retract. But Lark's. His was practically overwhelming. I marveled at how he kept it all bottled up inside all the time.

"Gambling dens," Rook announced as if he were some sort of Court of Rivals tour guide. He nodded down a crowded street we were passing full of bright lights and people running back and forth, smoke curling from the open windows.

"And bars," Cass added, nodding toward the opposite street.

"And that way?" I asked, pointing ahead of us.

"The fights," Rook answered.

I dropped my finger to my side, looking toward Lark.

"And that's where your brother is?" I asked.

"He regards himself as the immortal realm's finest warrior," he answered with a shrug. "Never lost a match."

The breath went out of me. Lark's brother, the one who would be hell bent on slaughtering him the moment their father died, was the Court of Rivals' best fighter? My jaw went slack.

"Never lost in the ring," Rook corrected, seeing the concern on my face.

"That's because the only people who get into that ring are foolish, pigheaded assholes drowning in toxic masculinity and unearned bravado," Cass snapped, crossing her arms as she glared at the establishments as if they had personally wronged her.

"Tell us what you really think, Cass," Rook said sarcastically in the silence that followed her declaration.

"I think my brother is a fool. I think he fights in this stupid arena because he knows he can win and he doesn't have a care in the world about whether or not it's actually fair to put up some Court of Rivals nobody against a member of the Bone Court's royal family. I think he's a coward and a prick."

It was quiet once she had finished. Rook stared at her with a raised brow. But then Lark chuckled, putting a hand on Cass' shoulder, and everyone relaxed.

"And I think you shouldn't say any of that when we meet with him, sister," Lark said.

Rook grinned but Cass just kept glaring at the fighting dens as we walked toward them. No one got in our way. No one tried to stop us. Hardly anyone even noticed us as we passed, making our way with the rest of the crowd toward the largest area at the end of the street.

I tried my best not to feel small and suffocated amidst the growing throng of powerful Fae but I couldn't help but feel like a fish thrown into a tank of sharks. Though none of them were looking at me. They were too busy standing on tiptoes, craning their necks to see into the ring. But I was far more interested in the spectators than the fighters. The crowd itself was diverse. Some with skin as white as porcelain, others a glowing ebony. Hair and eyes of every shade imaginable, even those which I wasn't sure occurred naturally in this realm. Tattoos and piercings adorned bodies more often than not and various styles of clothes were present as well. From shirts cropped above bare midriffs to long, flowing shapeless robes, every type of Fae I could imagine crowded the gates just outside of the arena, clamoring for their chance to enter.

Only my group appeared unenthusiastic. Rook's eyes were darting about the crowd, less from excitement and more to be on his guard in case anything might happen. Cass was muttering constantly about how much she hated this place and how ridiculous it all was. Lark just stood as still as a statue, jaw tensed, eyes glazed over as if lost in thought. And I, well, I was certain I had the appearance of a deer caught in the metaphorical headlights.

But then the gates opened and the crowd surged forward, rushing us into the arena whether we wanted to or not.

We found seats near the front, reserved, apparently for high-ranking noblemen and families of the fighters. I supposed we were both. Or, at least, my companions were.

A group of girls was chattering nearby about the champion fighting today and I heard Taurus' name on their lips along with the words sexy and powerful. The amused grin on Rook's face told me he had heard them as well and, when our eyes met, we couldn't help but both snort. Neither of our companions seemed to notice. Cass' and Lark's gazes remained on the arena where someone was emerging slowly from the darkness at the other end.

It was starting.

I fell silent, held captive by the display as a man strode into the ring, raising his arms high above his head and grinning broadly. The crowd erupted into cheers while, all around me, my companions tensed. I turned back to the man and narrowed my eyes in examination. Sleek black hair cut just above his shoulders, cruel, dark eyes, the unnatural beauty of a royal Fae. So this was Taurus.

And he was naked.

I blinked in surprise as my eyes traveled from his broad, muscled chest to... lower.

"Should have warned you about that," Rook said with a grin. Mischief was dancing in his eyes as he barely held back his laughter. I cut him a glare and turned back to the ring as his opponent emerged, just as enormous, just as naked.

From somewhere in the distance, someone shouted a word I didn't understand but it seemed to have been the signal to start.

Taurus' opponent charged him first and Taurus waited patiently, facing him, bouncing on the balls of his feet. There were a series of moves and countermoves, punches and dodges. They were moving so fast that I could hardly keep track of them even from my good vantage point. His opponent landed a blow and bright red bloomed from Taurus' nose. He wiped it away and charged again and they were back to landing blows upon one another. The crowd cheered louder than thunder, their stomping feet shaking the stands so that little flecks of dust rained down on those on the lower levels who hardly noticed as they leaned forward, out of their seats, and jeered at one man or the other.

"Why doesn't he just—" I started without looking away but Rook seemed to expect my question before I asked it.

"Magic is forbidden in the ring," he told me. "It's a test of strength, not of blood."

I didn't have time to respond before Taurus punched upward, sending his opponent reeling, and then drove down with his other fist, pummeling him into the dirt. He did not move again. Not even when Taurus strode over to the untouched weapon's rack, lifted a dagger from the display, and went back to slit his throat.

Horrified, I closed my eyes and looked away as the crowd went berserk.

"It's done," Rook whispered kindly but the intent in his tone was clear. I needed to look. I couldn't appear weak. Not in this crowd.

So I opened my eyes and turned forward again in time to find Taurus now stalking straight for us, a wicked grin on his lips as his opponent bled out in the sand behind him. Rook shot to his feet in the same instant that he hurled the dagger toward us. It stuck in the wood of the stands just in front of Lark, blood dripping from the blade and onto his shoes. To his credit, Lark didn't even flinch.

Taurus' gaze darkened as he nodded his head briefly in greeting and spoke, his voice low and gravelly.

"Brother."

Chapter Fifteen

A Fool's Bargain

We waited below the arena in an open room that seemed like it used to contain cages of some sort. I shuddered to think what those cages might have contained and didn't have the stomach to ask even though I knew Rook would probably tell me. I just stayed in the shadows, standing near the wall, close to where Rook stood. No one had said outright that he was to guard me but I understood his attention for what it was and allowed myself to be guarded, thankful for the protection for the first time.

"Brother," Taurus announced in his booming voice as he entered the room they had instructed us to wait in, having finally torn himself away from his adoring fans. "Tell me, how is exile treating you?"

Rook tensed but Lark only tapped his fingers on the table that he and Cass were seated at and frowned.

"It hasn't been the vacation father promised it would be," he answered in a low tone.

"You seem to have brought back a souvenir anyway," Taurus replied, dropping into the seat across from them and reclining easily, his eyes flicking up to where I stood. The corner of his lips quirked upward and Rook took a step in front of me.

"Speaking of father," Lark drawled, ignoring his brother's unasked question regarding the strange mortal in the room, "is he recovering well?"

"Why wouldn't he be?" Taurus snapped, his gaze darting back to his brother fast. Too fast.

Lark raised a brow and Taurus' jaw snapped shut. He leaned back in his seat again, this time folding his arms across his chest.

"What happened, Taurus?"

"Maybe you should ask Ursa."

"Why?" Cass intervened then, narrowing her eyes to a glare. "Because she stayed by his side while you ran away to these dreadful pits?"

"I did not run away," Taurus snarled. "And if you're pissed at me because of what I did to our sister, you might remind yourself that it was she who came for me first. Besides, I'm not the only one who ran."

Cass' lips curled, her glare intensified, and I could feel the heat of their combined power thrumming throughout the room.

"Alright," Lark interrupted their stare off with a tone of attempted mediation. "This isn't getting us anywhere. Just tell us what happened, Taurus."

Taurus' eyes flicked to Rook and I where we stood in the shadows.

"It's family business," he growled.

Cass barked a bitter laugh.

"So now we're a family?" she asked, collapsing back into her seat with a huff and a roll of her eyes.

Taurus gritted his teeth and cast a glare in her direction.

"Fine," he snapped. "It's Morningstar business. Court of Blood and Bone royalty business. Children of our father business. Take your pick."

"Whatever it is," Lark began, "you can trust them with it."

Taurus' eyes remained on me for a moment but, eventually, he relented.

"Fine," he grumbled. "The assassination attempt wasn't an assassination attempt at all. Or maybe it was. I'm not even certain anymore. But the main attempt, I think, wasn't to kill father but to curse him."

"Curse him?" Cass asked, sitting forward in interest.

"It's powerful magic, Lark. Ancient. Whoever did this has to be... old."

Taurus was staring into his brother's eyes as if trying to get him to understand something from the simple look that passed between them. It seemed to have worked. Lark cocked his head to the side.

"You don't mean—" Lark began but Taurus was already nodding.

"Who else? I've never seen anything like it, Lark. Even Ursa couldn't undo it and you know about her... specialties."

"What's the curse?" Cass asked, her jaw tense for an entirely different reason now.

"It's his power, his magic. It's been... funneled out him somehow, like locked away. He can't use it, Lark."

I felt the silence in the room in my very bones. A powerful Fae, a King of a Major Court, unable to use his powers, cursed so that he could not access his magic? What force could have such a capability to lay such a curse at the King of the Bone Court's feet? And, if they could do that, what else were they capable of?

Cass was openly gaping at her brother. Lark was quiet, contemplative, as if thinking about every consequence of such a thing. Rook didn't say a word but his jaw clenched and I caught the worry in his expression, the fear. I felt it like a bitter taste on my tongue, permeating the room, the fear.

"Rifts between the planes," Lark finally said, his voice sounding older, more tired, "ancient curses wreaking havoc on Fae Kings, beasts awakening from their slumber. Taurus, when is the last time you checked on Hellscape?"

Taurus frowned at that.

"It's been... a while," he admitted and Cass muttered a curse.

"You were appointed its warden five hundred years ago," Cass reminded him. "How many times, in all those centuries, have you actually done your duty?"

Taurus reached up with one hand to rub the back of his neck, uncomfortable.

"I've been busy," he said but Cass was already shaking her head, blowing out a breath, incredulous. "Besides, why would I need to pop down there time and time again just to check on a prison that's stood for millennia?"

"Because, you bastard, one of the minotaurs escaped into the mortal realm and killed at least a dozen soldiers and would have killed more if Ren hadn't stopped it when she did," Cass snapped.

"Ren?" Taurus asked, and must have noticed the sidelong glance Rook passed my way because his eyes were drawn up to mine once more. "Her? The mortal? She slew a minotaur?"

No one answered.

"Lark, come on," Taurus said then, his tone almost pleading, much less impressive than the booming bravado he had displayed before. "You know the title of Warden means nothing. Not really. Not when those beasts have been down there for generations."

"Except they're getting out," Lark drawled slowly, his gaze narrowing as well. "And it's your responsibility to lock them back up again. You need to go down there, Taurus. Now."

Taurus was rubbing the back of his neck again.

"Yeah, see, that's not possible," he said, his face turning as crimson as this court.

"What do you mean it's not possible?" Lark asked, his tone taking on a measured fury which grew larger with every word he spoke.

"I sort of... lost the key at one of the gambling dens around here."

Cass gaped.

"You lost the key?" she asked, stunned. "You unbelievable bastard."

"Who?" Lark asked simply, his voice now simmering with rage.

"He didn't look like much. I knew he couldn't get in anyway, not without the magic of a Fae, so I figured—"

"Who?" Lark asked again and even I knew that tone brooked no disagreement.

"Some gorgon," Taurus blurted.

"A gorgon!" Cass shouted, leaping to her feet in her rage. "You lost the key to Hellscape to a gorgon?"

I blinked, searching my memory for what a gorgon was. When I realized, I visibly paled. Because I knew the most famous gorgon who had ever lived. Even in the mortal realm, we had heard tales of the horror she had wrought. Medusa.

"He can't get in!" Taurus was shouting back in defense of himself. "He can't get in without a Fae, you know that!"

"Had you ever considered that he might have been working with one already?"

Taurus paled this time, his eyes widening, his jaw slackening.

"Why—why would a gorgon want anything to do with Hellscape?" he asked, still trying to justify his actions, still trying to lessen the need for any immediate concern. "His kind, they go crazy down there. Gorgons hate Hellscape. They would never set foot—"

"Take us to him," Lark interrupted him with a primal growl that set my teeth on edge.

"I can't. After I lost the key to him, the next day when I'd... sobered up and realized what I'd done, I went after him myself. But then he crossed into the Court of Peace and Pride."

Another silence descended upon the room and I knew, again, that I was definitely missing something.

"Given the state of our relations with that court, I didn't chance it," Taurus muttered and then, looking up at his brother as if he could sense the direction of his thoughts already, added, "and you shouldn't either."

Lark's jaw was set, firm. His gaze was narrowed, his lips curled in anger.

"You haven't given me much choice. We have to get that key back," he said simply.

"Lark—" Taurus tried.

Inexplicably, suddenly, Taurus' eyes flicked to me and he blinked once in recognition.

"Oh," he said with a sigh, collapsing into his chair.

My brow furrowed with confusion. I turned to Rook to find that he was taking great pains not to look at me. Even Cass had her eyes closed. Panic gripped me then. Sheer mortal panic. I hadn't understood half of what they had been talking about all this time but I had understood the tone, the body language. Things were tense. Lark and Cass were angry, almost desperate, and, in the end, somehow it all related to me. Somehow, I was a part of this. Though I couldn't fathom how.

"Where did you find her?" Taurus whispered a moment later.

"We will get the key," Lark snapped, ignoring him and rising from his chair.

Cass rose again with him, folding her hands in front of her and keeping her mouth firmly shut as Lark leaned menacingly across the table so that he was mere inches from Taurus' face.

"And when we do, you will take us to father yourself."

My lips parted slightly. This was it. This was how Lark won his way back to his realm. This was how he earned the end of his banishment.

Taurus gave one silent nod, and then we were leaving. Rook and I followed the royal brother and sister from the hall, up a narrow set of rocky stairs, and out into the fresh air once again. It was disorienting. During the hours we had spent underground, day had turned to evening and the sun was setting over the horizon.

"Does anyone want to tell me," I spoke when we were all far enough away from any potential eavesdroppers, "what just happened in there?"

They all froze. Rook cleared his throat and peered out at the horizon. Cass looked to Lark.

"Taurus lost the key to Hellscape to—" Lark began.

"No, I understood that," I snapped, annoyed at how much of a simpering fool he apparently believed me to be. "I'm not an idiot. I know what a gorgon is. I know what Hellscape is as well and yes, I can see why a monster having the key to it would not be ideal. I can put all of that together myself, thank you. What I don't understand is how I fit into all of this."

Rook was staring at the ground now. Whether his averted gaze was due to the knowledge he had that I did not, or because he had just witnessed a mere mortal scolding his future king, I wasn't sure. But I knew even Cass wouldn't meet my eye and that was what made this situation seem far more precarious than I might have assumed otherwise.

"The Court of Peace and Pride is ruled by the only other man in this realm older than my father. King Alban Dawnpaw," Lark told me, his mouth a grim line. "He's the only one ancient enough to possess the magic it would have taken to level such a curse upon my father. Now, it is his territory that the gorgon has entered while a war is brewing between our courts. He is the one who tried to kill my father. He is the one who cursed him. And Ren, he is your grandfather."

Chapter Sixteen
Without A Trace

I had never known anything about my mother's side of the family tree. I had never asked my uncle for any information regarding where I had come from on that side, the Fae side. Because it was easier to ignore that part of me completely while living in a world that historically hated magic so vehemently. It was easier to pretend that it didn't exist, that she didn't exist, because there was never any chance at all that I might see her again.

Now that had changed.

And not only might I be meeting my mother but I might meet my grandfather as well. My grandfather who was a Fae King, ruler over the largest territory in the immortal realm, the Court of Peace and Pride. They were the protectors of the realm, the sowers of the fields, and the defenders of the plane. They prided themselves on hard work, determination, and an iron will. They tilled the fields in their expansive territory and used the harvest to feed all the immortal realm. They honed warriors in their barracks, military schools, and training grounds, creating a new class of soldier, immortal men who had dedicated their unending lives to the defense of all courts, to protecting all Fae.

I had learned all of this from Cass during our daily lessons back at the Court of Light and Life. She had had nothing but respect for the brown court when she had told me about it. About the property of its people, about the dedication to such a noble cause, even about the Bronze Throne. And in all that time, in all that teaching, she hadn't told me that my grandfather was the king. She hadn't even mentioned him. Not once.

So the betrayal I felt at that revelation was sudden and it was great. So much so that I narrowed my eyes, glaring right back into that intense gaze of Lark's, those dark, brooding eyes, and I snapped.

"Take me back."

He blinked at me, truly stunned for a moment. It was the first time I'd ever actually seen him genuinely surprised.

"Ren," he said and the way he spoke my name, the strained pain of it, almost made me change my mind right there.

But the anger won out.

"Take me back," I spat again. "Now."

"Ren, please. Just wait," Cass tried but I whirled on her next.

"You knew," I barked at her. "You all knew and you didn't tell me. You lied to me."

"We didn't lie," Cass said, holding up her hands in a show of surrender and stepping slowly toward me. "You didn't ask."

"Oh, I'm sorry. Next time you teach me about the courts and their thrones, I'll be sure to ask if any of the royal asses that sit upon them happen to be related to me."

I stormed away from them then, stomping down the street, back through the city. Cass called out after me but I didn't so much as glance backward as I strode away, fists clenched at my sides, teeth gritting so hard they ached. But I didn't care. I was so furious I could hardly see straight.

For all their talk of wanting to be my friend, wanting to give me the time and space I needed to learn about this place and to figure out if it was somewhere I might want to remain, they had lied to me about what it meant for me to be here, for me to return. I was a princess.

It was hard to breathe as I turned blindly down an alley and continued storming through the streets, putting as much distance between myself and the others as I could. A princess. I was royalty, a member of a Major Court, an heir to the largest court in the land. My grandfather was a king, an ancient king. My fists clenched at my sides and I squeezed them tight. They had known who I was all along. They had known exactly what court I belonged to, exactly who my family was, and they let me parade around in gray. The hapless mortal so far out of her element that she was willing to blindly trust the first supremely magical being that showed her a hint of kindness. I could barely contain my rage as I whirled around another corner in one of the most dangerous territories in the immortal realm.

But anger is blinding and, in that moment of rage, I forgot.

I forgot I was a mortal trapped in the immortal plane, surrounded by powerful creatures of magic, predators lurking in the corners, watching me as if I were their prey.

My steps faltered when I realized I didn't know where I was anymore. This street wasn't familiar, nor was the scent of burning sage undercut with cloying jasmine. If I listened, I could hear the sounds of soft moaning interspersed with various grunts. I blinked, eyes widening as I took in the open shutters of the windows above, candlelight sputtering in the cool night breeze, and the bodies writhing upon a mattress beyond. I averted my gaze, cheeks heating as I stared down at the cobblestones and willed my feet to move on quicker.

I dared a look back, hoping to see that my companions had followed, but they must have taken my silent request for some space seriously. That or I had actually managed to shake them amidst these winding alleyways and crowded streets. There was no sign of them behind me.

I turned back around just in time to run straight into a solid chest. I stumbled back a step but the male caught me with a hand around my wrist, gripping me harder than was necessary to stop my fall.

"Hey there, pretty," he muttered, slurring his speech. I could smell the alcohol on his breath as he smiled wolfishly down at me. "You happen to know what time it is?"

My heart plummeted to my stomach.

"No," I said quickly and made to step around him. But he sidled to the side and blocked me, our bodies colliding as he coiled an arm around my waist and held me there against him.

"Oh," he whispered against my neck and I felt the cool tip of a blade pressed against my abdomen as he did, "I think you do."

He was toying with the ends of my hair. My breathing was coming in quick, ragged gasps. I wanted to run, to scream, anything but, as if he sensed my thoughts, his blade pushed even firmer into my stomach and I froze. At the same time, I felt an unfamiliar thrum of magic coil around me, binding my arms, my legs.

"Why don't you run in there and get us a room?" he asked, nodding his head toward the nearest pleasure house. "And I'll be along shortly."

I nodded my agreement, if only to get him to let me go. He loosened his hold on me and I darted away. The moment we separated, Lark appeared between us and the male Fae was blasted off of his feet by some invisible force. He went flying a few meters away, sprawling in the dirt, clamoring back to his feet a moment later.

Lark prowled toward him, his eyes a darker shade than I had ever seen them, narrowed into a glare of pure, unadulterated hatred. My lips parted in shock at the sight. He lifted a hand and a crack reverberated through the streets. The male who had been holding a knife to me just moments ago was on the ground again, howling in agony. I gave a soft gasp and then Cass was in front of me, cradling my head in her arms and turning me away. She was hushing me, wiping tears away that I hadn't realized I'd shed. The next crack was even louder and I jumped against her as I turned into her, breath coming in hitched, shaky gasps.

Lark muttered something I couldn't hear from this distance and then there was one last crack before the man's screaming stopped entirely.

"Is he—" I started to ask when Lark approached us, frowning.

"He will wake up," Lark answered before I could finish my question. "And when he does, he will remember not to touch a lady without her consent."

I shuddered at the darkness in his eyes, the cold cruelty, the memory of how easy it had been for him to shatter the man's bones and leave him unconscious in the street. And I couldn't help but think of Cass' words from before.

We let everyone believe we're so evil, so wicked. We aren't.

Weren't they?

Lark's frown deepened as if he understood where my train of thought had gone but before either of us could say a word, ten men appeared surrounding us. Cass gasped and pulled me closer, protectively. Rook fell back, drawing one of the two swords he kept crossed at his back, and took up a defensive stance. Lark didn't even look surprised. He just kept his eyes on mine, searching.

"Canis Morningstar," one of the men formally announced but Lark did not remove his gaze from me even then. "You have been found in violation of your sentence of exile. Come with us willingly to face your punishment."

Lark's jaw twitched but he held out his hands, eyes still on mine. They stepped forward and clasped chains around his wrists made of some metal I couldn't identify. But I could feel it. Even from here. The suffocating heaviness of the material made my eyes droop as if I were suddenly more exhausted than I'd ever been. Lark didn't look away from me but I saw his power dim, that bright, pulsing purple glow lessening, retreating within him and my lips parted slightly as I understood.

The trace. They had found him because he had used his powers to protect me, to save me.

I gaped at empty space as they were all gone as suddenly as they had appeared, taking Lark and Rook with them. Rook had violated his own exile as well.

Cass and I were alone now, huddling together in the street. She took a deep, shaky breath and then let go of me, slowly, carefully, as if afraid I might break apart if she moved too quickly.

"What—" I stuttered. "Where—"

"I have to speak with my father," Cass interrupted me, pacing away on the street, "before he punishes Lark. I have to go, Ren, now. So if you want me to take you back to the mortal plane first, I need to know—"

"No," I answered, shaking my head. "No. This is my fault. He only used his magic because of me. They only found us because of me. I want to help, Cass. Just tell me how I can help."

She watched me for a moment, warily, considering my plea. But we were running out of time and she knew it. We didn't have the luxury of distrusting each other. Not anymore.

So she gave one quick nod and strode back to me, grabbing my hand and giving it a squeeze.

"Don't say anything," she warned. "When we get there, no matter who speaks to you, no matter what they ask, don't say anything."

Before I could so much as nod my agreement, we were hurtling through space and time toward the Court of Blood and Bone, toward her home.

Part Three
Ruin

Chapter Seventeen
A Halfling and A Cursed King

"Casseiopia. Why am I not surprised?"

"Father, please. Just listen."

They were already talking before I could even right myself. I stumbled sideways, reaching out blindly and finding a table to brace myself upon. Once the room stopped spinning, I looked up from where I leaned against an enormous mass of obsidian molded into the shape of a dining table to find Cass, with arms outstretched, imploring a middle-aged man with salt and pepper hair and immaculate thick eyebrows. I fought the nausea roiling in my gut to stand up straighter and keep my mouth shut, as instructed.

"Your sister told me you'd go to him," the man said in a tone that seemed utterly exhausted. "That you'd help him find his way back somehow."

"I didn't," Cass argued. "I didn't help him back, father. He called me when he was back and I went to him. Of course I did. But I didn't break the banishment. I didn't bring him back. But father, please—"

"Forty more years, Casseiopia. That's all he needed to stay away for. Forty more years and his sentence would have been up. He could have returned to open arms and welcoming embraces."

"A welcoming embrace. Is that what you call Ursa trying to slit his throat?"

Her father frowned.

"I can't control the succession," he muttered, glancing around as if looking for a seat. He found one at the dining table by which I stood, his eyes flashing over me with disinterest before settling into the chair at the head of the table.

"What succession?" Cass bellowed, throwing her arms up in annoyance as she strode forward and he sat down. "You're here. You're alive. There is no throne to ascend to, no succession to take place."

"Not yet."

Cass stilled, halting mid stride in the center of the room. Her father's frown deepened and she resumed her walk until she stood beside him again.

"What do you mean?" she asked, her tone lowering.

His eyes slid to me.

"Who is your friend, Casseiopia?" he asked, shrewd gaze examining me from head to toe.

"This is Ren," Cass introduced simply, with no further explanation. But that did not satisfy the King. He raised a brow and she sighed. "Lark brought her with him from the mortal realm."

The King slammed his hand on the table.

"See?" he bellowed, pointing a finger at his daughter, jaw clenched in a way that reminded me of his son. "He goes too far! Always too far. I told you. I—"

"She is Ariadne's daughter."

He faltered, finger dropping as he turned to face me with fresh interest. "Half Fae," he muttered, jaw slackened.

"Welcome here," Cass said as if in reminder, "by your own decree."

He blinked at me, lips still parted in surprise.

"Yes, yes," he agreed, waving his daughter off and pointing, instead, at me. "The last I saw you, you were but a babe. How old are you now?"

"Sixty," I told him.

"Sixty," he repeated, taking me in again, no doubt examining my appearance, the way I looked nineteen or twenty. "Fascinating."

"It's a real head scratcher," Cass said then, obviously irritated at the change in the course of the conversation. "But father, about Lark—"

"Canis."

"Yes, Canis."

"I always hated that Lark business. Doubtlessly, he came by that wretched name from that boy he was always hanging around with. The one I banished too."

"Father, please. Forgive his premature return. With you falling... ill, and Taurus having run away to the Court of Rivals and Ursa off doing God knows what—"

"I know what. I know what she's doing. I sent her there myself. I don't need your lecture, Casseiopia. I'm still the boy's father. I know what's best for him."

"Canis hasn't been a boy for four hundred years, father."

I balked. Four hundred years.

"Leave us, Casseiopia," the King commanded then, his gaze firmly on me. "I wish to speak with the Halfling."

Halfling. I flinched. That was almost as bad as hybrid.

Cass' gaze flicked to me, uncertain. But I gave her a solemn nod and she departed, the skirts of her dress billowing like the night itself behind her.

Neither one of us spoke until she was gone. Then, the King was smiling up at me.

"Sit," he said, gesturing toward the table. "Are you hungry? My servants should be here any moment with dinner. Please, join me."

I blinked at him for a moment, wondering if this was a trick, but then decided that even if it was, it was too late for me to get out of it now. So I sat in the chair across from him, staring at him over the endless table between us. It was the most distance I could put between us while still meeting his request. Without my companions, I wasn't comfortable interacting with another Fae, specifically a King, whether what Taurus had told us about him having lost his magic was true or not.

"I'm hoping you'll tell me how you find yourself here, dining with the Fae King of the Court of Blood and Bone," he said and I did not respond, Cass' words echoing in my head.

No matter who speaks to you, no matter what they ask, don't say anything.

"Loyalty is a funny thing," he continued after a moment of waiting for my answer only to find that I wasn't going to give him one. "It can be so easily misplaced and, once it's dug in too deep, it can be nearly impossible to root out. I see my son has inspired such loyalty within you."

I did not answer as a servant appeared and placed trays of roasted meats and steaming vegetables in front of us. The King gestured for me to eat so I reached hesitantly for the serving spoon sticking out of the stack of carrots.

"I wonder, though, if he has told you why he was banished."

I stilled, my hand hanging frozen over the plate in front of me, my eyes flicking up to the king. He smiled at my surprise.

"I thought not," he said, pleased with himself. I averted my gaze, busying myself with piling more food onto my plate than I truly intended to eat, if only to keep my eyes away from his. "Since it has something to do with you."

My hands were shaking so I hid one under the table and lifted my fork with the other.

"Sixty years ago," he added, clearly intending to tell the story whether I asked for it or not, "a council of every King of every court was called to determine whether we might reach out to the mortals. Sentiments were changing. Some Fae among the leadership, myself included, were relaxing our laws against your kind, relinquishing our hold on some of the hatred we'd felt for you for millennia, and we thought it might be time to offer the mortal plane an olive branch of sorts. An ambassador. Someone to go back and forth between the planes for purposes of communication, to open access to our realm to your people by only the tiniest sliver and see what they made of it, if they could be trusted to attempt a peace."

I stared at my hands, now busy cutting through a thick slice of beef, and refused to look up at him as he continued.

"Canis offered himself for the job. He campaigned for it. He wanted it more than anything I'd ever seen him want in his life. And, in the end, when it went to your mother, when Ariadne Dawnpaw became our ambassador to the mortal plane, he raged and raged. He made every claim he could against her. That she wasn't fit for the role, that she couldn't be trusted. But he didn't tell any of us why he felt that way. Not until he had proof. Not until she was pregnant."

My fork stilled again. I was trying very hard to remember to breathe.

"It could have been taken care of quietly. He could have told me, or he could have gone directly to Alban. But instead, he decided to announce it at the next council meeting to all who had gathered. Alban had no choice but to punish her on the spot. To strip her title from her and worse. And when the news traveled that the baby had been conceived by a mortal, every bit of work we had done to extinguish the hate the Fae held for your people crumbled to ash."

I took a deep, shuddering breath.

"He is my son, Seren. I hope you can understand that. I should have stopped him. I know that now. I should have known that he wouldn't be satisfied with Ariadne's punishment, with her humiliation. He wanted to destroy her. So he did it the only way he knew how, the only way to truly crush a new mother's soul. He stole you."

The breath went out of me and I raised my gaze, slowly, to meet the King's. I shook my head slowly, tears welling up as I processed what this powerful Fae King was trying to tell me.

"So I banished him," the King finished then, leaning back in his seat and drinking deeply from his goblet. "One hundred years in the mortal realm, living among you and thinking about what could have been, about what he ruined when he lashed out at having not gotten what he wanted like a petulant child."

I blinked once, twice, trying to clear my mind, trying to think through every ounce of information I had just received. Lark was the one who had delivered me to my uncle so many years ago. He was the one who told Professor Xavier Belling that my father was dead, that my mother was Fae, that there was an entire plane of existence full of magical wonders we could not even imagine. I had grown up thinking that man was my savior or, at the very least, just the messenger dispatched to deliver me to my only remaining mortal family. But he was my kidnapper.

A shudder went through me as I took in a shaky breath and gripped the edges of the table. The man that had come to me, flirted with me, joked with me, protected me, and promised me. He had promised me. My heart pounded.

I had grown up believing that my mother had abandoned me, that she had never wanted me, and he let me. He let me believe that. He brought me here and gave me that whole bullshit speech about finding my way and learning about my people when he knew. He knew he was the one who took me away from it all in the first place, who took me from her.

"He's the one who left you in the mortal plane, Seren," the King told me, his voice sympathetic, almost pitying. "He's the one who sent you away."

I went completely rigid. I was an intelligent person. I was an academic, a professor, a scholar. And yet, my feeble mortal brain couldn't comprehend what this ancient, immortal king was telling me.

Lark, the Fae prince who had closed the rift and used its power to bring us here. Lark, the one who had stood before me and promised me he wouldn't drag me anywhere against my will, that it was my choice whether to stay or leave. Lark, the man who had protected me, just moments ago, from another Fae that wished me harm. The powerful Fae who looked at me like I might be something more to him than a mere mortal.

But it was all an act.

The pieces of the puzzle I hadn't realized I had been looking at started falling into place all around me. Why he had come to me that day, why he had allowed me to stick around ever since. It wasn't friendship. It was guilt. Or maybe it was some last ditch effort to right the wrong he had committed and win himself an early release from his banishment. And he hadn't told me. None of them had. Just as they hadn't told me about my grandfather being the King of the Court of Peace and Pride. Just as they still, even now, weren't telling me everything they knew about my past, about who I was or what I might become.

I gripped the edges of the black table with white knuckles. How foolish had I been? To believe such a powerful Fae, the Prince of the Court of Blood and Bone, and his immortal friends would ever want anything to do with me, would ever care about me at all.

"I am certain they have instructed you not to speak to me," the King said then, with a tone that was more understanding than I could ever have expected. "Which has Cassiopeia's name all over it. But you should know I decreed long ago that any being with so much as a drop of Fae blood in their veins is always welcome in my court. For any wrong my son may have done you, I sincerely apologize. You will be treated as an honored guest just as much as any of our kind would for the duration of your stay at my court."

With that, he clapped and two servants emerged from the shadows. I just stared at them for a moment before realizing I had been dismissed. I rose mechanically, hardly making the conscious decision at all, and followed them toward the exit.

"And Seren," the King called out behind me. My escorts froze so I did as well. "I will try not to take it to heart that your grandfather is the one who did this to me."

His smile had fallen from his face completely. Gone was the compassion he had shown me moments ago. In its place was a stone cold glare, a cruel frown, and the twitch of a hand. My blood ran cold as I followed the servants out of the hall, now completely surrounded by enemies I had thought were my friends.

Chapter Eighteen
A Fall From Grace

The King of the Bone Court had kept his promise. My room was lavishly decorated and equipped with any imaginable luxury I might want during my stay, however long that may be. But I didn't take as long to explore it as I might have done before when academic curiosity got the better of me.

Instead, I paced across the plush black carpet, chest heaving with the deep, shaky breaths that I was forcing myself to take. Was I truly his guest? Or was I his hostage? Because of my blood, because of who I hadn't even known I was related to, he would hold me here. Maybe he would even use me to get revenge on his would-be assassin, on the ancient king that had cursed him, on my grandfather.

I felt ill. I slid to the floor in front of my bed, keeping my back to the mattress, and stuck my head between my legs. I focused on my breathing, trying to calm down, trying to rid myself of the nausea passing through me. It might not have mattered if I vomited all over their fine carpets but it couldn't possibly make things any better either.

Lark had known. They all had. He knew it was my mother who he had betrayed over half a century ago. He knew who I was from the moment he met me. He knew exactly how I would fit into his plans, how he could use me, and I had let him. I had gone along with it, all of it, and I hadn't even questioned him. I'd felt so lucky to be allowed in his exclusive group, so exhilarated to be studying the people I had spent my whole life wondering about. I hadn't allowed myself to really question why he was letting me get so close, why he was convincing me to stay. But he'd known. He had known all along who I was. I only wondered what he had intended to trade me for. A certain gorgon jumped to mind and I shuddered.

"I've been looking everywhere for you," a familiar feminine voice spoke suddenly and I froze, still sitting on the floor beside my bed, knees up to my chest, as Cass entered the room.

She glanced around, taking stock of the amenities, before striding to the decanter in the corner and pouring herself a glass of the sloshing amber liquid.

"Sorry it took so long," she muttered, annoyed. "Father can be so irritating when he wants to."

I didn't say a word, didn't even breathe. At my silence, she looked over and, when she saw me there, her head cocked slowly to the side.

"Ren?" she asked, taking a step forward.

I scrambled to my feet, pulling from my sleeve the only thing I had found in this room that could be used as a weapon. A hairpin made of sharp bone.

"Ren," Cass said again, more slowly this time, her brows furrowed in confusion.

"Stay back," I snapped.

To her credit, Cass stopped, raising her hands slowly.

"Ren, what are you doing?" she asked.

My chest was heaving, my eyes darting around the room for an escape, as if I had any chance of outrunning a Fae princess. As if this insignificant little hairpin could actually offer me even a sliver of defense against her might. She knew that too but she was playing along, always playing along.

"Why didn't you tell me?" I asked, my voice barely a whisper as a tear slid down my cheek.

"Ren, please. I didn't realize you didn't know. I mean, she was your mother. I thought—"

"Not that," I snapped. "About him. Lark."

Cass blinked, her lips parting slightly as if in genuine confusion.

"About what he did," I spat. "About why he got banished in the first place."

"Oh."

"Oh? That's all you have to say? Oh?"

"Ren, listen. I don't know what my father told you but I'm sure it isn't the whole story. If you would just—"

"Take me back."

She blinked at me again.

"Take me back!" I shouted.

"I... can't," she said and I deflated, shoulders slumping. I dropped the shard of bone to the carpet and sank to my knees. "I'm so sorry, Ren. If it was up to me, I would take you back right now if you wanted to go. I swear it. But my father has... forbidden it. He sent word to your grandfather. The King of the Court of Peace and Pride knows you're here. Your mother knows you're here. You are—"

"A hostage," I breathed the word with all the hopelessness I felt in my heart.

I had known it. I had known it would go this way. I was too valuable a piece for the King of the Bone Court to let slip through his fingers. I might have avoided it if I had known, if they had told me.

"No," Cass tried to argue. "We're going to get you out. We're going to—"

"You have done enough," I hissed, glaring at her. "You're the one who brought me here. I thought you were my friend. I thought we were all becoming friends but I was never free to leave, was I? If you couldn't have convinced me, you would have just trapped me. It would have been easy enough."

"No," Cass was arguing, shaking her head. "No, Ren, that's not true. You are our friend."

"No, I'm not."

Cass' lips opened in surprise. She started to say something, but changed her mind.

"Get out," I spat.

"Ren—"

"Get out!"

That time, she obeyed. She turned on her heel and left my room, setting her glass on the table as she left. And when she was gone, I finally let myself sink back onto the plush carpet below and collapse into a puddle of tears.

No one but my servants came to see me for days. They washed me, fed me, dressed me, and hardly said a single word the whole time they did. I bore it all in a silence of my own and, when they were gone and I was alone again, I crawled back between the sheets in the fine dresses they put me in, hoping I would venture out into the court.

I slept, mostly. When I got restless, I paced or plucked a book from the shelf and tried to read it in those rare moments when I managed to remind myself that was I still a scholar, that I could still study something even if I didn't have the courage to actually walk about the court itself.

But most of my energy was spent on keeping the thoughts at bay, distracting myself long enough that I wouldn't let my mind wander to the mother I had never met and the shock the news of my sudden appearance in the immortal plane must have given her. Nor did I wish to consider my supremely powerful grandfather and whether he cared about the threat of my capture or not. Because I imagined it was the latter and my heart simply couldn't take any more abandonment from these people.

Mostly, I stood out on my balcony when the night grew deep and dark and stared up at the stars, identifying constellations. I drew them in journals, on any scrap of paper I could get my hands on, anything that my servants brought me. I named them all and counted their connections. An entirely new sky, a whole new set of stars, and I was the only astrophysicist here to see them. Maybe they already had names. They probably did. But I didn't want to know them. I just wanted them to be mine. I wanted something to be mine.

Cass didn't try to see me again. Nor did anyone else though I imagined the males were imprisoned somewhere for their crime of returning and unable to venture about the palace the way the princess could. It didn't matter. I did everything in my power not to think of them at all.

After a week of never setting foot outside of my room, the door opened again and I didn't even look up to see who had entered. It would be my servants. It was always my servants. So I stayed where I was, sitting cross-legged on the floor, surrounded by my dozens of drawings of stars and constellations and cosmos, staring down at one that looked peculiarly like a hummingbird, rather than standing to greet the King.

"My children are named after the major constellations of your world," he said and I stilled, holding the hummingbird picture in my hand. "A tie that binds them to the mortal world, to remind them of where we came from, where we all come from."

I did not respond.

"I had hoped a week of luxury would convince you to speak to me, you know," he told me, settling into the black sofa nearby and crossing one leg over the other. I had seen that posture before in his son. The reminder of the man set my blood boiling and I snapped a glare in the King's direction.

"Yes, you treat your hostages quite well," I snarled.

"Who said you were a hostage?"

"For someone who banished his son for kidnapping an infant, you seem to have no trouble holding a woman captive yourself."

"I take great issue with it, I assure you. But I take even more issue with being cursed by a fellow King and a man who I believed, frankly, was my friend. I am sorry, Seren, to make you a pawn in our political game. But he has given me no choice."

I frowned, deflating somewhat at his rational argument.

"Have you heard from him?" I asked even though I hated myself for caring.

"No," he answered and I hated myself even more for the disappointment.

I turned away from him then, back to my drawings.

"You are half Fae, Seren," he said then, leaning forward and getting on with whatever business had brought him to visit me in the first place. "Have you ever attempted to use magic?"

I shrugged.

"Once or twice when I was a teenager and the whole thing had a Sabrina vibe," I told him and watched as his brow furrowed at the pop culture reference of a world separate from his. I sighed. "No. I haven't tried it. Not really."

"Why not?"

"I wanted no part of this, of you. I didn't even want to be one of you. So trying to use magic felt like admitting to what I was. And if I tried and failed, then... it would be proof that I wasn't actually special. That I truly had no connection to my mother. That she had given me nothing at all."

He nodded, considering.

"Try," he said then and my gaze snapped back to him.

I blinked.

"Excuse me?" I asked, uncertain if I had heard him correctly.

"Try," he repeated.

"I—I don't know how—"

"Do you see the glass on the table here?"

My eyes flicked to the glass, half full of water.

"Move it," he told me.

I stood, brushing myself off.

"No," he said, stopping me. "With magic."

"But I don't understand how I—"

"You're thinking too hard. Just move it."

I sighed, letting my shoulders droop. Then I turned to face the glass and focused. I imagined it moving from one side of the table to the other. I narrowed my gaze and emptied my mind. I thought of nothing but the movement of the glass, the water inside. Nothing.

"Keep trying," the King said, standing from the sofa and walking toward the door. "Tell me when you manage it."

When. Not if.

I watched him, lips parted slightly in surprise, as he wrenched open my door and stepped through the threshold to the hallway beyond.

"And Ren," he added, turning back over his shoulder before he left. "You're expected to be in the throne room this afternoon when I sentence my son."

Chapter Nineteen
A Royal Mess

I stared at that glass of water for hours. I stared at it while sitting, I stared at it while standing, I closed my eyes and envisioned it. I waved my hands around, wiggled my fingers, tried different facial expressions. Nothing. Not even a slight shake enough to stir the water inside. Mentally drained and physically exhausted, I collapsed on the bed, closing my eyes and finally allowing the thoughts I had been fighting against all day to filter in.

Lark was being sentenced today. I had to be at the hearing. Would he be aware of what I knew now? Would his father or Cass have warned him of my fury? Would he even feel guilty for what he had done, for lying to me all this time? Did any of it matter?

My servants arrived not long before the court was to be assembled, before the time that the King had commanded my presence. They washed me and dressed me in a long brown dress. It was plain and unembellished, thick and slightly itchy. The true garb of a prisoner. But I made no complaints as they shrouded me in the uncomfortable fabric and piled my blonde hair atop my head. When they tried to dust me with makeup, however, I turned them down and they merely strode away, leaving me to ruminate in peace until I marched to my kidnapper's doom.

I didn't know the woman who came to get me but I recognized the facial features. Dark hair, dark eyes, high cheekbones, the glowing power of a royal Fae, and that insidious black.

"Ursa," I guessed the moment she appeared on my threshold.

Her lips quirked up into a grin that simultaneously told me I had been right and reminded me of her siblings. I looked away quickly, turning back to shut my door as I stepped out into the hall with a would-be murderer. I couldn't even summon the energy to fear her as we strode forward together.

"My reputation proceeds me," she said, amused.

"Something like that."

"He told you I tried to kill him, didn't he? Did father tell you he's a liar?"

"Cass actually told me you tried to kill him. But don't worry. I know she's a liar too."

Ursa snorted.

"She trips all over herself trying to follow in his footsteps," Ursa told me, the cruel condescension clear in her tone.

"And you?" I asked, raising a brow in her direction. "Who do you follow?"

She grinned again.

"Never mind," I said. "You'd probably just lie to me."

"You're better equipped for this place than I thought, Mortal."

I am now, I thought but I kept my mouth shut as we reached a massive set of double doors and the guards on either side pushed them open. I expected to emerge at the end of the hall, facing the throne and the man upon it. I expected to be able to merge into the back of the crowd, unseen.

But we had entered from the front, through doors directly behind the throne, where all eyes were directed.

Everyone was already gathered and I became very aware of three things at once. One, the King had provided me with a time later than the true start of court so that I could make this dramatic entrance at his behest. He was grinning from ear to ear as the onlookers, the entire gathered court, stared at me in a mixture of shock and awe. Two, that I was wearing my family's colors, Court of Peace and Pride colors. And three, that a very familiar intense gaze was burning into me from where I stood on the dais.

Lark was standing directly in front of his father, his wrists still bound in the magic-suppressing chains which they had captured him in. His eyes were darker than usual, bruised a deep purple around the sockets. He had a cut on his bottom lip that looked fresh. It dripped bright red onto the black onyx floor below. Nearby, Rook knelt on the cold floor, his hands bound behind him in the same chains, his face gaunt and haunted.

I tried not to think about how Rook had saved me from falling off a cliff or how much I had worried for him in those weeks he had to stay away from the court we all took refuge in. Tears pricked the corners of my eyes and I turned away from the kneeling Fae.

"Father," a familiar voice gasped.

I did my best not to look at Casseiopia but I couldn't help it. Her dress was a shimmer of black diamonds when she lurched forward, toward the dais, toward me, and was blocked by her sister. Ursa was there in a flash, holding her back with a lip curled in disgust. Cass looked from her to her father, her eyes wide, pleading, as a tendril of hair fell down the side of her face in a dark curl.

"Silence," the King commanded and the hall obeyed. He rapped his fingers against the arm of his throne, gaze narrowing in examination of his son, the traitor.

All attention went to the king. All but Lark's. His gaze bore into me until it forced me to meet it. The emotion in those dark eyes hit me like a punch to the gut. I sucked in a quick gasp. The torturous pain he was in, the deep well of sorrow he was feeling, the hopelessness, the despair. He wanted me to know it. He wanted me to feel it. He didn't look away. Even when I schooled my features into a glare to convey as much hatred as I could, even when I looked at him like I had never known him and never wanted to again. He held my gaze, firm and strong and full of meaning

"Canis Morningstar," the King cried out into the silence, "you were banished for a term of one hundred years sixty years ago. And yet you're back."

Lark did not respond and behind him, kneeling on the ground, Rook hung his head.

"What do you have to say for yourself?"

At that, Lark's gaze finally turned away from mine, his eyes narrowing, jaw setting, lips thinning, as he faced his father.

"Nothing that I haven't said before," he growled so lowly that the onlookers were leaning forward so that they could hear him.

My heart threatened to beat straight through my chest but I fought to maintain my composure as the sound of his voice ricocheted around my heart.

"You have nothing to offer in your own defense?" The King asked and I could hear the hint of surprise in his tone. Maybe he was so used to arguing with his son that the possibility of Lark going to his fate without a fight was more stunning to him than anything he could possibly say instead.

"I have plenty to offer," Lark answered. "But none could penetrate your sheer determination not to believe me."

The King's lip twitched in annoyance.

"Try," the King barked.

My gaze snapped to the man on the throne. He was radiating anger, white-hot rage at his son's disobedience, at his impertinence. But there was something else just beneath that fury. A desperate affection. He was a father, this was his son. He was giving Lark a chance to justify his actions, to save himself. And it was only infuriating him more that the man wasn't taking it.

"I made my arguments against exile when you passed your last sentence. I told you why I did what I did. I told you my justifications. You chose not to hear them," Lark said and I felt rage burning inside me at the casual nature in which he was discussing my kidnapping. "I imagine this time will be much of the same but, if you're so insistent, I'll tell you. I came back because a full grown and heavily armed minotaur fell through a hole in the sky of the mortal realm. I came back because my sister showed up and tried to kill me. I came back because things are changing in our plane, things that the mortals are noticing, things that impact all of us. And I'll be damned if I'm going to ignore the signs like everyone else."

A grave silence met his words as the entire hall fell quiet. Then they whispered among themselves and I could hear the questions, understand the confusion, even from where I stood beside the King. Minotaurs? Murders? Mortals?

"Damned, indeed," the King replied with a sigh. He closed his eyes and shook his head. "Canis Morningstar, you are aware of the punishment for circumventing banishment."

"Death," Lark answered and the whispers stopped.

I couldn't breathe. My gaze snapped to Lark's to find that he was already looking my way. That sorrow from before intensified a thousandfold. Execution. That was the punishment for his return home. He had known that. He had known the punishment was death and he had saved me anyway, had used his magic to protect me knowing that they could trace him from it, to find him and bring him here to face trial, to die.

Why would he do that? Why would the man who kidnapped me almost sixty years ago go to such trouble to save me now?

I blinked and looked away, to Cass who was weeping on the onyx floor, to Rook who had visibly paled as he awaited his own death sentence. No. I didn't want this. I would never forgive them, any of them, for what they did, for what they hid from me. But I didn't want them to die. I didn't want them to be executed.

"Kill me," Lark said then and my gaze snapped back to him, though he was looking at his father now, hands raised, imploring. "But do not kill Rook. He was just following orders, serving as my protection as you assigned him to centuries ago. Do not punish him for my insolence."

The King looked from his son to Rook and back. He frowned deeply, eyes widening as he took in the boy pleading for his friend's life before him. His son. A man he had loved for centuries. And now he was considering killing him. Because he had to. Because it was the law. I closed my eyes, took a deep breath, and tried to push the feelings away.

They were strong, thrumming into me and against me from every angle. Anguish, sorrow, dread, fury, desperation. No one was happy about this. No one was pleased. Even Ursa's lips were set in a grim line. This was a family tragedy. This was an unforgivable choice. And yet...

"Canis Morningstar, I hereby sentence you to death," the King announced with a heavy voice and Cass collapsed with a horrific wail, "for the crime of circumventing exile. You will be hung in the courtyard tomorrow morning at sunrise."

"No!" Cass was screaming, clinging to Ursa's legs, tears streaming freely down her porcelain cheeks. "No, father, please! Don't do this! Don't do this! No!"

Ursa leaned down and whispered something before gripping Cass under the arm and hauling her to her feet.

"Lark," Rook said quietly.

The warrior Fae had finally looked up, his wide, wet eyes on his friend. Lark gave one solemn nod as the guards stepped forward to lead him away.

"Father, stop this!" Cass was screaming again, clawing against Ursa to get to the King. "You can stop this, please!"

But the King's jaw was set as he watched his son being taken from the room in chains, the crowd of onlookers parting as he went, courtiers and courtesans from places I didn't know, places I had never heard of. They watched with wide eyes, slacked jaws, as their prince was led away to await his execution.

Lark didn't look back. Not once.

I stared into the back of his head as hard as I could but he disappeared beyond the pillars and was gone. The others began to file out quietly, blinking away the shock of the events that had just transpired and moving along automatically, putting as much distance between themselves and the grieving royal family as they could. Cass was still wailing, still begging for her brother's life. Rook was being unshackled. He stared down at the chains as they fell away with cold, dead eyes.

"Come," the King whispered under his breath as he passed me on his way toward the doors behind us. "Now."

Ursa was busy with her sister. Rook was surrounded by guards. I just turned my back on all of them and followed the King through the doors from which I had entered. I didn't dare to stop to catch my breath until I made it all the way back to my room.

Tears were streaming down my cheeks but they were hidden in the dark of the hall as I walked swiftly down it. I wiped them away with a shaky hand as I opened my door and plunged inside. Shutting it tightly behind me, I crossed the room until I was standing in the center, pacing back and forth at the foot of the enormous bed. I clutched my stomach, bent over slightly, chest heaving. A sob escaped me, wracking my body as I shook with silent grief. My knees buckled and I slumped to the carpet, shuddering as the whimpers I was fighting to hold at bay escaped in desperate clusters.

I should be glad. This was justice served. The man who had stolen me from my mother when I was only an infant, the man who had determined my fate in a way he had no right to do, the man who had lied to me for weeks, who had kept secrets from me while claiming we were friends. He was going to be executed for his crimes. After sixty years, my kidnapper was seeing justice.

But the words he had spoken gave me pause.

I made my arguments against exile when you passed your last sentence. I told you why I did what I did. I told you my justifications. You chose not to hear them.

Justifications.

He'd had his reasons for stealing me away. He'd had excuses. Did it matter what they were? Could anything make up for what he'd done? Even if they could, they didn't make up for the lies he told for six weeks, the way he didn't tell me who I was the moment he knew.

I hated him but I ached for him. I hated him in the way that you could only hate someone you had loved.

But what right did I have to claim I'd ever loved him? I didn't even know him. We had only just met. But there was something there, something that even I couldn't define. Everything felt bigger when I was around him. Emotions were stronger, colors were more vibrant, power was more evident. So maybe I had never had a choice. My uncle used to always talk about fate. That sometimes there were bigger things in store for us and sometimes we just wanted to believe there was. That was what astrology was about, the small science, the people who looked up at the stars and believed they foretold their future. Because they needed to feel that they had a future.

Lark was my past but he also felt like my future. I couldn't explain it. I couldn't define the connection between us but it was there and now, losing him, it felt like losing a part of myself too. A part I should hate. A part I should revile and want to be rid of. But I didn't. Because that part kept me alive. That part made life bigger, brighter, more vibrant. And that part was dying.

I screamed then, unable to contain my emotions any longer, sinking into the carpet in a puddle of sorrow and despair as Cass had done in court only moments ago.

So I screamed and screamed and, when I was done, when my face was wet with tears and my voice was hoarse and there was nothing else in me to break, that glass of water, the one that the King had told me to move, it shattered into a million pieces.

Chapter Twenty
At Death's Door

I had no desire for the King to know about my newfound ability but I hadn't been given the choice. Ursa had entered my room moments after my screaming had stopped to ensure I hadn't attempted to end my life in some way or I hadn't screamed myself into oblivion and fell unconscious. She'd found the glass shards dug deep into the plush carpets, so deep that they couldn't be removed. I hadn't just shattered the glass; I had turned it into a million tiny projectiles. They had shredded the carpets so thoroughly that servants were now cutting it away for replacement. I watched them work, numb, tired, too exhausted and emotionally spent to do much of anything else.

I stood by my bed, arms crossed, and stared at a male servant I had never seen before as he used a blade to cut a circle around the coffee table, extricating the shredded fabric and carefully placing it into a nearby bin. Another servant paced around with a dustpan, cleaning up all the smaller fragments her companion missed, the ones she could remove, at least.

"Remarkable," the King was muttering from where he stood in the threshold.

Ursa was by my side, watching me from the corner of her eye as though afraid I might shatter the entire room and take us all down with it at any moment.

"I told you to move it," he told me, finally looking away from the mess to the one who had caused it.

"And I told you I didn't know how," I snarled.

But he only grinned.

"How?" he asked.

"I don't know," I answered.

"You must know something. What were you doing when it happened?"

I didn't answer so Ursa did for me.

"Screaming," Ursa told him. "She was screaming at the top of her lungs."

The King's gaze snapped to me.

"Emotion," he said, thoughtfully. "Your power is tied to emotion. How interesting."

"Don't you have a son to execute?" I snapped.

The servants stopped. Even Ursa tensed. The King's gaze narrowed to a glare. He pursed his lips, clenched his jaw, then snapped his fingers. All the tiny shards of glass that the servants hadn't finished cleaning up rose as one from the ground, hovering in the air like some strange hesitating rain, glimmering in the light from the chandelier above.

"Control," he said, striding toward me, "is power."

I tensed as he drew nearer, those tiny puncturing projectiles still hovering in the air behind him.

"Simple control will always defeat raw power used recklessly. No matter how great that raw power might be. You made this mess. Now, clean it up."

He snapped and all the glittering shards of glass fell back to the floor below. The servants turned away to avoid being struck by the deadly rain.

The King turned on his heel and stormed from the room, Ursa following in his wake. The servants exchanged wide-eyed glances before scurrying away themselves, leaving me to clean my own mess as the King had ordered. I let out a roar of frustration and kicked a nearby pillow that had been removed from the couch area while they cleaned. Then I threw myself onto the bed.

I didn't clean up my mess. I didn't even look at the little shards of glass for the rest of the night. I just laid in bed and stared at the ceiling, unable to even sleep.

I turned toward the window beside me and stared outside at the moon and stars, at the dark night sky that grew lighter and lighter as the day approached. I wondered if Lark had slept or if he had waited for the sun as well. If he had stared outside and thought about his exceedingly long life and his ultimate demise. I wondered if he had regrets and I wondered if I was one of them.

Before the sun crested the horizon, Ursa came to fetch me. There was no servant to dress me, no gown hung in the closet, no one to fashion my hair. Just a soft brown coat and matching pleated pants, just a quick brush through my tangled knots and simple brown flats. No glitz, no glamour. This was an execution, not a ball, not court.

I tried not to look at myself in the mirror, at the red rings under my eyes from a night spent without sleep, at the puffiness of my cheeks from the tears I shed all alone. My hands were shaking so I put them in my pockets as Ursa and I left my room and headed down the hall toward the courtyard.

I had never been outside at the Court of Blood and Bone. When we had arrived, Cass had shadowstepped us right into the royal dining room and I hadn't been allowed the freedom to venture beyond the palace walls. So when we stepped outside, it was a shock to see a vast tundra set out before me. Snowcapped mountains in the distance, fresh billowing snow blowing around our ankles, frigid air freezing my face as I blinked against the rising sun. I took a deep breath and saw my exhale in the air before me.

"Are you ready?" Ursa asked quietly beside me as we stood in the threshold.

"Are you?" I snapped.

"I didn't want it to be like this. There is honor in dying for the succession. But this... I loved my brother. For all his faults and all our disagreements, I did love him."

Loved. To Ursa, Lark was already dead.

I held my breath as we stepped forward, leaving footprints in the snow as we made our way toward the platform erected in the center of the yard. I wondered absentmindedly if it had always been there or if they had placed it there the night before, or even so soon as this morning.

The crowd from the night before wasn't here. The King himself was standing off to the side. Cass was beside him, her eyes staring into the snow in front of her, blank and unseeing. They were red rimmed and raw, much like my own. Her lips were cracked. I wasn't even sure she was breathing.

Ursa pulled me to the opposite side, close to the platform. Too close. I tried to squirm away, to make some excuse about not being family, not needing to have a front-row seat to this, but she held me firmly at her side and the intention was clear. I wasn't just a witness. I was still a hostage.

A few important men stood around, solemn faced and stoic. Some soldiers were scattered about the field behind them. Rook was at the back of the crowd, as pale as the snow beneath his boots, eyes just as cold, just as dead, as Cass'. He didn't even glance at me.

Suddenly a loud groaning sounded from somewhere nearby and I looked over my shoulder to find a gate at the base of a tower I had assumed long abandoned was opening, rolling upward. Beyond it stood two men, one of them in chains. I flinched, digging my trembling hands further into my pockets, and waited, with everyone else, for the gate to open completely.

It took some time and, in those few horrible moments, nothing could be heard but the ancient mechanisms that moved the iron. I closed my eyes and felt that sound grating against my very soul.

Then the gate was open and silence fell once more as the man without shackles dragged the other one forward. They strode together, leaving footprints of their own in the untouched snow behind them, as they made their way toward us. Cass let out a sob as I let my eyes fall, finally, on Lark.

He wore a cloak as black as night with the hood drawn up over his face so that only his smooth, pale neck and the uppermost part of his chest were visible. A small mercy to his friends, to his sister, that they wouldn't have to look upon him yet. I waited for that wave of emotion to pass over me, to drown me in his sorrow, his desperation, his anger. But it did not come.

The lack of sensation caught me off guard. I had expected a flood and was getting only a trickle. Just an inkling of the deep sadness he was harboring within him. Had he cut me off? Could he even do that?

I wasn't even certain how this connection worked. The King had said that my magic was accessible through emotion. It had been a small cognitive leap from there to realize that all these emotions I was feeling weren't always mine. I had always been empathetic. My uncle had raised me, saying that I had the biggest heart of anyone he'd ever met, that I had some heightened awareness of other people's feelings. But now I was beginning to suspect that it wasn't just empathy that had me so tuned into the feelings of those around me. It was magic. I felt Cass' sorrow, Rook's anger, Ursa's disgust. But Lark's emotions, I had always felt those the most. They were always the strongest, overwhelming even my own from time to time.

And now, I couldn't feel them at all.

The executioner was leading him onto the platform and I saw the noose for the first time. I hadn't paid attention to it before but it hung above the platform, right at average height. He would have to stoop to loop his neck through.

The King said nothing. He just stood, his lips set in a firm, grim line, while the executioner led his son forward and slipped that rope around his neck.

My palms were sweating, itching. Something sharp was carving a hole in my chest, leaving it so hollow that I couldn't tell what had been there before. I made a fist, relaxed it, made a fist again. I fidgeted, kicking the snow beneath my feet, swaying with the morning breeze, anything to distract myself from what was coming, what was going to happen any minute now.

And then it did.

There was no lever, no machinery, nothing like the ancient gate and the decrepit tower. The executioner simply stepped off of the platform and raised his hand. A moment later, the platform was gone and Lark was dangling from the rope around his neck, that dark hood still hanging limply, obscuring his face.

I heard the moment his neck snapped. Watched as his feet stopped twitching.

Cass fell to the snow, wailing. Ursa took a deep breath she thought no one heard. The King just stared at the body, at his son.

Rook was gone. I wasn't sure when he had left. I hadn't seen him go. The soldiers were leaving as well, their duty as witnesses completed. I couldn't stop staring at that hood. Like if I stared hard enough, I could see through it to the face beneath. I didn't want to see it, not really. I didn't want to see him dead, his eyes opened in some macabre imitation of that intense stare he had always had, his lips parted in the shock of death, his neck bent at some unnatural angle.

But I did question that connection that had felt so raw, so real, the night before. I had felt every ounce of his grief then, every inkling of his sorrow, his fury. I had expected to feel the moment Canis Morningstar's soul left this plane, the moment he died imprinted upon my heart forever, but I didn't.

I felt nothing at all.

Nothing but an overwhelming sense of loss as a tear froze upon my cheek.

Chapter Twenty-One
A Different Kind of Fae

"If it's fear you need, then feel it, but block this one."

Ursa flicked her wrist and another half dozen shards of hardened night materialized in thin air and shot toward me at high velocity. I focused on their approach, lifting my hand to block them, and hissed when I failed to produce an adequate shield and the black daggers pierced my skin, slicing me from wrist to elbow on my left arm and piercing my right shoulder. I staggered back a step, biting back the curse on my tongue.

"No," Ursa barked. "Again."

She waved her hand and the daggers from before disappeared, the skin of my arms healing itself, though the pain remained. I grit my teeth and faced her again, fighting back tears as another round of knives shot forth, one of which plunged deep into the tissue of my thigh. I roared in agony, falling to my knees.

"No!" Ursa snapped, a thick cloud of darkness emanating from her in her fury. "It's just a shield, Seren. This is the most basic thing I can teach you and we've been at this for two weeks."

"I just... I need a break," I wheezed, kneeling.

She just shook her head, turned on a heel, and stormed from the training room. She waved her hand on the way out and the dagger was gone from my thigh, the gash already closed and healing. I rubbed the spot where I'd been struck, staring down at my arms where they had bled before, again and again.

The King had disappeared after his son's execution, the last of his orders appearing to have been for his daughter to train me to use my newfound magic. But Ursa only knew one way to train, through torture, and it wasn't working for me. It was exhausting me, all the healing, the split second concentration, the agony. I wasn't able to use any of my emotions because she wasn't allowing me to feel anything but hurt.

I wondered if they had trained Lark like this, in this court, if they had cut him apart just to piece him back together again, stronger than ever. Cass too. I wondered if Rook had suffered the same strict regiment from Ursa or perhaps even the King. I wondered if this was the only way the Bone Court knew; pain and torment, exile and executions, blood rights and sacrifice. And then I remembered what he had said, so long ago, when we had sat across a dinner table in the Court of Wanderers and looked to the future with bright eyes and high hopes.

If Taurus or Ursa took the throne, things would get even worse than they have under my father. I can't let that happen.

Would he have been a better leader? Would he have been kinder? Would he have taken away the suffering, made the world a better place? Now, we would never know.

The moment he died, Rook had disappeared and no one had seen him since. That fact seemed to irk Ursa. She had gone on a tirade the first day of our training when I'd brought him up, claiming that he should have known he would always be welcome at the Bone Court, with or without her brother. I had made the mistake of pointing out he had been banished for sixty years and she made me pay for the remark with a shining black spear through my calf.

Cass was gone too. They had taken her to her rooms afterwards. The guards outside claimed they'd heard sobs for hours but then they suddenly stopped and, when they entered the room to check on her, she was gone. And that was that.

So all the people I had believed once were my friends were gone, had abandoned me again as they had before. And I was here, under the tutelage of Ursa and the dominion of the absent King, a hostage because of my blood, because of my ancestry. I spent my days training with Ursa and my nights staring at the stars, trying to shatter them into a million pieces as I had the glass before.

But my magic hadn't returned to me since that day, not even a trace of it. I hadn't even felt it coursing through my veins. And that emotional connection, those visions of auras and feelings of spiritual bonding with the people and the world around me, they were all gone. As if Lark's final breath had stolen all my power away. As if his death had been mine as well.

I felt more mortal than I ever had.

And I felt more lonely than ever before as well.

I grabbed the rag from the nearby bucket of water mixed with cleaning solution that the servants had learned to leave behind for all of mine and Ursa's training lessons. One of her more tedious lessons was that I had to be the one to clean up the blood left behind from my injuries. She healed the skin, the muscle, the tissue. But she didn't wipe away the blood. That was for me to do at the end of a failed lesson. To get on my hands and knees and scrub my own blood from the obsidian floors. So that I would remember the consequences of my failures as if I didn't feel them in my burning limbs enough as it was.

"The method works," a deep voice spoke and I froze, white rag turned red beneath my palms. "You may consider it barbaric, something you once called our succession rites as well, I believe, but it works."

I plunged the rag into the bucket and watched the water turn red.

"It isn't working for me," I snapped.

"So what would?"

I turned to face the King, wiping my wet, blood-stained hands on my borrowed tunic, and stood.

"You said it was interesting that my power was tied to emotion," I said. "Why is that interesting?"

He clasped his hands behind his back and strolled forward to meet me in the center of the room.

"Because your mother's is tied to thought," he answered. "And thought and emotion seem like two sides of the same coin to me."

I cocked my head to the side, brow furrowed.

"Thought?" I asked, because I knew he wanted me to.

"Yes, thought," he said, nodding his head and circling me, looking down at the puddles of my blood on the floor. "The strength of one's thoughts, the strength of their will, she pulls her power from that. She's amassed quite the collection of cunning advisors over the years. She can identify them easily enough, read the patterns of their minds and compare them to others."

"She can... read minds?"

"No. She can read the patterns."

My lips parted as I went to ask another question but wasn't sure how to phrase it. He seemed to anticipate my confusion, though, and continued his explanation.

"Alban explained it to me once," he said. "They both have the same ability, you see. He said he can see the patterns of thought like a musician might identify notes. There's a particular flow, a rhythm. Everyone's rhythm is different and the directions of their thoughts can indicate the state of their mind. Short, staccato bursts might mean someone is angry or impulsive. Cautious rests and holds might mean someone is paranoid or calm. A steady, thrumming rhythm is usually happiness and so on. I confess I can't envision the matter myself but he says he sees it in the air around a person, it flows from them."

I froze.

"You've experienced something similar?" he asked, raising a brow when he noticed my hesitation.

"You... glow," I said, trying very hard not to think about this very similar conversation I'd had with his son not so long ago.

"A glow?"

"Yes. It's—I thought it was tied to your power. The brighter the glow, the more significant the power. But your glow isn't so bright and you're the King—"

"A King without his magic," he corrected me.

"True," I said, "but Ursa's isn't that bright either. Lark's could be blinding. Cass' was radiant. Even Rook had his own signature. Maybe it was connection, maybe it was how well I knew each of them, maybe—"

"Maybe it was emotion."

I stopped, watching him as he rested his chin in his hands and paced before me.

"These auras, are they different in ways besides brightness?" he asked.

"Yes. Some are more solid, some are flowing. Their rhythm is different too. Some pulse, some are constant. But it's not just that. It's—"

I stopped myself, watching the King, unsure if I wanted to tell him this much. I was his hostage, not his citizen. I wasn't just some half Fae he was training to see what she could do. I was the daughter of his enemy, the girl he had exiled his own son for stealing. And I didn't trust him. I didn't trust anyone, not anymore. But I was thinking about this relationship in terms of what I could gain from it. So maybe I would give up a secret but I would gain answers in return, a better understanding of who I was and what I was capable of. That benefit seemed to outweigh the cost. At least, for now. And I was growing used to living moment to moment.

"I can feel other people's emotions," I told him then, my voice hardly above a whisper.

I had never spoken it aloud before, the suspicion I had that my sensitivity to other people's feelings was more than just heightened mortal empathy. I knew exactly what the people around me were feeling, particularly those closest to me, and I was never wrong. Because I didn't just feel it. I saw it. Radiating from them in waves of living color. Anger and sadness and excitement and love. All of it at once, all the time. I hadn't known it wasn't normal, this almost omnipotent empathetic awareness, until I was a teenager and all of those raging hormones from my peers had become so much that I would go home and shut myself alone in a dark room just to feel my own feelings for a while. But I had grown with it and learned how to tune it out, how to ignore it, and I'd gotten so good at it that I hardly saw that glow at all anymore.

And then Lark came.

He and Rook were so foreign, so strange, so other. Their power called to mine and drew it outward in a way it hadn't been pushed in decades. It had been dormant and they had awakened it. The colors had returned and I had found them beautiful and ethereal just like this strange place and its strange people. But it had dimmed again when Lark had died and, even though I was trying now, even though I wasn't trying to hide it away again, I couldn't find it. I couldn't reach it. It had buried itself within me somewhere so deep even I couldn't find it. And Ursa would not unearth it with her daggers and the King would not unearth it with his questions. I knew that. With all of my heart, I knew that, but I wanted him to try anyway. Because I couldn't allow myself to believe that I needed Lark for anything, that he had stolen this from me as well.

"Can you control them?" he asked, curtly.

My brow wrinkled.

"I've never tried," I answered, horrified by the very suggestion.

"Try."

He stood in front of me, arms raised in surrender, showing me it was okay to try. My chest heaved and I took a deep, shaky breath. The King of the Court of Blood and Bone was standing before me, commanding me to manipulate his emotions, to try to control them.

"I don't know how," I told him, feeling a disappointment in myself for how often I was speaking those words to him lately.

"I can't tell you," he replied. "Because I don't know either. But if you can see them, you can try to manipulate them. Reach for them."

I focused on that dim glow coming from him, closed my eyes and searched the darkness. It wasn't nothing, like I had expected. When I turned my full focus to one person, to their aura, their emotions, I felt something. It was quiet, still, a whisper like a caress against my soul. I reached for it, gave it a tug. The King grunted.

My eyes flew open to find him watching me, hand on his heart and gaze boring into me.

"Again," he snapped.

I closed my eyes, widened my stance, and focused. His feelings were there, buried beneath the thick veneer of his authoritative shell. I prodded his anger. He pushed me aside. I searched for it because I knew it was there and I needed to see it for myself. The sorrow, the despair, the horror at what he had done to his son, what he had ordered himself. It was there, buried deep, hidden away and locked so far within him I knew he wasn't feeling it now. I reached for it, brushed against it lightly. He tensed. Then I snatched it and yanked it forward.

The King crashed to the obsidian floor on his knees. Guards in the shadows that I hadn't even realized were there charged forward, half of them running to his aid, the other half grabbing my arms and pinning them behind my back. Foolish, since I hadn't used my limbs at all in the assault.

The King waved them all away and, when he looked up at me, I saw the tears streaming from his eyes.

"Take it away," he begged through gritted teeth.

I didn't remove it. I pushed it back within him, back into that locked box, back into his favorite hiding place, where it could lie dormant until he needed to feel it, until he deserved to relive it.

He gasped for air as he rose to his feet on shaky legs.

"How did you do that?" he asked. "How did you make me feel that?"

"I didn't create the feeling," I told him. "It was already there. I just pulled it out of you."

His wet eyes were wide, his lips parted in a perfect O, and he was watching me as if I was something he didn't recognize, something he didn't understand. A chill ran down my spine at that look.

"Well, you're right about one thing," he said then, clearing his throat and straightening his lapel. "Ursa's training will not work for you."

With that, he and his guards left me standing alone in the training room, a bucket of bloody water by my feet and now-dried blood to clean from the floors.

Chapter Twenty-Two
A Shot In The Dark

"Now, Ursa," the King bellowed and I turned my attention away from the three soldiers writhing on the ground to the princess. She stood still, waiting for me.

I turned my focus to a pinprick, a precision instrument, diving into her heart, her soul. Anger was first. Ursa always had anger lurking on the surface. I waded through the ocean of it, letting it lap over me, try to pull me under. The King had been unguarded before, when I had brought him to his knees in the training room, but now I was finding out just how powerful these royal Fae were.

Ursa didn't just guard her emotions. She used the baser ones against me, weaponizing them. All of her fear, her sorrow, her doubt, her happiness, the little silver linings she celebrated and clung to, her love, her pride, it was all hidden behind a gleaming fortress built up in her mind. It was impenetrable. I had tried for five days now to breach it and every day before, she had used her rage, her ferocity, her ambition to drown me before I could. She had amplified and intensified that anger so that it wasn't a weakness anymore. It wasn't something I could use against her; it was her own weapon. Honed from centuries of stoking, nurturing. And she unleashed it when I delved inside her mind until it overwhelmed every one of my senses and broke my focus, pushed me out.

The soldiers on the ground hadn't been able to guard against me, these new ones no more of a challenge than the last. I had found their deepest sorrows, their fiercest doubts, and had preyed upon them with it until they succumbed. The first time, it had left me cradled in a ball as well, wracked with guilt for the suffering I had imposed and for the trauma of another man that I had experienced all at once. But the King had explained they were only doing their duty. That they had agreed, even volunteered, to help me hone my skills. And they would recover. Like I said, I created none of those feelings myself. I just brought them to the surface.

But Ursa's surface was already overflowing with emotion. There was no room for any more. Her chest heaved, her lip curled. She glared at me with a hatred I couldn't fathom. And I wouldn't even try or else I would get lost in it and never find my way out as I had on the third day. But not this time.

I planted my feet and closed my eyes, narrowing my focus to that impenetrable wall. I let the red rivers of her anger flow around me, push against me, but I waded into the mud and muck that was her surface. I stuck there, immovable, like a parasite on a host trying desperately to flick it away. And I moved. Slowly, so slowly, but I moved. I felt her tense the closer I got, felt her control slip slightly and the waters recede a bit. She was building up a wave, a tsunami. I knew it was coming for me again, as it always did before. I was running out of time. If I could just get within those walls, if I could just breach her defenses.

I shot out with hope and it ricocheted off like a fly buzzing in a window. I shot out with despair and it didn't even make a dent. I thought for a moment, weighing my options. I could already feel the current shifting, the wave forming. I sensed the daggers in her hands now, aimed at me, materialized and waiting. There was one thing I hadn't tried. One thing that no one would ever think to try, not in a battle, not while fighting a war.

I shot out with love.

And that impenetrable wall gained the tiniest chink in its armor.

My surprise was so great that she was able to pull me out and toss me down. I fell to the floor in a heap, stuck there by some invisible force as Ursa stormed toward me, eyes alight with something that might be mistaken for anger but I knew it was fear.

"How?" she snapped and the hall fell silent.

I pulled and pulled, but to no avail. I couldn't rise. I couldn't defend myself from those daggers she had created, the obsidian knives rotating slowly around her hand, waiting to be thrust out. And the King did not intervene. He waited, stroking his chin in interest, to see how this would play out.

"Everyone has a weakness," I said. "Even you."

She bristled.

"How?" she asked again, this time in a scream.

"Love," I snapped. "Love is your weakness, Ursa. Not because you want it but because you have it and you want to be rid of it."

Her lips curled into a hateful snarl and she let out a low growl before turning away and storming from the room, letting the door slam behind her.

"You should know," I called out to her even though she was gone. "Love is a not a weakness."

"For some of us, it is," the King said finally, waving a hand so that I could move again. I shook out my wrists as I rose, shooting an annoyed glance to where Ursa had vanished. "Very impressive, Seren."

"Can I stop hurting people now?" I asked, rubbing my wrists and glaring at the King.

"Is that what you think you're doing?"

I gave a pointed glance to the one soldier still curled up in a ball in the corner of the room.

"I told you he is doing his duty—"

"I'm done."

I turned and strode toward the door that Ursa had vanished through.

"You came here afraid," he called out behind me and I stopped. "You were a frightened little rabbit when you appeared in the middle of my dining room with my meddling daughter. Wide eyed and terrified, you were looking at all of us as if we were predators and you were just waiting for us to pounce. Do you remember that feeling, Seren? The hopelessness? The doubt? The knowledge that we could pick you apart at any time without lifting a finger?"

I took a deep breath. I remembered it well.

"You aren't that little rabbit anymore," he told me. "You aren't a mere mortal. When they look at you with scorn, you can glare right back. You can hold their minds. You can break them even more efficiently than they could break you."

"I don't want to break them," I said, my voice soft.

"No, maybe you don't. But at least you have the choice now."

Then he was gone. I didn't see him go, just felt his absence, felt my own loneliness. I closed my eyes and took a breath before pushing through the doors into the hall beyond.

I followed the familiar tapestries to my room. The servants had lit the glowing orbs of light for me when they had gone for the evening. I couldn't light them myself. I was a powerful empath, capable of feeling and altering emotions and auras, but I couldn't manage even the most basic practical magic. I couldn't clean the shards of glass I had made. I couldn't light my room or change my clothes. I couldn't even form a passable physical shield. The King hypothesized that my power was temporal rather than physical, that I might never manage the type of physical magic that others seemed to use with such ease. Likely because I was only half Fae and therefore did not have as privileged a use of magic as full Fae. Though personally, I believed my connection to emotion was a gift bestowed upon me by my mortal side. Humans felt more, emoted bravely. Fae hid their feelings behind impenetrable walls and empty minds.

I bathed, stripping from my brown tunic and thin leggings and changing into the silk beige nightgown. I brushed through my wet hair and tried in vain to dry it with magic to no avail. I padded, on bare feet, through my room, letting my toes sink into the soft carpet as I reached for a book written by some Fae astronomer from the Court of Scholars. I read the names of the constellations, compared them to my own, and ran a finger along the detailed drawings of each, much finer than mine, much more intricate.

I turned to the stars and stared up at the blinking night sky, memorizing the view of it so that someday I could return and tell my uncle all that I had seen. I could paint him a picture of the stars from memory and show him all the constellations in this book, their real names and the ones I had made for them myself. I could show him what I had accomplished and who I had become. I could tell him about magic, about how it was used and what it felt like.

I closed my eyes, feeling the thrum of it in my veins. A steady, near-silent hum I had ignored my entire life, that I had never heard over how loud I was being, how loud I was thinking.

I had begun a new practice lately, when no one was around and I was all alone. It was difficult to practice an ability tied to emotion when the only emotions I had to investigate were my own. But it was possible. I had found that much. I kept my eyes closed and narrowed my focus, organizing my feelings into buckets. Pride here, sorrow there. Happiness here, anger there. Some feelings were associated with people, some with places, and some were just a haze, an intangible and undefined concept flitting between the others. I arranged them, bucketed them, bracketed them out using the methods of a true type A academic.

I sifted through them all, recognizing them for what they were, memorizing the feel of them, the conceptualization of them, so that I could recognize them in others. I studied them, played with them, held them, and let them go. I dug deeper than I ever had before until my fists were clenched in the blanket beneath me, until tears were flowing down my cheeks and I gritted my teeth against the strain. I let myself feel it, truly feel it, all of those emotions I had been avoiding.

My abandonment, I toyed with that for a moment, indecisive over whether to place it with sorrow or anger. My mother I held firmly in hand, not wanting to let it go. Lark, I gripped him tightly and then dropped him to sorrow, to grief, one of the more potent emotions. Cass and Rook followed. My uncle, I missed him but he made me happy. These things, these people, they weren't easy to categorize. They had made me feel so much, so many different things, but nearly all of them ended up in sorrow because of the betrayal, because of the hurt, the death, and the absence.

I picked up every broken piece of me and started to make it whole, started to help it mend. The categorization helped. But toward the end, I picked up a piece that didn't go to my puzzle.

I didn't recognize it. It wasn't just hazy; it was obscure. It was dark and dismal and unrecognizable. I caressed it, held it, examined it. And, when I had almost given up on identifying it, I reached out with my whole heart and gave a firm tug.

My eyes shot open.

Because that piece, it had tugged back.

Chapter Twenty-Three
A Court of Conflict

The Lord of the Court of Friends was visiting.

Ursa had stormed into my room the next morning and roused me from where I had fallen into a fitful sleep on the couch, a book of astronomy laid open across my lap. She had informed me of the noble visitor and demanded that I rise and dress for the occasion.

I questioned her thoroughly the whole time. Why was I expected? I wasn't even of this court. She explained that word had spread far and wide of my stay here since her father had sent notice of it to the Court of Peace and Pride. I had become a bit of a wonder to the lords of the minor courts, a marvel to stare at and whisper about the implications of my being here.

"Why is he visiting?" I asked as a servant worked on my hair and another powdered my face with that shimmering substance Cass had used on me before, the one that left my natural skin tone but gave me a bit of a glow.

"The Court of Friends is always the one that reaches out first when it looks like there might be a conflict between courts," Ursa explained in a tone of irritation without even looking up from her nails which she examined while leaning against the door frame of my bathing chamber. "They always think they can help both sides make amends, mediate the conflict before it turns into something bigger."

"Something like a hostage situation?" I asked, turning back to her with a raised brow.

She frowned, slipping off of the wall to stand at her full height as if expecting me to lunge at her. I rolled my eyes and turned forward again for the servant working on my face. The royal family didn't care for it when I mentioned the truth of my situation here, that I could not leave even if I wanted to. And her shields were up. They always were around me now. I wondered if it was mentally exhausting, locking your emotions away from someone who lived with you. But they still had that chink in them, the one I had carved away with a simple expression of love.

"I will not go begging for asylum," I muttered and watched through the mirror as her shoulders visibly relaxed. "Why trade one prison for another? Particularly one I know nothing about. My only interest in leaving is if you agree to take me back to the mortal plane, back to my uncle."

"We've been over why that's impossible now, Seren," Ursa reminded me with a sigh. "Now that the Court of Peace and Pride knows that you're here, that you're... alive, they would find you. Anyone could find you."

I frowned. Every bit of information I learned about my kidnapping from infancy made bile rise in my gut. They had believed he had killed me, killed a baby, rather than taking me to live with my uncle. Lark had been so wicked that it was easy for the entire realm to believe he would commit infanticide. That explained the looks of fear and disgust he had received everywhere we went, the warnings of behavior Sophierial had issued to our group at the Court of Light and Life, and Cass' declaration that the world thought the people of this court to be evil. I could see why. I wasn't so certain myself that they weren't.

"My uncle?" I asked.

"Protected," she assured me. "By the wards that Lark placed over the university after he delivered you there. Alban and Ariadne, they could tear them down with their magic, easily. But that would be too much work just to get at your uncle. You, however..."

"I understand."

"Princess Ursa," a servant spoke then and Ursa whirled around with a growl, conjuring a dagger from thin air. The maid went wide eyed, backing away from her in terror. I didn't recognize her, which meant that she was new, that she wasn't aware of how greatly Ursa hated her title. "I—the King requests your presence, both of you."

Ursa snapped and the dagger disappeared.

"Do not," she said, her voice a low warning, "call me princess."

The servant nodded vehemently and then scurried away.

"Don't be so prickly," I chided, standing and brushing myself off.

I stared into the mirror for a moment in one final examination. This brown dress did not look so much like a burlap sack. It was a deep, dark chocolate with a sweeping train beneath a poufy tulle skirt which slimmed at the waist and rose in glittering applique to a halter around my neck. It was backless and cut low in the front, displaying my cleavage amidst the glittering jewels. My hair was a waterfall of honey around the sides of my face, down my bare back. My makeup was dark and heavily lined, just as Cass had made it before, the preferred style of the Bone Court. The appearance alone was a statement. I wore my family's colors but I wore my captor's face.

"Don't be so vain," Ursa snapped because I was still admiring myself in the mirror.

I turned, grinning, and strode toward her.

"Off to breakfast then?" I asked and she groaned before turning away and stalking toward the door to the hall.

I followed and we made our way, together, to the dining hall set at the other end. We entered to find that the King was already seated, leaning back in his chair at the head of the table, sipping on some amber colored liquid that I thought it might be too early in the morning for. Across from him, on the opposite end of the long table, sat a man dressed head to toe in an immaculately embellished emerald tunic, matching wide legged pants, and green leather loafers. He was dark-skinned and wore a simple cap atop his bald head. He lowered his head in a sort of half-bow that they expected lords of minor courts to give the royalty of the upper courts. I blinked for a moment before I realized I was one of them as well.

Ursa settled into the seat beside her father. I sat beside the visitor as I had been instructed. He turned to smile at me as I settled in and I beamed right back at him. He was ancient, I could tell that just from his eyes, but his skin was smooth and unwrinkled, his body straight and not stooping. He appeared to be in his early thirties but his eyes held whispers of a millennium. Kind, bright eyes. The sort of eyes one might convince themselves to trust.

"Seren Dawnpaw," he said with a voice as thick as honey. I cringed at the name but did not correct him. Ren Belling was dead, it seemed, and rising from her ashes was Seren Dawnpaw, more Fae than mortal. "I am Lord Koa Oaksky from the Court of Friends. It's a wonder to meet you."

"The pleasure is mine," I replied with a smile, because I wasn't sure what else to say.

"You must have quite the tale. Would it be too imposing to ask you to regale us with it?"

The food arrived then. Plates upon plates of buttered biscuits, assortments of jams, fruit from all over the realm, piles of eggs and sausage. My mouth watered at the sight of it but I let my gaze wander to the King. He let down his shield only a fraction to send a feeling my way. Approval. I could answer this question.

"I'm afraid it's a rather boring story as far as I know," I told him. "I was raised by my mortal uncle, my father's brother, at a university. I grew up studying the stars and the cosmos, knowing what I was but never really wondering what it meant. I thought I—well, I believed myself to have been abandoned."

Lord Koa's eyes widened just a fraction.

"It must have been quite a shock to learn the truth," he said.

I grit my teeth and stared down at my plate, remembering that feeling, the utter betrayal.

"Yes," I agreed. "It was."

"The Bone Court has sent a clear message that kidnapping is an indefensible crime," the King bellowed then, reminding us all of his presence, his authority here.

"By executing its heirs," Lord Koa said and the dining hall fell into a tense silence.

I could feel the emotions being held at bay. These were very powerful Fae. Each of them had a shield around the cores of their souls but their surface emotions were readable and they were rampaging in a way that was nearly overwhelming. Anger and frustration from the Bone Court, disgust and dismay from Lord Koa. It rose and swirled, rising to a breaking point, as I closed my eyes and waited for someone to speak, hoping it would diffuse the tension.

"And holding hostages," Lord Koa added with a pointed glance in my direction.

"If you traveled all this way just to insult us—" Ursa snapped but Lord Koa held up a finger and she fell into an enraged silence.

"If it is an insult to hold up a mirror and allow you to see your own reflection, perhaps you should question what the root cause of that truly is," he said simply and cut her off before she could respond. "But I have not come to bicker about your actions. I have come to inform you of how they are being perceived."

"The same way they are always perceived, I imagine," the King replied easily, dabbing his mouth with a napkin and tossing it upon the table. "Evil, wicked, vile. It's what you all think of us. It's what you've always thought of us. Why should that change now?"

They were all speaking easily, calmly. The tone of the conversation was the same as it might be if three friends were casually discussing some mutual interest or current event. But I felt the undercurrent of emotion all the same. The tides washing over one another, vying for supremacy, roiling and raging. I closed my eyes, gripping my fork and knife until my knuckles turned white, taking deep, concentrated breaths to clear my mind, to push them out.

"You executed your son for a crime that occurred sixty years ago, for kidnapping a baby and for ending that baby's life," Lord Koa said, tone stiff. "And yet here she sits, dining with us, wearing your fashions, hale and whole. But not free, is she? You exiled Canis for capturing her but you've captured her yourself. You are hypocrites and murderers, the lot of you."

Ursa's fork clattered to her plate a moment before her chair was scraping against the onyx floor and she was rising to her feet, shards of obsidian already swirling around her wrists. The Court of Friends' guards lurched forward, surrounding their lord but remaining a few feet away, awaiting his orders. The Bone Court's own soldiers stepped forward as well and it appeared we had reached a standoff of sorts.

"I'll remind you to watch your tone, Lord Koa," the King spoke with a tone of authoritative warning.

But Lord Koa did not even look up at him. He reached across the table, plucking a strawberry from the platter of fruit before him. He held it aloft for a moment, examining it, turning it. Then I watched as, right before my very eyes, it grew plumper, redder, bigger. He bit into it and juice dribbled down his chin. He let the silence intensify for a moment before he spoke again.

"Right your wrongs, King Perseus," Lord Koa said, those kind eyes becoming menacing as they flicked up to the King. "Send her home."

The King's lip curled. His jaw clenched as he leaned slowly forward, staring Lord Koa down from across the table. I had never seen two powerful Fae face off before but I knew in that moment that I had no desire to.

"The King's actions are a response to politics beyond his control," I said then, my tone measured, calm.

Lord Koa's gaze flicked to me.

"With all due respect, Princess, you have not lived among us for long. You cannot comprehend the intricacies of our politics or—"

"I can comprehend the idea that a King cannot appear weak before his own court. That idea reigns supreme even in the mortal realm. He exiled his son, gave him every opportunity to stay away, to keep his life. So, when he returned, he gave him no choice. I know that my mother's court has made moves against this one, moves that I imagine even you are not aware of Lord Koa, and the King has responded in kind. I may not be able to leave if I choose to but I am treated well and I am cared for. So before you try to use your righteous indignation to free me of this cage of my own making, please ask me if I want to leave."

Lord Koa froze, his lips parted in surprise as he blinked at me. I could feel the King's satisfaction as it seeped into my bones. I held my head high. If I was the heir to the Court of Peace and Pride, a princess as Lord Koa had called me, then I would act like it. Peace, I was learning. Pride, that was easy.

"You call me a princess," I continued, leaning forward as I spoke. "So heed my instruction. You've made your attempt. You can leave with your head held high knowing that you tried. But I will remain here until my mother herself deigns to stoop so low as to collect me."

Lord Koa sat back in his seat, eyes widening, jaw slackening at my sincerity. I felt a swell of pride inflate within me and couldn't help my grin as I settled back in my seat, turning my attention back to the eggs piled on my plate. But that feeling of pride grew into approval and it warped and shifted until it wasn't my own at all. Smile faltering, I searched for that feeling, rooting for its source, and found that fragment again. That deeply buried dark shard that I couldn't identify, the one that had tugged back when pulled upon. Now it was invading me, spreading its own feelings into me.

Panic gripped me and I fought not to let it show as I pulled away from that fragment like wrenching my hand away from a nest of vipers. I schooled my features into an expression of the arrogant princess, as I had just masqueraded as before, and focused on my breakfast.

"Perhaps the Court of Blood and Bone is as persuasive as they say," Lord Koa muttered, rising from his seat and throwing his napkin down on the table.

In four long strides, he had left the hall, his guards following close behind him. I watched them all go before I turned back to the King and Ursa.

"So much for attempted mediation," I grumbled, poking into my eggs.

"That wasn't mediation," Ursa snapped, turning to her father. "That was an assault. The Court of Friends has just made their position clear. If it comes to war, father—"

"It will not," the King snapped. "No one would be foolish enough to declare war on the Court of Peace and Pride. Particularly when the rest of the world doesn't seem so inclined to understanding as Princess Dawnpaw here."

I wrinkled my nose, finally understanding Ursa's hatred of the title.

"Lord Koa is conceited, self-satisfied, and annoyingly virtuous," the King said. "But he isn't a fool. The Court of Friends wouldn't dare make a move against us. None of his council members would agree to such a thing even if he attempted it. He's harmless. The public opinion that he is alluding to, however..."

"You did the right thing, father," Ursa assured him. "Canis circumvented exile."

"He did," the King agreed, lost in thought. "But I'm not so sure."

Chapter Twenty-Four

An Evening Star

Alone in my room, I searched for that fragment. I dug deep, searching through feelings I hadn't felt in decades, sorting through the ignored trauma of my past, the pain of watching those around me age while I remained the same, the dawning of my understanding that I was truly different, truly other. The doubt, the ignorance, the fear of myself, of who I was. Tears streamed freely down my cheeks, my fingernails punctured half moon holes into my palms, my jaw ached. Even so, I searched.

Because I had to find it. I had to examine it again, to find a way through it, to figure out what it was and why it was a part of me, a part buried so deep there was no chance of extricating it. I had to understand why it felt like I had in the mortal plane, different, other, alien. It was within me but it wasn't me. So who was it?

"Get ready," Ursa said suddenly and my eyes snapped open to find her standing at the foot of my bed, watching me.

Her arms were crossed, her lips set in a grim line. I wiped the tears away and then the blood off my palms and wondered how long she had been standing there, how much she had seen. I threw my legs over the side of the bed and stood, already padding toward my washroom.

"Where are we going?" I asked. "It's late."

It was. It had been three days since breakfast with the Lord of the Court of Friends and Lord Koa had long since departed the Bone Court to return to his own. I had spent every waking moment since training or searching for that fragment within me. One was proving far more successful than the other.

"There's someone who lives in the city, someone we trust," she told me. "If anyone can help you access your physical magic, it's her."

My eyes snapped to her momentarily while I washed off my hands. Then I turned back to the foaming soap and finished my task, wiping my hands on a towel nearby.

"Just let me change and then—" I started but Ursa cut me off with a wave of her hand.

A moment later, I was wearing a brown racer back tank and matching leggings, the look I had worn during all of my hand to hand combat training. The King had claimed I didn't need to know how to fight but Ursa had insisted. I thought it was just her way of justifying cutting me up some more in the training room, coating that obsidian floor with my blood in vengeance for our other training drills when I invaded her soul. But it was strengthening me. I wasn't the thin wisp of an academic that I had arrived as. My muscles were becoming more toned, my stomach flattening, my curves more pronounced, more feminine.

"We don't have time," she snapped. "Let's go."

Before I could object, she reached for me and we were hurtling through contorted darkness, away from the palace and toward some undisclosed location in the city. I stumbled on the other side, taking a few steps down the cobblestone road behind me, gasping in the frosty night air.

"I hate that," I growled, gritting my teeth against both the nausea roiling through me and the frigid air creating goosebumps on my exposed skin.

"It's the quickest, safest way to get you out of the palace," Ursa snapped, grabbing me by the arm and pulling me quickly from the alley in which we had emerged. "Gemini Morningstar wards against anyone shadowstepping right into her home but the alley by the pub nearby is fair game."

"Morningstar?" I croaked, rubbing my arms to keep warm as my breath froze in front of me. "Who—"

"My aunt. Father's sister. And one badass Fae."

My eyes widened as we stepped out of the alley onto the wider cobblestone road beyond. We were indeed outside of a pub. I could hear the loud jeering of drunken men as they whistled at the women making the rounds inside, clapping each other on the back and laughing in deep, booming voices. One man stumbled outside, still holding a pint, and fell face first into a freshly piled snowdrift, his ale spilling out and dribbling down the side, turning the snow a deep gold.

I looked above the shutters of the tavern and saw the sign, beaten and faded, swinging in the faint arctic breeze. The Evening Starr. A play on the royal family's name and a hint at what could be found inside.

"She trained me," Ursa told me, still talking about her aunt, the elusive Gemini Morningstar. "She trained all of us and she can train you, too. I'm sure of it."

Ursa led me onward, toward a large and looming house at the end of the road. If we were in the mortal plane, it would be the kind of home that started rumors among the neighbor kids, the kind of place that everyone would assume was haunted simply because of the dreary color scheme and the lack of proper landscaping. It wasn't the immaculate manse that I had expected for the sister of a King. It was a modest home, two stories and thin. The land around it was fenced as if to keep any loiterers out and I wondered what happened if one tried to shadowstep into a place that was warded against it as Ursa and I passed through the physical gate. The surrounding air shimmered as we passed and I glimpsed a glowing, magical shield enveloping the house and its grounds as we entered.

"Aunt Gemini takes her privacy seriously," Ursa explained, noting my observation.

"How does your father have a sister?" I asked, suddenly realizing something else as well. "I thought the succession rites—"

"Gemini was thought dead already at the time of my father's succession. She only came to light afterwards and then she bent the knee and promised not to usurp him."

"Thought dead? Why—"

But the sound of the front door swinging open interrupted us. No one, however, stood on the other side. Eerie haunted house indeed.

"Come on," Ursa instructed and then we hurried along the path, up the steps, and into the foyer. Once inside, the door slammed shut tightly behind us and I tensed.

"Is this the mortal?" a disembodied voice asked from somewhere to our left. I whirled to find a woman emerging from a darkened room, her dark eyes heavily lidded, bags beneath them. Her long dark hair was graying, frayed and tied behind her in a loose knot.

"Yes, Aunt Gemini," Ursa spoke with a tone of respect I thought she reserved only for her father, the King.

Gemini Morningstar looked over me with a shrewd eye, crossing her arms and glaring at me as if I were something insignificant, hardly worth her time.

"Explain to me, dear niece, why my brother deems it wise to train our enemy's heir," she said.

"Hope for a new generation?" Ursa guessed with a shrug. "The king's intent is not for me to reason out."

"No, you just follow his orders."

Ursa bristled.

"Come, dear, let us see what you can do," Gemini said and led me further into the dark house.

I followed her through narrow hallways, past room after room, and realized that some magic was at work here, making this place much larger inside than it appeared from outside. It was a manse, some ancient ancestral home complete with dusty old paintings of long dead royal Fae and their families. Or maybe they were still alive. It was hard to tell with immortality.

We reached a larger room at the end of the hall. It was in the shape of an oval. Its walls were made of windows that opened into the night sky beyond. A greenhouse sat nearby, a path to which led right up to the only door in this room. It reminded me of what the mortals might call a sun room but this one seemed more fitted to worshipping the moonlight than basking in the sun.

Gemini Morningstar positioned herself a few feet in front of me and waited.

"Show me," she said simply and I complied.

Narrowing my focus, as I had before, I delved into her soul. I found that impenetrable wall around her core, like all the other powerful Fae I had encountered had, but before that, her surface. It was still, calm, and dark, much like her home. There was no trace of any emotion here. No anger, no sadness, no happiness. Nothing. Wrinkling my brow in confusion, I withdrew.

"An empath," she said simply. "How incredibly rare. Tell me, girl, what did you find?"

"I—nothing," I confessed and Ursa pushed slightly off of the wall she had been leaning against in surprise.

"You cannot fight an empath," Gemini said and I knew she was teaching her niece at the moment. "Because fighting an empath is fighting yourself. Silencing yourself, your baser emotions, shielding the ones that matter. You will not overwhelm an empath, not forever, but you can kill her with quiet."

I shuddered at the choice of words but Gemini was smiling as she turned to face me again.

"So try something physical," she commanded. "You cannot hurt my soul. So pierce my body."

"I can't," I told her.

"You can try, can you not?"

And so I did. For hours. I focused, I employed every method they instructed, imagined every scenario they detailed for me. Nothing worked. Gemini was about to tell me she was convinced I could not utilize physical magic because of my mortal heritage when Ursa interrupted to inform her I had shattered a glass in my room. Then the old woman watched me with renewed interest.

In the end, our attempts utterly exhausted me so Gemini instructed us to return in a week to try again. She would research what existed of my "condition" and have a new training regimen ready when we returned.

Discouraged, I followed Ursa from the home, pushing through the gate and back onto the city street beyond. The tavern was even more raucous at this hour, the patrons inside growing louder the more they drank. I was in a foul mood. What little hope had bloomed within me at the possibility of accessing my physical magic with the help of this ancient Fae had vanished. So now I stormed through the streets, a few steps ahead of Ursa, with a scowl.

"We will try again," she was assuring me, though I could tell that she was just as disappointed as I was. "Gemini is the best trainer in the realm. She will have answers. She will—"

She was cut off by the sudden appearance of a dozen men in flowing green robes as they emerged from the darkened alleys around us. The light from the tavern slanted over the road, illuminating Ursa's stunned expression as they arranged themselves in a circle surrounding us. With a flick of her wrist, Ursa's daggers appeared and I shrank against her, searching the souls of the men around us. Hints of fear overwhelmed by an honorable sense of purpose. These were soldiers. Ursa palmed a blade.

"I wouldn't do that, Princess Morningstar," a familiar voice spoke from the darkness.

Ursa went completely still as Lord Koa emerged from the shadows, hovering just outside the circle of his men.

"Hand over the hostage and we will not hurt you," he told her.

"Over my dead body," Ursa spat.

"It didn't have to be this way," he replied, raising his hands as he shook his head.

Vines from nearby fence posts, shutters, and potted plants reached toward us, snaking along the cobblestones and stretching out to meet us, clawing at our heels. Ursa raised a boot and stomped down on one, sending her blades spinning for another that was only inches from my face. I reeled back but one of the vines caught me, pushed me upright. I scrambled forward, spinning around to see Ursa throwing her blades at rapid speed, faster than I could have imagined.

In a matter of seconds, those obsidian daggers had cut through three of the largest vines, slashed the throat of one soldier and hurtled towards two more who were scurrying out of their way. She took a moment, between knife throws, to slam her hands down to her thighs. A cloud of darkness rose around her, obscuring the fight, making it difficult for the soldiers to flee. But still, those vines reached. One of them had me by the wrist.

I slashed out with magic but I hadn't mastered the physical forces and nothing happened. It pulled and dragged me with it, kicking and screaming. I lashed out again and this time, the vine cleaved deftly in two. I blinked at it as it slithered away, part of it still wrapped around my wrist, in awe at what I had accomplished. But then Gemini stepped forward out of the shadows, hands raised, and I realized I hadn't done anything at all.

In a moment, three more soldiers fell, choking on something I couldn't see but, when they turned purple and fell to the ground, unmoving, I noticed the wisp of black smoke escape their lungs at their dying breath and turned to find Gemini watching them, her head held high.

Ursa was locked in battle with Lord Koa, having successfully distracted him long enough that those vines were no longer reaching for me.

"Run, girl," Gemini hissed, throwing out her hands to block another soldier that was hurling my way.

I didn't have to be told twice. I ducked under her arms and sprinted past the tavern, hearing the sound of Lord Koa roaring in fury as I disappeared into the dark alley.

I couldn't shadowstep and I did not know where I was but I kept running, my feet pounding against the pavement, turning away from any opening at which the fight grew louder, nearer. I resurfaced on a main road after a few twists and turns in the alleys and found it utterly deserted. I turned and followed it up the slight incline toward the hill on which I knew the palace sat. If I could only get to the gates, they couldn't reach me. Not there.

I took two steps and then stopped, chest heaving from all the running. A figure had appeared right in front of me, only a foot away. I faltered back a step, nearly tripping on a loose stone. Cassiopeia's eyes were wide and full of sorrow when she reached for me.

"I'm so sorry," she whispered, and then her warm hand gripped my cold wrist and I didn't even have time to scream as the world below spun away from us.

Chapter Twenty-Five

A Bitter Blade

I threw a punch before the world even stopped spinning and bruised my fist deeply as it connected with something hard on the other side.

"Ouch," a familiar voice grunted and I came to, blinking rapidly to clear my vision, to see Rook holding a hand to his bleeding nose, hissing in pain as red spots dotted the white snow beneath our feet.

"Ren, please—" Cass begged but I whirled on her next lashing out blindly, violently. She evaded me, shadowstepping a few feet away and holding her hands up in front of her in a sign of peaceful surrender. "Just stop for a second."

I turned, my braid swinging over my shoulder, and reached for the blade I knew Rook always kept holstered at his side. The warrior was too busy examining his injury to guard against me as I wrenched it from its sheath and trained it on both of them. I held it out, pointed at their throats, and backed away so that I could see both of them at once, so that I could assess the entirety of the threats surrounding me.

"Ren," Cass said again as Rook looked on in stunned horror, "don't do this. Just listen to us, please. Give us a chance. We can explain everything."

"I don't want any more of your explanations," I snapped. "I don't want any more of your lies."

"Just one more, then," Rook said, his gaze fixed on a point over my shoulder.

I whirled around and all the breath left my lungs. I faltered back a step, then two. I froze, keeping the knife aloft as my mouth fell open and my eyes bulged from my head. I shook my head slowly at first and then viciously.

"No," I whispered. "No, it's not possible."

"Hello Ren."

Lark's voice was the same. That deep, intoxicating drawl that drew me in like a warm fire on a frozen winter night. His dark eyes remained on mine as he watched me closely and I squirmed under the weight of that intense gaze I had thought was lost to me forever. He wore the same dark, embellished cloak, stark black against the backdrop of the snowy landscape we found ourselves in.

I aimed for his neck when I slashed out with Rook's blade.

He dodged the blow expertly. Rook stepped forward to intervene, already drawing his other weapons, those two swords crossed at his back.

"Don't," Lark warned and Rook hesitated as I swung again.

Lark dodged and then dodged again as I lashed out wildly with the blade. I used the training Ursa had given me, placing my feet where they were supposed to go, using my momentum to my advantage. But he had endured the same training as my trainer and had done this for far longer than me.

I raised my arm high, intending to slash down at him, but he caught me by the wrist and spun me so that my back was up against him and he was holding me tight. One hand was around my wrist, holding the blade away from us, the other was around my waist, pressing me against the hard planes of his body. I felt a flush of heat creep up my neck and screamed in frustration.

"Yield," he whispered, his breath warm upon the shell of my ear.

Hand shaking, I released the dagger and it plunged into the snow below.

Rook scrabbled forward to collect it as I shot into Lark's soul to find an impenetrable dark wall guarding his emotions. He spun me around so that I was facing him, our noses just inches apart, frozen breath mingling in the frigid air. He cocked his head to the side, dark eyes boring into mine.

"You've learned a new trick," he drawled.

I lifted both hands to his chest and gave him a firm shove backwards.

"Traitor!" I shouted, slicing a hand through the air.

The snow behind him tumbled, rolling forward until it reached a boulder in the distance. That boulder split in two as if it had been slashed, the top sliding off of the bottom and rumbling down the hill beyond. Lark watched with a raised brow.

"Two new tricks," he said.

I tried my best not to appear just as surprised as they were at my sudden display of physical magic as I glared at him.

"Are you going to tell me why you captured me against my will?" I snapped. "Again?"

He cringed at my tone, at the hatred I was pouring into it. His eyes widened slightly with sorrow. I felt a pulse of sadness plunge into me and knew he had allowed that wall to open, just a little, just enough that I could feel his pain. But I gritted my teeth against it and kept my gaze narrowed at him.

"My father has told you his side of the story," Lark said then, his voice low, expression grim. "Let me tell you mine."

"And why should I hear it? Why should I listen to what my kidnapper has to say?"

"Because you deserve to know the truth."

I barked out a bitter laugh.

"Oh now, suddenly, I deserve the truth," I scoffed. "You didn't think I deserved the truth during those weeks we spent together in the Court of Light and Life, or when you pulled me through that rift into this immortal plane without my consent, or when—"

"Yes, I did. But knowing the truth puts you in danger. I thought I was protecting you from that."

I strode forward until I was inches away from his face again and narrowed my glare, arranging my expression into a sneer.

"I can protect myself," I growled. "I don't need you."

His gaze flicked over me, from my dark, kohl-lined eyes, to my brown training attire.

"Maybe not," he muttered with a frown.

"Just let him tell you what happened, Ren, please," Cass was pleading with me from where she stood beside Rook.

Rook hadn't relaxed entirely, not yet, not until he could determine for certain whether I was a threat or not. His hands still rested on his weapons but relaxed as my gaze flicked to his. I looked over at Cass once, noting the bags under her shining eyes.

"And how do I know that this time he's telling me the truth?" I asked, crossing my arms and raising a brow.

"I'll let down my wall," Lark drawled from behind me.

I froze, every muscle in my body going rigid. When I turned back to face him, he was already staring back, that intense gaze boring into me. He meant it.

"You'll let me in?" I asked.

"Entirely," he told me. "No tricks. Nothing hidden. You can see for yourself that I'm not lying. You can feel everything I felt when I did what I did."

"Lark—" Rook started to argue but quieted at one quick glance from his master.

I watched him warily. He stood in front of me, still as stone, jaw clenched but dark eyes aflame with that familiar determination.

"Fine," I said in agreement. "Where can we go?"

He reached out a hand and I knew what he was offering. Shadowstep. With a shaky breath, I took it.

Part Four
Redemption

Chapter Twenty-Six
A Confession From the Heart

The world blinked away and returned. Some of the dizzying sensation was diminishing. I supposed that meant I was getting used to it. But it still nauseated me, the feeling of being ripped out of the world and tossed back into it.

It took me a moment to realize that we were in the horrendous orange-covered apartment from the Court of Wanderers, the first place he had ever taken me in this realm, the place where he had offered me his friendship, his understanding, and the chance to figure out who I could be here. I had felt fear here and even a bit of hope, excitement at the scholastic opportunity. Now, I looked at that orange leather sofa and felt only hate.

"The Court of Wanderers?" I asked with a raised brow, hesitating in the center of the room while the Fae spread out all around me.

Rook wandered into the kitchen where he leaned against a counter and waited, giving us space but remaining near enough to intervene if necessary. Cass strode away to the windows, looking down at the city beyond and averting her gaze as if that might make this easier for her. Lark kept his eyes on me, mimicking my movements so as not to appear threatening.

"I'm going to tell you everything and, when I'm done, the choice will be yours. The portal to the mortal realm is just down the street. You can walk yourself there and step through it and I'll never darken your doorstep again. Or you can choose to stay with us, to find a place in this realm that is entirely your own, wherever that may be."

I tensed, hope clawing at the door of my heart, begging to be let in. But I couldn't trust him, couldn't tell if he was lying or not.

"Shall we begin, then?" I asked, instead, remaining calm, remaining distant, as I strode forward and took a seat on that hideous couch.

Lark gave a nod and settled into the armchair in front of me, leaning forward in preparation. Rook tensed in the kitchen and even Cass loosed a breath that fogged up the windows. I focused, narrowing my gaze and peering into his soul. The wall was still there and I almost said as much aloud but then I watched as it crumbled away, one piece at a time, brick by brick, until nothing was standing between us.

I felt the rush of his emotions then. Some fresh, some centuries old, cascading into me. It was so much that I had to grip the seat beneath me, knuckles turning white as I gritted my teeth and faced the onslaught of centuries worth of feeling.

His sorrow hit me first, a wave that pulled me under, drowning me in countless losses, untenable grief, a sea of mistakes and failures. Then came the anger, always an easily identifiable base emotion. His father, his sister, his brother, even Rook from a time long before they shared such a close bond. Other people too, people I didn't recognize, people I had never known. Anger always clung to those who had caused it. They wore every color of the rainbow and marched forward in a dizzying haze of blurred lines as I was still trying to resurface from the sadness. Rage followed, a fiery inferno with no particular direction, encompassing me in its swirling heat.

Then came fleeting moments of happiness, laughter, light. Memories associated with some of the same people who had preceded in anger and more, far more. He let me see them, flashes of them, dreams of living color, waking jubilance. It filled my veins with calm, clarity. A sampling of others followed. Doubt, pain, fear, disgust, trust, joy, anticipation. It was too fast and too much to follow. I closed my eyes and tried to feel it all, tried to focus on it all. Then I felt it, a light blossoming, growing larger and stronger. Love. I recognized it the moment I felt it. My breath hitched as I prepared to be overcome by it. But he pulled it back, at the last minute, and my eyes snapped open to find him watching me.

"Ask," he said simply.

"What happened?" I replied.

"Ariadne Dawnpaw has been the heir of the Court of Peace and Pride for over a millennium now. I've known her name since I was born. She has a reputation for being manipulative and deceitful. I never cared to get to know her personally or to intervene in any of her schemes, despite how much I heard of them from members of other courts, people she had wronged. I would not go against the heir to another Upper Court, not when she had done nothing to me," Lark spoke and I measured his emotions. So far, he was telling the truth, or at least the truth so far as he believed it. I grit my teeth against the accusation that my mother was manipulative and deceitful as he continued. "But then the council announced their intention to test the possibility of revealing our existence to the mortal plane. They said that they were in search of an ambassador, someone who could be trusted to represent us and our interests to the mortals. I had no interest in the job but that was before I heard Ariadne did."

I tensed, remembering what the King had told me about this part of the story. That Lark had wanted it, had desired it more than anything he ever had before. I searched the Fae sitting in front of me, however, and found no trace of desire, no inkling of dissatisfaction that he had not been chosen for the job, not a hint of the devastation his father had suggested he had exhibited on finding out that Ariadne had gotten the gig. My shoulders slumped as I realized, again, that I had been lied to.

"I went to the Court of Peace and Pride," Lark continued and I snapped back to attention. "I talked with Alban, asked him about his daughter's sudden philanthropic interests. He was pleased with her, practically beaming with pride. He said he was happy she had finally found purpose and that she was throwing herself into this so wholeheartedly. He even told me she had been visiting the mortal realm doing research for months. But I knew the council had only made their announcement weeks ago."

His pulse remained steady, his emotions calm, collected. There was no hint of deception when he spoke.

"I knew Ariadne did nothing that wouldn't result in some personal gain so I took it upon myself to investigate. I couldn't send anyone else. If anyone but a high-ranking member of another royal family were caught spying on another member of another royal family, they would be executed. So I went. I waited in this apartment, watching for her. And one day I saw her walking right towards the portal. I followed her to the mortal realm, all the way to New York City to a dingy apartment in a dark, forgotten part of town."

I was leaning forward in my seat, I realized, and attempted to right myself, to focus on examining his emotions as he spoke. But they were still level, still consistent. And that wall was nowhere to be found. There was nowhere for him to hide.

"She had a man chained up in the basement," he said then and I felt a rise of anger within him at the memory. He clenched his jaw, looking away from me as he spoke, as if remembering it all vividly now that he was saying it aloud. "I heard her talking to him but I couldn't hear what she was saying. When she left, I sneaked down there myself. When I stepped into that basement, he didn't even move. His eyes were open but he wasn't seeing me. They were glazed over, his pupils a fog of gray. I should have freed him. I should have cut through those chains and helped him escape. But I couldn't break him out of that fog and I knew that even if I broke the chains, he wouldn't leave."

I was starting to feel sick and, from the signals I was receiving from the rest of the room, the others were too. But Lark grit his teeth and went on.

"I returned home in a daze, confused. The Dawnpaws could sense thought, maybe even read it. There was never any sign that they could manipulate it, could control it. But it was the only thing that made sense. I researched their family lineage, your family lineage, for any mention of mind control and found none. But it was eating away at me. I had to know. I declared my intentions to run against Ariadne for the position of ambassador just to keep it away from her a little longer and I went back to that apartment. I sneaked into the basement and I used my magic to flood that man's mind until my own ability crowded out hers. When that fog broke, I released him, and he started screaming the second he was free of her control. He grabbed my collar, shook me, begged me to help him, to save him. He verified my suspicions, saying she was controlling his mind, forcing him into a relationship with her, saying she loved him, that she was making arrangements so that they could be together. He said she had... used him too."

Lark's eyes slid closed as a wave of sadness and disgust washed through him.

"I broke his chains, I helped him up the stairs, and I took him all the way to Hadley University where he said his brother worked in the astrophysics department. I promised him I would take care of Ariadne, that I would see her punished for what she had done to him. I put up protective wards around the university and I left. I rushed home to tell my father all that I had discovered but arrived to find a feast in progress, celebrating Ariadne's victory over me for the position of ambassador to the mortal plane, allowing her full, unobstructed access to the mortal plane. I lost it. I destroyed half the feast in my rage. My father assumed I was angry that I had lost and, when I told him about what she had done, he accused me of petty jealousy and told me not to dare breathe a word of that nonsense to anyone else."

My hands were shaking so I gripped the couch below me even tighter. He wasn't lying. I could feel it. He wasn't lying. But this couldn't be true.

"I went silent," he continued, the memory pulling him under, shrouding him in anger, in bitter sorrow. I wanted to reach out to him, but held myself at bay. Not yet. I couldn't trust him. Not yet. "I did as my father said. I didn't tell anyone because if my own father heard that tale and accused me of making it up out of jealousy, everyone else would too. And besides, the mortal was safe, hidden at the university, and protected by my magic. For a time, the world moved on. Ariadne seemed happy with her new position, keeping busy with the council as they sought to define her role. She was in and out of meetings every day. She hadn't even set foot in the mortal plane. I knew because I'd had her tracked."

Lark glanced Rook in the corner and he gave a solemn nod. My breath caught in my throat.

"But that mortal, he was never one to stay in place. He thought he was safe. He didn't understand that my wards only protected him when he was at the university. He ventured off campus and she found him," Lark said and I stared at him, wide eyed. I couldn't breathe. "She dragged him back to our realm, put him under her spell again, and locked him in the dungeons of her court. I couldn't reach him, not without invading another court, not without starting a war. I tried to tell my father again but he wouldn't hear it. Ariadne was doing a great job of convincing the council they had made the right choice. That she was the shining representation of the Fae race and I was an unhinged lunatic from the darkest court. She held him for two years."

I hissed in a breath.

"Then she announced she was pregnant and I knew whose it was. I knew she had sired a child with that mortal captive of hers. It was horrific, repulsive, and I knew he wouldn't want it. I knew I couldn't break him free of her control, not while he was so close to her, but I also knew that he wouldn't want her to have his child. That he wouldn't want his son or daughter to be raised by that woman, controlled by that woman, never really knowing if what they were doing was their mother's will or their own. So I told the council. When they were all gathered for a meeting, I burst in, despite having been asked not to attend, and I told them all that she had become pregnant by a mortal. That, alone, was against our laws. It should have been enough. I shouldn't have even had to make any other claims. But her father stood and gave some rousing speech about there being no better way to establish an alliance with the mortals than through commingling blood. After all, that was how it had been done for centuries. Arranged marriages and the like. The council bought it and chose not to punish her. I went stark-raving mad. I started screaming to anyone who would listen what she had done, how she had the mortal locked up in the dungeons, how she had been raping him for years, how she had him completely under her control. And because there was no history of mind control in the Dawnpaw family, because that magic was unverified and unknown, no one believed me."

I withdrew from his emotions to face my own. I knew what was coming. The writing was on the wall. The picture he was painting was only missing one key piece and I knew what it was before he said it.

"I fought for the entire duration of her pregnancy. I made multiple attempts to access those dungeons, to save that mortal, but she beat me at every turn. She was always one step ahead," Lark said and I noticed Rook tensing again as he looked away, jaw clenched against the reminder of their failures. "I got close once. When she was in labor, I thought I could use her pain as a distraction. It was enough to break her hold on his mind, enough for him to say three words to me that I will never forget. Save the child."

His eyes flicked to mine and I crumbled. I lifted one shaky hand to my mouth as a sob escaped me. Cass was there in an instant, holding me against her as I wept, as Lark continued because he had to, because I had to hear the end.

"We made a plan. Rook tried to break the mortal free or, at least, he made a good enough attempt to draw Ariadne's attention away from the baby. Then Cass and I sneaked in, dispatched the guards, and we—," his voice broke as his eyes bore into mine, "we took you."

My lips trembled, tears streaming down my cheeks.

"I brought you right to your uncle, the man I'd taken your father to before. I told him only what you needed to know. I reinforced the wards around the campus and added a few more in the surrounding areas. I burnt that dingy apartment to the ground. And then I came back and I—" he closed his eyes. "My father was waiting. Alban and the other council members were there. Ariadne was distraught, half naked and wailing. They asked me what I did and I told them I killed you."

My whole body shook with sobs.

"I told them I killed you so they wouldn't look for you, so she wouldn't find you. And they believed it because it was exactly what they had already convinced themselves I was capable of, anyway. She started screaming. She fell to the floor, clinging to her father. Alban snapped at my father about doing something with me. So he banished me. And I disappeared before I could hear anymore."

In the silence that followed the culmination of Lark's story, I wept. I turned into Cass and let the tears flow freely as my mind reeled to understand every version of this tale that I had been told.

"Ren," Lark tried and I did not have to target his soul to identify every emotion in his broken voice.

"Give her time," Cass said, looking up at him from over my shoulder.

So he did.

Chapter Twenty-Seven
A Wound That Heals

Lark and Rook left the very next morning. He had looked at me in a way that made my heart go out to him. I knew he wanted to talk to me, to ask questions, but I wasn't ready to answer them and he knew that. So he took Rook and they left to continue their hunt for the gorgon with the key to Hellscape and Cass stayed home with me. But that monstrous orange apartment was too small to hold everything I was feeling so I took my chance to get out of it once a day when the market opened and Cass had made a list of what we would need to nourish ourselves for the next few hours.

On the first day, I had only retrieved a quarter of the list before all the stares had gotten to me and I had rushed back to the apartment in a full-blown panic attack leaving Cass to finish the list herself. It was the gray, I knew it. I had opted for the gray color scheme that signaled I did not belong to any court. Ever since Lark had told me what had really happened with my mother, I couldn't stomach the thought of wearing brown. But the gray stuck out even more in a sea of orange and that first day I had let that sense of unbelonging get to me.

The second day I returned, it was with my head held high. I was determined to finish the list, to not let the stares get to me. They did but I finished the list anyway and rushed home as soon as I did.

By now, three days since I'd begun, I was browsing the market stalls at my own pace, feeling the discomfort of the stares and letting it pass on through me like a warm breeze on a summer day. I enjoyed the few precious moments of the day in which I escaped that apartment. It wasn't Cass. She was doing well to treat me normally, not to hover over me too much or give me too many pitying glances. It was the feeling of freedom, no matter how small.

I was aware now, more than ever before, of the threats I faced. Both from my mother and from external sources as well. The Court of Friends had tried to abduct me. The King of the Bone Court had held me hostage for weeks. I needed to be careful about where I went and who I spoke to. But I also needed to get out into the world. I needed not to feel like I was a captive anymore. I needed to make my own decisions.

I didn't necessarily want to go to the market. I just wanted to be able to say I was going to the market and have no one stop me. And Cass hadn't. I was grateful to her for that, more grateful than she would ever know.

We were unpacking the produce that I had purchased late that morning when the door to the apartment burst open and Lark came through carrying an injured Rook. Cass threw down the vegetables and ran to assist him as he lowered Rook onto the couch and the warrior let out a yelp of pain.

"I've summoned a healer we can trust," Lark was saying, rapidly, as he pulled away from Rook who was bleeding from a long gash in his left leg. Cass had fashioned a strip of fabric from thin air and was replacing the blood-soaked tourniquet Lark had placed around Rook's thigh with a new one of her own.

"What happened?" Cass snapped, not daring to look away from the wound as she pulled the knot tight.

"We found the gorgon," Lark said.

Cass' eyes snapped up to her brother's but Lark just kept his jaw clenched, gaze firmly on his injured friend. Rook was pale, his breaths becoming shallower.

"Move," I snapped, stepping forward to examine the wound. I wasn't an expert by any means but I had spent a few years following around a med student I had a bit of a crush on in my early twenties and had learned proper field protocol from the soldiers I spent time with at the camps under the rifts.

"A healer is coming," Lark repeated.

"We have to stop the bleeding or he won't make it that long," I snapped. I jerked my head in the direction of the fireplace behind us. "Light that fire. Cass, get me the cooking weight from the kitchen."

Sensing where I was going with this, Rook began to whimper and writhe beneath my fingers.

"Stop that or you might puncture an artery," I snapped and he fell still. "Cass!"

She was at my side a moment later, handing me the flat metal press used to weigh down meats and vegetables in grilling. Lark snapped his fingers and flames roared to life in the grate. I turned and set the press inside, letting it heat.

"Rook," I said then, turning my attention back to the patient. "I need you to take some deep breaths for me, okay? Can you do that? Close your eyes and focus on my words. Breathe in for five seconds, okay? One, two, three, four, five. Good. Now breathe out for five. One, two, three, four—"

I reached for the press and grabbed it from the fire, pinching his wound closed with my fingers and pushing the hot press against his skin a moment later. He howled in agony, kicking his uninjured leg wildly. Cass muttered a curse and turned away as the stench of burning flesh filled the room.

"Okay," I said, examining my work. "One more time, okay? Just one more. Breathe in for me. One, two, three—"

Rook screamed again as I clamped the press down a second time, holding it still as he writhed. But when I pulled away, the bleeding had stopped. I exhaled, wiping the back of my hand against my forehead as I fell back and let Cass fill the space I had occupied, holding him close and cradling his head against her chest.

It took another ten minutes for the healer to arrive. He never would have made it that long. Lark seemed to sense the same thing when the woman burst into the apartment, the skirts of her yellow dress flowing behind her as she ran to the patient, examined the cauterization wounds, and gave us a grim nod of understanding before getting to work with her magic. I let my shoulders slump then, breathing easily now that a professional was on the scene, and left to find the bathroom so that I could wash the blood from my hands and from where I'd rubbed it against my forehead.

I felt his presence as I leaned over the basin, scrubbing the blood from my skin.

"You should be in there with him," I said without looking up.

"He has enough support for the moment," Lark answered, his voice that intoxicating low drawl I hadn't realized how much I'd missed. "Are you ready to talk about it?"

I turned off the faucet, dried my hand on the hanging towel, and turned to face him, leaning back against the sink as I did.

"Do I have to be?" I asked.

"No," he answered.

We stood there in the silence for a moment, watching each other.

"I know we didn't come back in the best way," Lark said, gesturing toward the living room where an injured Rook was recovering with the help of healing magic. "But I was relieved to see that you had stayed."

I didn't answer right away because I wasn't sure what to say. I had stayed and I wasn't even sure why myself. I could have left, could have taken that portal home and never looked back. He had said as much. But I hadn't.

"You told me the truth," I said, simply, with a shrug as though it didn't matter.

"Ren," he said my name sweetly, like a prayer, and took a step toward me.

"I watched you die," I blurted and he stopped short. "I watched you hang for the crime of stealing me from my mother and then daring to return with me again. I grieved for you. I spent days coming to terms with the fact that I would never see you again, hating myself for even wanting to after what I believed you had done to me. Finding out that you were going to be executed, it was the first time I ever used magic, the first time I felt connected to what I was. And your father spent time that he didn't have, time that he could have spent on anyone else, training me to use that magic. So he may not have known the truth of what happened and he may have been wrong about your intentions. But he didn't have the audacity to claim he was keeping anything from me to protect me. He was honest with me. Even honest about the fact that I was a hostage."

"You're right."

"It wasn't your call, Lark. It wasn't your decision to determine what I did and didn't know."

"You're right. It wasn't."

"Because you wanted to protect me? All of this to protect me? You lost your reputation, you got exiled from your home and then, when you returned, you got caught because you were saving me. Always saving me. Why? Why am I worth it to you?"

"You know why," he growled, taking another step toward me. I faltered, reaching back to brace myself against the sink. "I know you feel it too, Ren. This connection between us. Like there's a part of you firmly embedded into me and a part of me within you."

I blinked, chest heaving as I thought of that dark fragment, unidentifiable but with a mind of its own, pulling at me, feeling.

"What is it?" I whispered in awe.

"I have my theories. But none of them matter as much as yours. When did you find it?"

"After you died. Or after I thought you died. I was... sorting through myself and I found it. I didn't know what it was so I gave it a tug and it, you, tugged back."

"I felt you then but I knew before."

"When?"

"When I broke that man's arms for touching you."

A shiver went through me but I held his gaze as I asked again, "What is it?"

"They call it a soul bond," he told me, that intense gaze of his boring into me as he did. "It's incredibly rare and no one really knows how it's formed. Some people think you're born with it, that it draws you to the other person, some people think it's formed when you meet. There are only a handful of them in recorded history. It's a connection between two people like no other. Part of your soul is within me and part of mine is in you. The mortals have a version of it that isn't so mysterious. Soul mates."

My breath hitched as I stared back at him, the angular lines of his beautiful face, those pronounced cheekbones, deep, dark eyes, full lips. He was staring at me as well and I felt his desire coursing through him, heightening my own with its presence.

"You—you think we're soul mates? Or, um, soul bonded?" I asked, trying my best to focus on the conversation and not how close he was to me now.

"I think there's a part of me that calls to you," he answered. "And a part of you that calls back."

I stopped breathing.

"But this," he said then, gesturing between us, "like everything else, is your choice. I know you don't trust me yet. And I know I've done damage to what little trust I had managed to build before. I'm willing to do everything in my power to rebuild that trust, to make you comfortable around me again and, maybe then, we can... revisit this, whatever this is between us."

Because I didn't trust myself to speak, I clamped my lips shut and nodded.

"For now," he drawled, looking down at my hands and taking them in his own, running one thumb over the backs of them and hesitating, holding himself back, "I'm going to check on my friend, the one you saved. When you're ready, I'd like for you to join us. We have much to discuss."

He gently let go of me, turning away and striding toward the door.

"At some point," he called out as he reached the threshold, "I look forward to hearing what sort of training my sister gave you."

"At some point," I called back, able to breathe again because of the distance between us, "I'd like to hear how you survived your own execution."

He grinned that broad, dazzling smirk back at me once before striding through the door and leaving me alone in the washroom, knees weak and heart heavy.

Chapter Twenty-Eight
A Cave of Nightmares

Rook was in much better spirits when I finally emerged from the bathroom. I had taken a shower first, telling myself it was because of the bloodstains still visible on my hands from helping Rook but really it was because I was trying to buy time before I had to face them all again after the bombshell that Lark had just dropped on me regarding our connection.

So I had taken a particularly long shower and an even longer time selecting the dark gray denim pants and loose gray sweater that I threw on before exiting into the living room again. I was so lost in thought that I hadn't heard the revelry taking place just outside the bedroom door.

Rook was entirely healed, the magic having done the trick, and he was drinking heavily, smiling as Cass laughed uncontrollably at some story they were recalling. Even Lark was grinning, raising a glass to his lips which he paused when he saw me, that penetrating gaze sweeping over me from head to toe, drinking me in as if he could never get enough. Heat rushed to my cheeks and I lowered my head, pretending to fix my hair as I settled onto the settee next to Cass.

"You are so lying," she was saying, though she was grinning from ear to ear.

"I swear to you, I'm not," Rook boomed back. "That gorgon took one look at Lark and shit his metaphorical pants."

Cass snorted into her glass as Rook reached behind her to hand me one of my own. Our eyes met and he gave me a solemn nod of thanks. It was enough.

"He's not used to a Morningstar actually taking the job of Hellscape warden seriously, I bet," Cass replied, rolling her eyes as she took a drink. Rook nodded his agreement. "Did he give you the key?"

Rook grinned, looking at Lark.

"It took some convincing," Lark drawled before taking a deep sip of that amber liquid.

His eyes flicked to mine and I squirmed in my chair, internally cursing myself for the physical reaction. But the smirk on his lips when he noticed how he had affected me was almost worth it.

"He didn't turn you to stone," Cass said, brow creasing in confusion as she looked over her shoulder at where Rook lounged beside her. "But he stabbed you through the leg. How did that happen?"

"Turns out, he wasn't working alone," Rook told her and he wasn't smiling anymore.

Neither of them were.

"Lark?" Cass asked, glancing at her brother as if hoping he might tell her it wasn't true.

But Lark's smirk fell into a frown.

"Fae appeared before we could grab him," Lark said, swirling the contents of his glass and staring down into them. "Dressed in brown."

I froze.

"Peace and Pride," Cass muttered.

"My ass," Rook snorted.

Lark cut a glare to him and he fell silent, raising his glass to his lips instead.

"Do you think she's behind this?" Cass asked, her voice wavering as she did. "That she could be... recruiting gorgons to do her bidding? And why would she want the key to Hellscape anyway?"

"My guess?" Lark asked. "Access to minotaurs she can drop into the mortal realm."

I dropped my glass. It shattered against the rug, brown liquid seeping into the orange shag. But Cass waved a finger, without even looking my way, and the mess was gone and Rook was handing me another drink, which I took with shaking hands.

"You think she's behind the rifts," Cass breathed, so in awe that her voice barely rose above the whisper.

"Who else would have such power, such ambition? Who else might want to see our planes collide? Who else might want to tear down the division between mortal and immortal?"

"But even she doesn't have the power to tear through the Divide. Even she cannot control beasts or access Hellscape."

"Sixty years ago, we claimed she couldn't control minds either, Cass. Truthfully, we don't have the slightest idea what she is capable of. And we have been underestimating her for far too long."

The group fell silent at the implications of what Lark was suggesting. That a single woman, my mother, might be capable of ripping holes into the temporal divide that separated the immortal plane from the mortal, that she might be sending monsters of lore and legend back into the mortal world once again, was almost too much to take, particularly given what I had learned about her only recently.

"Is it even possible?" I asked in a whisper when no one else was speaking.

"It... would be the first time," Lark said. "I can't think of a way, but if anyone could..."

He left the rest unsaid. That it would be my mother. That she could feel justified in creating that much chaos, that much destruction. I felt sick to my stomach and set my drink on the table beside the settee, taking a deep breath.

"What's your plan?" Rook asked. "Storm into the Court of Peace and Pride and ask her? I don't really think she would be all that forthcoming, considering the last time you saw one another."

"We don't need to ask her," Lark said. "When there's the matter of the gorgon."

"They captured him. We won't be able to get to him."

"All gorgons report their actions to their queen."

Silence descended upon the group once more. I sensed an overwhelming feeling of doom surrounding them.

"You don't mean—" Cass started but Lark interrupted.

"It's been a while since we visited Medusa."

Wrapping my mortal mind around the fact that Medusa was real, let alone still alive and thriving as a self-proclaimed Queen somewhere in Hellscape, was proving nearly impossible. I had been quizzing Cass on what to expect for the last half hour as the men armed themselves to the teeth and prepared to leave again despite my suggestion that Rook take some time to recover. Even if he was healed physically, nearly dying and experiencing the pain of cauterization was a mental wound that would need time as well. But he waved me off and armed himself alongside his prince.

"Does she really have snakes for hair?" I was asking as Cass strapped a knife to her inner thigh and handed one to me to do the same.

"No," she answered with a snort. "That's a mortal myth. She can turn you to stone, though. That's sort of a gorgon's whole deal. She's also a raging bitch."

"Cass! Ren!" Rook called from the next room and I quickly slipped the knife beneath my waistband before joining Cass and the boys in the living room.

"Not that it would be a problem... again," Lark said, his gaze flicking to Rook, "but don't let her kiss you."

Cass rolled her eyes and then disappeared.

"One time, Lark," Rook argued with a sigh. "I kiss a gorgon one time and you never let me live it down."

"You were paralyzed for six hours," Lark reminded him.

Rook raised a particular finger in Lark's direction before disappearing as well. Lark chuckled, shaking his head, and extended a hand to me.

"She would talk to me, you know," I said softly. "My mother. So we don't have to go into Hellscape, so we don't have to face Medusa."

"I would rather face Medusa any day than Ariadne Dawnpaw," Lark replied with a frown, dark eyes boring into mine with significance. "Besides, unless you choose to go to her for yourself, she will have to drag you there over my cold, dead body."

Then he snatched my hand and we were gone, leaving behind the soothing warmth of the cozy orange apartment and emerging into a world of darkness.

It took my eyes a moment to adjust as I looked for the sky and could not find it. Everything around us was pure blackness. Not a trace of light to be found. But we were illuminated somehow. Just us, just our bodies. I raised my hands and peered down to find shining specks of light glinting from my fingertips.

"So you know you're not a monster," Cass whispered as I continued my examination. "And so you remember not to become one."

I shuddered as Lark approached an enormous door. He pulled a blade from his cloak and sliced his hand right down the middle. I gasped but Cass held me back as he pressed his palm to the ancient door. He muttered something in a language I did not understand and then pulled an obsidian block from an internal pocket of his coat and pressed it against where his hand had been, the bloody print left behind glowing red against the endless night.

With a groaning hiss of a mechanism that had gone mostly unused for centuries, the doors pushed inward and we strode inside. I stuffed my hands into the sleeves of my sweater, trying not to shiver. It was cold here and damp. Like a cave, but darker. Somewhere, far away, a beast I couldn't see let out a howl that chilled me to the bone. Shivering increased, I hastened forward to walk closer to Cass who had waved her hand and summoned a ball of light which she was using to light our way through the dark passages. Lark led on ahead as though he knew the way so well he didn't need the light.

Snarling emanated from a pit below, accompanied by hissing and the savage gnashing of teeth. I gasped, stumbling back a step and tripping on a rock. Rook caught me against his chest as I righted my footing.

"Careful there, beautiful," he warned lowly. "Wouldn't want you getting lost in here."

"Don't be a prick, Rook," Cass called out from up ahead.

"Wouldn't dream of it, princess," Rook muttered back, falling in beside me as we continued our walk.

He ushered me to the inside protectively, against the rising cliff of rock rather than next to the drop off into an enormous dark pit. I glanced up at him, wondering if his protective nature was instinctive or if Lark had commanded him to treat me this way.

"Thank you for earlier by the way," Rook said a moment later, so quietly I had to look up to make sure I'd heard him correctly.

"You don't have to thank me," I told him. "I imagine I owe you a great deal more than a healed leg."

"You don't owe us. None of us. We did what we did because it was the right thing to do. And I would do it again."

"Even with the banishment?"

"Especially with the banishment," he said and then turned to me, grinning mischievously. "Mortal women can be pretty fun when they let loose."

I snorted, the sound echoing around in the cave. Lark glanced back over his shoulder and I fell silent, Rook grinning like a fool all the while.

"Medusa isn't so bad," he whispered then, sensing my discomfort. "I'm sure whatever you've heard about her is worse than she really is. Mortals have a tendency to exaggerate."

"But she can turn people to stone."

"Delights in it."

"So should I avoid looking her in the eye or—"

"It doesn't work like that. It's magic, same as everything else. I won't let her get to you."

"Thank you."

"Let's stop thanking each other now, agreed?"

I smiled up at him.

"Agreed."

"Lights out," Lark called suddenly from the front of the line. The darkness seemed to close in on us even more so than usual as we stopped at the foot of the incline we had been descending. And Lark's voice was just as dark when he made the announcement that brought all of my fear and anticipation right back to the surface. "We're here."

Chapter Twenty-Nine
A Warden of Hell

Our narrow walk along the cave wall ended abruptly at a craggy opening and we entered a chamber bathed in soft moonlight, though there was no moon to be found and no opening above us. Stalagmites rose from the floor, some of which were nearly touching their stalactite brethren hanging above them. They were formed from a mineral that looked strangely volcanic. I brushed a finger along the smooth surface and froze.

"Is this—" I started, eyes widening as I looked around in wonder. "Are we inside of a volcano?"

"A hollowed out one," Rook answered, grinning broadly at my realization. "So don't go worrying about lava and all that. This one died a long, long time ago."

"A hollowed out volcano as a prison for ancient mythical beasts. Incredible."

"We can probably dispense with all that mythology business now, can't we? I mean, it isn't exactly a myth after all, is it?"

I opened my mouth to answer, but was interrupted by an ethereal female voice floating into the chamber from somewhere off to the side.

"To what do we owe the pleasure of a Morningstar's presence?" She cooed, floating into the chamber in a gown of ombre gray. As her skirts shifted, they changed color. From white to gray to black and shades in between.

Her skin was cracked and splintered and of a grayish-green hue. Her hair, which seemed perpetually wet, was roped and hanging in strands around her face. At the base of her throat was a deep cut all the way around, as if her head had been severed from her body and reattached long ago. Her lips were full. Her eyes were both dark and bright. Everything about her screamed unnatural and yet I could see she had been beautiful once, before whatever had occurred to her, before time had taken its toll as it did for all things, even the immortal.

"Which one are you?" she asked, coming to a stop in front of Lark and raising her chin while narrowing her gaze in examination. It wasn't an act of intimidation, but mere curiosity. She folded her hands demurely in front of her and awaited an answer.

"I am Canis Morningstar," Lark announced. "Son of Perseus Morningstar. This is my sister, Casseiopia."

She looked from Lark to Cass and then swiveled her head around to peer at Rook and I.

"And your friends?" she asked, quirking a manicured brow. "Or... foes?"

"Friends," Lark answered quickly at the look she was giving us. "Rook is a Fae of the Court of Blood and Bone. Seren is—"

"A mortal," Medusa hissed, nostrils flaring as if she had just caught a whiff of my mortal scent. Her tongue snaked out and flicked once and I realized, with horror, that it was forked.

"Half Fae," Lark corrected and Medusa's gaze whipped to him. She cocked her head in surprise and raised a brow again.

"Yours?" she asked, simply.

"Uh," he hesitated, clearing his throat. It was the first time I had seen him flustered and it was nearly as shocking as the ancient woman of mythical lore standing right in front of me.

Medusa's cracked lips spread into a grin and she clapped her hands together so suddenly that I couldn't help but jump.

"It's been so long since we've had visitors," she cried, suddenly excited. "Come on out, everyone. We have new friends to get to know."

At her encouragement, dozens of gorgons began to slink closer from the shadows. Without making the conscious decision, I leaned closer to Rook, so close that it pressed my heaving chest against his back.

"You're safe, Ren," he told me under his breath. "But you may want to take just a tiny step back. I'm not in the mood to be gutted by Lark today."

Cheeks heating, I stepped away. I couldn't help but gape at the creatures crawling toward us. Their skin was much like Medusa's, cracked and splintered, coarse like stone itself, and various shades of pale red and light yellow, even blue and green, but all faded and grayish. Their hair was roped, their teeth sharp and dripping with some blue venom. Most shocking of all was that they had no legs. Unlike Medusa's moderately humanoid form, the surrounding gorgons had the upper body of a human and the lower body of a snake. They slithered forward rather than walk and I shuddered at the hissing emanating from all corners of the room.

"Tell me, Canis, what situation is so dire that a Morningstar would dare to treat with me?" Medusa asked as her people hissed their approval.

I narrowed my focus to her, seeking her emotions. But I was met with silence as solid and sturdy as cold stone.

"You won't be able to read her," Rook whispered under his breath, divining my intentions. "She's—well, she's technically dead."

My eyes bulged from my head as I turned my gaze to him.

"Dead?" I croaked.

"She doesn't like to talk about it, of course. But yes. She's... not alive, not really. You know the story, don't you? Medusa was the only gorgon born mortal, the only one passably human. She had a rough go of it and then Perseus, not Lark's father, another one, killed her by cutting off her head. Then her sons sprouted up from her blood and he took the head as a trophy."

"So how—"

"Some necromancer came along and, well, it's really not worth getting into. But these gorgons still see her as their queen down here. They follow her word like its law. There isn't anything a gorgon does that she doesn't know about, in or out of Hellscape. The point is, you won't be able to read her. But Cass will."

"Cass? What do you—"

A sudden hissing sound interrupted me as a blinding white light shot suddenly from Medusa's own eyes toward Lark. I let out a scream but Rook didn't even move as Cass flung out a hand and silver smoke flew from her, colliding with Medusa's strike and landing on the cave floor with a soft thud, smoke turned stone, silver, gleaming rock.

"How did she know?" I asked, gaping at what had just occurred in front of me.

"Premonition," Rook whispered back. "That's her gift. But she should tell you about it herself sometime."

I didn't have time to respond before Medusa was speaking again.

"I had to try, you know," she said, putting her hands on her hips and raising her chin as she stared back at Lark and Cass. "They wouldn't respect me if I didn't."

The gorgons hissed their assent.

"I'm here about a gorgon named Lycurgus," Lark said, steering the conversation back on track and getting to the point of our visit. I could feel his impatience. At least I wasn't the only one who wanted to get out of here as soon as possible. "I assume you know who that is."

"Is he dead?" Medusa asked flatly.

"Captured."

"Pity."

She raised a hand and examined her nails as if the matter was of no consequence.

"I know he bargained with my brother to procure the key to Hellscape," Lark said.

"Procure," Medusa scoffed. "Is that what you call a rightful gain from your gambling addicted brother?"

Lark's gaze narrowed.

"Very well," Medusa sighed, rolling her eyes. "Not that it mattered. He needed Fae blood to use it, you know that. Though I imagine the one who conscripted him for the task in the first place might have sufficed."

I tensed. This was the information we needed. This was why we were here. And she knew it. She was playing with us, I realized, letting her eyes roll over her nails and flick up to Lark who stood completely still in the eerie moonless light.

"What do you want to tell us who it was?" Lark asked. "And don't say you want to be set free."

Medusa rolled her eyes again and then twisted her head back and forth, as if rolling out the muscles of her neck.

"I want that Cerberus next door moved," she said, frowning. "Howls all night and whines all day. Makes getting one's beauty sleep a trifle more difficult. Not that I need it."

"I'll move your noisy neighbor," Lark promised. "Now. Who sent Lycurgus to get the key from my brother?"

"You already know, don't you? You just want me to verify your suspicions."

Lark's gaze narrowed. Medusa just smiled, those sharp, pointed teeth on full display. When she realized he wasn't taking her bait, however, she huffed out a sigh.

"Fine," she said. "It was the Dawnpaw. The younger one, not that any of us are young anymore, are we? Well, except you, sweetling."

Her gaze snapped to me and she licked the top row of her razor-sharp teeth with that forked tongue. I stood my ground, trying to appear unaffected by the obvious taunt.

"Ariadne?" Lark snapped, drawing the Queen of the Gorgons' gaze back to him.

"The one and only," she hissed.

"Why did she want it?"

"You already know that too."

"Humor me."

"She's been experimenting, dabbling in a bit of dark magic here and there. The sort that your kind always claims to abhor until you decide you want to use it."

"For what?"

"That."

Medusa pointed upward at the same time I and everyone else noticed a sudden ribbon of sunlight flowing into this otherwise dark world. The gorgons in the shadows hissed and withdrew into the dark. Medusa smiled even wider, turning her ancient eyes to the golden beams she likely hadn't seen for centuries and positively basking in them, holding her arms out wide and letting her eyelids flutter closed.

It was a rift.

My eyes bulged, lips parting in surprise as I stared up at the hole torn into the fabric between worlds. It was growing as we watched, turning from a pinprick of sunlight into a veritable skylight. And beyond, we could see a balmy beach, ocean water lapping up the coast, and scientists in white lab coats running back and forth, already searching for their instruments, already shouting instructions to one another. And then I saw him, staring up into the rift as if peering up at me from the surface of a lake.

Wyn Kendrick.

I felt his fear, his determination, his fury that another one of these things could blemish his world, become a blight upon his people, his department. He stared into the void with such intense hatred that I thought, for a moment, he might have seen me. But then he turned away, waving a hand and calling for someone else.

"Incredible, aren't they?" Medusa asked, pleased with herself. "A window into the mortal realm, a doorway back to where we're from, back home. If you're brave enough to claim it. I know a minotaur who was. Poor thing didn't make it."

Her gaze flicked to me and my breath caught in my throat at the realization. She knew me. She had seen me take down that minotaur. They could see everything from this side of the rift. Everything.

"Very chivalrous of you," Medusa quipped then, turning back to Lark, "kidnapping this one a second time to save her life."

"Is she here?" Lark snapped. "Ariadne. She must be nearby to perform this."

"That's the beauty of it. Whatever dark and ancient magic she's drawing from allows her to conduct this little light display from somewhere else, a fact she figured out after her one and only jaunt down here. I assume that's why she let you get your hands on the key so easily. She didn't need it anymore."

Rook muttered a curse. Cass hung her head. Lark just stood there, gritting his teeth and staring up at the rift.

Then, with one primal cry of rage, he threw his arms outward and began to steam. White mist rose from him and slithered against the cave floors. Medusa gasped and slid away. The gorgons hissed and retreated even further, as if afraid to touch such powerful magic. The mist thickened as it rose up the cave walls and came together to cover the rift above. There was a moment of struggle in which it seemed the Divide couldn't decide whether or not it intended to heal but Lark's magic won out and we watched as the rift disappeared, the mist dissipated, and we were plunged back into darkness, back into that dim, eerie moonlight glow.

"You can't keep us here forever," Medusa hissed, her melodic, narcissistic tone vanished and replaced by one of utter cruelty, genuine hatred. "If she doesn't free us, someone else will. We are eternal. Hellscape is not."

"It will be," Lark promised. "So long as a Morningstar sits the Obsidian Throne."

Medusa fell to hissing with the rest of the gorgons as Lark spun around and led us all quickly from the makeshift hall, his cloak snapping after him as he left.

Chapter Thirty
A Fire That Consumes

We strolled right out of Hellscape, locked the door behind us, and shadowstepped right back into that orange apartment in the Court of Wanderers before anyone dared to say a word. When they finally did, it was Rook of all people, and it wasn't exactly the most elegant choice.

"Shit."

"We have to stop her," I was speaking before I could properly think about what I was saying. "If she opens Hellscape up to the mortal plane, if she finds a way to make those rifts bigger, if more creatures attempt to escape like the minotaur... how do we stop her?"

Rook grimaced, rubbing the back of his neck. Cass looked to Lark. Lark was staring at the wall behind me, jaw set.

"Lark," I said his name gently and he came too, blinking as his dark eyes found mine.

"What she's doing shouldn't be possible," Lark said then, thinking aloud as he strolled into the living room behind us and we turned to watch. "She's hundreds of years old and she's never shown even a hint of such power before. The mind control, that's a part of her family's legacy, and I can understand keeping that hidden but this. This is something else entirely. It's not just dark magic. It's ancient magic. That kind of power was lost millennia ago with the Fae that put up the Divide in the first place, and it took scores of them. How is she able to pierce it alone? How—"

He stopped, his eyes widening suddenly in realization.

"What is it?" Cass asked, stepping forward.

"Do you remember what Taurus told us about father's curse? That it was like his power had been funneled out of him."

Cass' brow creased for a moment as she tried to remember but then they raised as she parted her lips in understanding.

"You don't mean—" she started but Lark didn't let her finish.

"All of that power had to go somewhere. Why wouldn't she funnel it into herself?"

"Is it even possible?"

"There are relics from the age of Altair and Andromeda, amulets instilled with dark magic to curse highly powerful Fae, to steal their magic away from them. Maybe they could be tinkered with to allow the use of that magic held inside. Maybe she found them. They were rumored to be hidden in her own court anyway. Maybe her family has even held them in their archives for centuries. Who knows? The point is, Cass, who else would be powerful enough to curse our father, the King of the Court of Blood and Bone?"

"We thought it was Alban but, if she had the amulet or if he helped her…" Cass whispered, thinking. "We need to tell father."

Lark was already nodding.

"My thoughts exactly," he agreed.

"Tell him what, exactly?" Rook chimed in at that. "We think we might know who's cursing him and even what she's doing with all of that extra power but we can't prove it?"

"The gorgon is the proof," Lark said. "Lycurgus."

He and Rook exchanged a glance.

"It's been a while since I attempted a prison break," Rook mused. "It's about time for another."

"Get permission this time," Lark warned, his gaze narrowing as he spoke to Rook before turning to Cass. "Talk to father. Tell him what's at stake. Get him to agree to an extraction mission to free the gorgon."

"You're not coming?" she asked, cocking her head to the side.

"I'm supposed to be dead, remember?"

She nodded.

"Father isn't easy to convince," she grumbled. "It might take time."

"However long you need," Lark replied. "Take Rook for protection."

"Protection?"

"Ariadne slipped into the Bone Court well enough to steal one of the most powerful living Fae's magic, leave him nearly dead, and escape undetected. I wouldn't put it past her to do even worse to you if she found out you were asking questions. Take Rook. I'll stay here."

"Lark, someone could recognize you here," Rook spoke up in sullen warning.

"I'll stay in the apartment," Lark replied and, when it was clear that no one believed him, he heaved a sigh and made his vow. "I promise."

"Good enough for me," Cass said with a shrug and then looped her arm with Rook's. They disappeared in an instant, leaving me blinking after where they had been just moments before.

"I'll never get used to that," I said and Lark chuckled.

"I'm going to shower," he told me. "Need to wash this darkness off me."

I nodded and did my best to look at anything but him as he disappeared into the bedroom, off toward the bathroom inside.

This group had come up with a plan and executed it so quickly that I hadn't had time to consider all the potential fallout and consequences of said actions. Cass was convincing her father to allow us to snatch the gorgon for proof of Ariadne's schemes. Rook was to be her guard while she spoke very dangerous words in a very precarious place. I wondered if he would pin her to his side like he did to me every time Lark commanded him to guard me and couldn't help but laugh at how I thought Cass might react to that.

But that left Lark and I alone in this apartment, an apartment we couldn't leave, or he couldn't leave, so that he wouldn't be recognized. And, since I had no desire to get him caught again, I wouldn't leave either. Because I knew that if I needed him, if I got into some sort of trouble that I couldn't fight my way out of, he would come just like he always did. And they would catch us.

I wouldn't do that to him. I had watched him die once already. I had no desire to see it again.

So that meant that we were trapped here, together, for as long as it took Cass to convince their father to let us sneak into enemy territory and retrieve the one creature who could verify what we suspected my mother to have done, to be capable of. I was stuck in an apartment, alone, with a man who had, just hours ago, told me he believed we were soul mates.

"Do you miss your uncle?" Lark spoke so suddenly that I nearly jumped out of my skin where I stood in the kitchen, making myself a pot of tea. He gave me a sheepish, apologetic grin. "Sorry."

"Uh, I—" I stuttered as I watched him tug the black t-shirt down from where it had ridden up below his chest. I got the briefest glimpse of hard, toned abdomen before it was gone and I raised my gaze to his face to find him smirking at me and my loss of words. "Sorry, what was the question?"

He snorted, shaking his head so that his wet hair fluffed up a bit.

"Do you miss your uncle?" he repeated. "I know I promised Rook I wouldn't leave the apartment but no one would look for me in the mortal realm so, if you wanted, we could go for a visit."

"No," I answered, quickly. "We shouldn't take unnecessary risks."

"Family is not unnecessary."

He was behind me now, so close that I could feel the warmth radiating off of him, smell the clean scent of his crisp cotton shirt. He reached over me to get a mug from the cabinet above my head and I ducked to the side and out of the way before any accidental contact could occur.

"No, they're not," I agreed with his previous statement, nodding as I poured the hot water into my own mug and then his when he held it out. "But we just promised yours we would stay put so that's what we're going to do."

"Yes, ma'am," he replied with a grin.

I just rolled my eyes, despite the flush creeping up my cheeks, and dropped two tea bags into our piping hot mugs. He watched me, that intense gaze returning. So I cleared my throat and turned away, heading out of the kitchen and toward the living room where I settled onto the couch and set my tea on the end table beside it. He followed but gave me the space I seemed to need, sitting in the armchair across from me instead of the couch beside me.

"So," I said, dipping my tea bag in and out of the water to avoid looking at him, "are you going to tell me how you survived your own execution?"

"It was Cass' idea," he told me, leaning back casually, not a trace of that smirk on his lips as he recalled the tale. He looked so saddened by the reminder that I almost regretted asking. "She convinced my father of a way to save my life and his reputation. There was another man locked up beside me. About the same height, same build. Cass has always been better at glamour than the rest of us. She made him look like me, or passably so, and, for anyone who might know me too well to buy the impersonation, we used the hood."

"Another man died in your place?" I asked, the horror of it like a punch to the gut.

I could tell that Lark was displeased about it as well from the way he clenched his jaw at the question.

"He would have died anyway," he said. "Or at least that's what I keep telling myself."

I frowned and took a sip of my tea because I didn't know what to say.

"You asked me a question," he told me then and I looked up to find him watching me again. "Do I get to ask you one in return?"

I nodded, sitting up straighter and waiting to hear what he would ask.

"Tell me about your training at the Bone Court," he said.

"That wasn't a question," I chided.

"Humor me," he replied with a grin.

"When your father found out what I could do, he made me practice on soldiers, common Fae without the power to truly protect themselves from my invasion of their souls. Then he made me try to break Ursa. It took me five days but I managed a chink in her armor and that really pissed her off so she spent all her time after that training me in the more traditional ways of the Bone Court."

My eyes flicked to his and his jaw clenched again.

"She cut you," he said.

"Yes," I answered even though it wasn't a question.

His fists were tight at his sides.

"She hurt nothing she couldn't heal," I assured him.

"But you were in pain," he told me.

"You cannot spare me from pain, Lark."

"I can try," he growled.

I watched him for a moment, so caught off guard by his fierce protectiveness. Was this what it meant to be soul bonded? Was this a natural reaction to the connection between us, that we would defend it until our dying breath, that we would tear apart the world itself just to keep each other from getting hurt?

I rose to my feet, slowly, letting the blanket I had pulled over my lap fall to the floor. He watched, eyes darkening as he looked at me from head to toe.

"Come here," I said.

He rose as well and hesitated. He wanted to approach. I could feel it. But he held himself back and I knew why.

I know you don't trust me yet.

He wouldn't make a move, not a single move, until I did.

"Touch me," I told him and his eyes flared a brilliant silver as desire surged through him so strong that I felt it through our bond without even trying.

I had to steady myself as he reached out, letting one finger trail slowly from my shoulder down to my wrist.

"I'm here," I whispered, gripping his hand as it dropped to my own. "I'm whole."

He looked away from me, down to where our hands were clasped together, and took a deep breath.

"Why do I feel like I'm always a moment away from losing you?" he asked, his voice just as low.

"I think," I started and then paused, considering my words. "I think we've lost each other enough to last a lifetime."

His eyes flicked to mine, craving me, devouring me. And I could feel every part of that ache in my very bones. I closed my eyes and let his desire consume me, the raging wind of his want swirling all around me, encompassing me in a warmth that was utterly, unapologetically his. I prepared myself to give into him, to surrender myself to all the barely restrained sexual tension between us, and I could tell that he sensed my surrender. He moved forward, leaning toward me as he wrapped an arm around my waist and I burned at his touch.

"Ren," he whispered my name like a prayer and I ignited.

But suddenly I could sense another presence in the room. Shadows I hadn't realized had formed faded away to reveal a familiar older woman standing a few feet away, her eyebrow arched and her wild hair swinging.

"Neglecting our training, are we?" Gemini Morningstar scolded with a click of her tongue as her nephew let out an agonized groan.

Chapter Thirty-One
A True Gem

Lark had extricated himself from me with what appeared to have been a monumental effort. He ran a hand through his still-drying hair as he paced away from his aunt, clearly unwilling to look at her while still in such a state. She watched him with something like amusement. If Gemini Morningstar ever allowed herself to be amused. He took a deep breath and then another, flexing his fingers and clenching them into fists. I bit my lip to keep from snickering at his behavior. Of course, I was disappointed at the sudden appearance of a chaperone as well but his reaction was borderline ludicrous.

"What are you doing here, Aunt Gem?" he asked, still not looking at her.

"You didn't think I'd recognize my own niece when she popped up in the middle of the street and snatched away my pupil?" Gemini chided, shaking her head so that her wild locks shifted back and forth on her shoulders. "I'm old, boy, not blind."

"We've been gone for days."

"I had other matters to attend to. Your father, for one. It was fairly difficult to convince him the Court of Friends hadn't stolen away his most prized hostage while keeping who it really was a secret. But I imagine you didn't think about that when you conspired to help her escape, did you?"

To his credit, Lark looked properly scolded at that. He blinked at her for a moment before allowing a sigh.

"I'm sorry, Aunt," he told her. "We meant to send word, but became a little preoccupied."

"Oh, I can see that," she rebuked, nodding her head toward where we had been standing, entwined, when she'd appeared. "Is this tea?"

She was reaching for my cup. I nodded and so she lifted it and took a sip.

"I hate traveling," she said. "Always leaves me parched. Now, what's all this? I thought you'd be halfway back to Ariadne by now, girl."

"I told her the truth, Aunt Gem," Lark said, his gaze narrowing.

"Which is?" she asked, brow raised.

"The same as I told it the first time."

"Ah, the truth then."

"You knew?" I asked, lips parting in surprise as I stared at the woman sipping my tea.

"Who do you think helped him get into the Court of Peace and Pride?" she asked. "My name still carries some weight in the royal circles, you know."

At my confused glance, Lark explained.

"Aunt Gem told Ariadne she was coming for a visit. Your mother likes to fancy herself friends with my aunt but the feelings are not mutual. So she packed us all in her trunks and set off. The Court of Peace and Pride doesn't allow shadow stepping in their lands, probably out of jealousy that they can't do it themselves, so we had to travel the old-fashioned way. Three days locked in a trunk with Rook, avoiding using any magic so that they wouldn't know we were within their borders. Once she was settled in her room, we set off on our mission and all hell broke loose."

"We didn't stay much longer after that," Gemini recalled, still sipping my tea.

"You helped?" I asked, staring at her as if seeing her for the first time. "You helped save me all those years ago and you didn't tell me?"

"I couldn't," she replied with a shrug as though it was obvious. "Ursa never left us alone once throughout the duration of our one and only meeting and my dear brother never knew I was involved. He exiled and then executed his own son for the crimes he committed that day. What do you think he might do to his sister?"

She raised a brow and I fell silent in realization.

"Thank you," I told her because I didn't know what else to say.

"Babies don't thank people for saving them," she snapped, waving a hand as she set down my tea. "They're defenseless. But you're grown up now and you're not. So thank me by learning how to properly save yourself so that I don't have to come running to rescue your ass again."

At that, a form, like liquid night, shot from her palm and slapped me across the back of my hand.

"Ow," I hissed, rubbing the offended hand with the other.

Lark chuckled, shaking his head.

"I want absolutely no part of this," he said, raising his hands in surrender as a broad grin split his face. "Call me when one of you is still standing."

With that, he disappeared into the bedroom.

Gemini waved a hand and all the furniture vanished so that it was just the two of us standing in an empty room, facing each other.

"The absence of that hideous orange really helps to clear the mind, doesn't it?" she said, lowering herself into a fighting stance. "Now, hit me."

We trained for four hours. We spent the first two on physical strikes. Punches, kicks, dodges, and attacks. Gemini was fast for her age, though I imagined Fae stamina never quite decreased at the same rate a mortal's did. She blocked every one of my attacks and dealt a few bruising blows of her own just to teach me a lesson.

The second two hours were a mental drain as she walked me through exercise after exercise, trying to get me to summon even an ounce of physical magic, but it was no use. And when I was exhausted, so tired that I couldn't even hold an arm up to attempt a magical gesture, Gemini waved her hands again and the furniture reappeared just in time for me to collapse onto the couch.

"I did it once," I told her as she took both mugs into the kitchen to fetch more tea. Then I corrected myself. "Twice, actually."

"Physical magic," she said to verify and I nodded even though I knew she couldn't see me. "When?"

"Once when I found out that Lark was— when the King sentenced him to death," I confessed, throat burning at the admission. "And again when he captured me. When I thought he was my kidnapper, when I hated him for what he had done to me and lied about."

Gemini stilled where she stood over the sink. It was quiet for a moment before she spoke.

"Do you feel as though your magic is stronger whenever you are around my nephew?" she asked carefully and I considered the question.

"I suppose," I answered with a shrug. "He was the first one to make me think that my ability to read emotions might be more than basic human empathy and now that... connection is so strong that I can hardly read anyone else when he's around. I don't even have to try to read him anymore. I just know without focus. And those few times I've practiced physical magic were because I was grieving him, a loss of him, of who I thought he was."

"You're soul bonded, aren't you?"

There it was. The matter that I hadn't even been able to admit to myself yet. My breath hitched as all the air was sucked out of the room. Gemini was leaning against the counter, facing away from me.

"I—I don't—" I started.

"Don't lie to me, girl," she interrupted but it wasn't angry, it wasn't snippy. She simply wanted the truth and, after what I'd learned about what she had done for me so long ago, how could I deny it to her?

"He seems to think we are, yes," I answered.

"And you?"

"I... think I can feel it as well."

"He thinks? You think? Do either of you know?"

"Um—"

"If what I nearly walked into was any indication, I think you already do. Both of you," she snapped then, whirling around to face me and approaching where I sat in a few long strides. "A soul bond is not something to be trifled with, girl. It's rare and powerful. It can make you both stronger. It can give you the strength you need to face what's coming."

My lips parted in surprise.

"What's coming?" I repeated. "What do you mean?"

"I've seen war before, girl. The writing is on the wall, same as it always is. One King gets his power stolen by another whose granddaughter was murdered by the son of the first. It's always the same, dear. Always the same. Countless more to die to make up for deaths long done or, in this case, never done at all."

I forgot to breathe as she loomed over me, the voice of reason, of warning.

"Whether it comes from Alban and Ariadne or Perseus and Ursa, I promise you, it will come. And my dear, you seem to find yourself in the middle of it. So you had better not think, you had better know when that time comes," she said. "And in the meantime, I'll be damned if you're to face it all untrained. So get cleaned up and get some rest because we're starting again in the morning."

She thrust a piping hot cup of tea into my hands and then disappeared into a cloud of smoke.

I stared after where she had vanished for a long time before I heard the telltale click of a latch as Lark emerged from the bedroom.

"Is she gone?" he asked, peering around.

My gaze snapped to him and then narrowed.

"So you are still here," I snapped. "You abandoned me to her!"

He shrugged his shoulders, taking the second cup of tea his aunt had left behind for him as he settled into the armchair across from me as always.

"She seemed rather intent on having you alone," he said.

"So did you," I snapped, bitterly. "Before."

His lips curled up into a mischievous smirk.

"And I always will," he drawled. "But you look exhausted."

"Oh, thank you," I muttered sarcastically, though I knew he was right. My eyes were already drooping from my exhaustion.

"You've had quite the day. Maybe it's time for a rest."

"A shower first."

I rose slowly from the couch, my muscles groaning out their displeasure as I did. I hesitated, stretching my back, cocking my head to the side, rolling my neck. And as I did, Lark waved a hand and the couch suddenly held a few pillows and a black fur blanket. I looked over the makeshift sleeping arrangement with a narrowed gaze.

"I'll take the couch," he told me, already moving from the armchair to the sofa.

"That's unnecessary," I replied. "The bed is big enough for the both of us. You'll be more comfortable—"

"If I get into that bed tonight, Ren," he started, already raising the blanket and settling onto the couch, "neither one of us will get the rest we need."

I turned away as my eyes widened and my cheeks blushed crimson, but not fast enough. He had seen and his deep chuckles reverberated against my chest as I scurried from the living room and shut the door tightly behind me.

Chapter Thirty-Two
A Lesson in Combat

I shouted a curse as I hissed and shook my hand to clear the stinging from the blow I'd just been dealt.

"Eyes up," Gemini snapped. "Keep your focus."

I gritted my teeth and refocused, resuming my fighting stance and preparing to strike again.

Lark knew what he was doing, lazing about in that armchair, nibbling on fruit as he watched me train, that dazzling smirk ever present on his lips. If I were intended to focus, he could try a bit harder not to be such a distraction. Though at present, I wasn't sure which was more distracting. Him or that peach in his hands. My stomach grumbled as my gaze flicked back to Gemini in time to see her lunge forward.

I protected myself, sidestepping her attack and coming up with one of my own. She blocked it, of course. She always did. But at least I'd delivered some sort of blow before she swept my legs out from beneath me and I went crashing down onto my backside with another curse.

Lark chuckled and I cut him a glare as I got back to my feet.

"Don't laugh, boy," Gemini snapped, "or I'll come for you next."

My glare turned into a grin as I stuck my tongue out at him. He smiled, raising a brow as he licked peach juice slowly from his thumb. My heart raged against my chest but then Gemini thwapped me on the side of the head and my gaze snapped to her.

"Enough of this," she barked. "If the two of you are going to behave like love-struck teenagers, you can work out that tension on the mat. Come on then, boy."

Lark licked his lips and stood, wiping his hands off on his trousers as he strode forward and positioned himself in front of me.

"Wide stance," Gemini was coaching me from nearby. "Balance on the balls of your feet, not flat, floating, like dancing. Okay, watch him now. He's got a tell."

"I do not," Lark argued, annoyed.

"His hands," Gemini told me. "He fights with his hands as much as he talks with them."

"What does that mean?" I asked but Gemini didn't have time to answer as Lark swung out and I slid sideways, narrowly avoiding the collision of his fist with my shoulder. My eyes widened as I faced him, stunned, and leveled my accusation. "You tried to hit me."

"I want you to live," he told me. "If I have to kick your ass to make that happen, so be it."

My gaze narrowed. I took up my stance again, readied myself for the blow.

It took a few swings from Lark and a few dodges from me before I realized what Gemini had been trying to tell me. Lark gesticulated more than anyone I'd ever known and there were hints, little tics, sudden flexes of his fingers, that told me when he was preparing to strike. Once I noticed them, I could anticipate the punches better. I could duck and roll away from them. He wasn't much for defense, choosing instead to keep me so busy avoiding his blows that I couldn't even attempt to land any of my own. We circled one another for so long that I was starting to believe I was actually getting the hang of this, that I was maybe even a quick learner, catching on so fast that I could already keep pace with the prince of the Bone Court. But then Gemini hissed another command, this one to Lark, and I realized how wrong I was.

"Quit playing with her, boy," Gemini scolded. "Your enemy won't."

Then, in one quick fluid motion so fast I hadn't seen it coming at all, Lark swept my feet out from under me, catching me before I could fall and holding me in his arms only inches above the mat. He leaned over me, that dark gaze penetrating my own, and grinned.

"Not bad, mortal," he drawled.

I pushed away from him, scrambling away and getting to my feet, turning to face him once more.

"Again," I growled and it was the first time I'd seen Gemini smile.

Time and time again, Lark knocked me to the mat. Sometimes he caught me, sometimes he pinned me down, sometimes he let me go tumbling down on my own, earning myself a bruised ass along with my bruised pride. Every time I fell down, I got back up even madder than before, tried a little harder, lashed out a little more. But he had been training for centuries longer than me and it showed. I could tell he was holding himself back, even as we spun around each other, evading and attacking, and that only made me angrier.

Gemini called out instructions from time to time, suggestions about how to dodge his more critical blows, where I might land my own, but I never even so much as touched him. He was too strong, too fast, and too smart. I failed time and time again but still; I tried.

I was sweating through my pants, my shirt. My hair was damp and stuck to my forehead. I took a moment to catch my breath, using the time to toss my hair up into a ponytail and pull my shirt up and over my head. I couldn't fight with the material clinging to my sticky body so a sports bra would have to do. I turned back to Lark to find him grinning like a madman.

"If you're trying to distract me," he drawled, his eyes flicking down to my breasts, "it won't work."

That comment earned him a smack on the back of the head from his circling aunt. He hissed in a breath, rubbing the back of his head and shooting her a glare as she made her way back to me.

"Don't be disgusting," she warned and I couldn't help but grin as she made her way to my side and lowered her voice. "You've figured it out by now. He won't hurt you. Use that to your advantage."

I raised my gaze to meet hers and nodded. Then I wiped my sweaty face with my shirt and tossed it aside, cracking my neck, my knuckles, as I resumed my position in front of Lark. Annoyingly, he hadn't seemed to break a sweat at all and I couldn't help but feel disgusted by the break I had needed to attend to my very mortal stamina.

I raised my fists and he lowered himself into his stance. I attacked with all I had, getting in close so that he couldn't simply bat me away. He actually had to fight back. He blocked the first punch, then the second, but the third landed squarely on his jaw.

He stumbled back a step, raising a hand and rubbing his jaw in surprise. When he looked back at me, his gaze darkened.

"Alright then," he said simply and strode toward me.

I swung again and then immediately with my other hand. He grabbed the first wrist, then the second, yanked me toward him so that the only thing between us were my hands, pressed against his heaving chest and my own. His gaze narrowed and flared, his face just inches from my own. His eyes flicked to my lips and a heat surged through me. I pushed out with all I had and a tremendous force of wind blew through the apartment, sending him skidding away from me. He braced himself against the counter to stop and I lowered my hands, taking shaky breaths and staring down at my twitching fingers.

"Finally," Gemini huffed from beside me and I swiveled to face her. "I'll admit, I thought pairing you two off would call that out of you a lot sooner. We've been at this for hours. But finally, some progress."

"This—this wasn't about fighting at all?" I asked, looking over to where Lark was smiling at me from where he now leaned against the counter. He had known.

"Who needs to use their fists when you can use magic?" Gemini asked, shrugging. "It's good to know how, in case you need it. But if you have magic, use it. Remember where you are, girl. This is not the mortal plane."

I fought to catch my breath, looking down at my hands, still reeling from what I'd done. I looked back up at Lark.

"I could have hurt you," I said, breathless.

"You never would," he replied, his voice low, soft, so sure that it made me certain myself and I smiled back at him, grateful.

"Enough celebration," Gemini snapped. "We're not done here. Back on the mat, boy."

We spent the next hour experimenting with what emotions brought out my physical magic. I didn't tell anyone what they were; I didn't identify them. But I was pretty sure Gemini and Lark could have guessed as, from that point on, every time he touched me an invisible force shot out from within me. Gemini taught me to channel it, to shape it. And when I had formed a passable shield, Lark and I faced off once more. But this time, as he stood across from me, I saw the dense white mist snaking around his wrists, his legs, waiting to be used. My eyes widened and I turned to Gemini.

"You must learn to fight magic with magic," she explained. "A big step, but a necessary one. No one you face here will fight you without it."

I nodded my understanding, taking a deep breath and turning back to face him. He flexed his fingers, letting that mist coil between them, writhe around him in a way that was almost a caress. I imagined what it might feel like to let the power caress you. Then I imagined what it might feel like to let Lark caress me and suddenly I was on fire, burning from the magic within. I flexed my own fingers and felt it there, hovering but invisible, ready to protect me.

He shot a spray of mist outward and I remembered the feel of his hands on mine, the smooth muscle of his chest beneath my clenched fists, his warm breath on the shell of my ear.

The mist hit an invisible barrier a few feet from me and dissipated.

"Well done!" Gemini exclaimed, clapping her hands together in approval. "Now me."

I didn't have time to ask what she meant before she sent that dark ink of hers outward. It filled the room around me, blotting out the sunlight streaming in through the windows, so dark and so complete that I could see nothing at all. Not her, not Lark, not my own hand in front of my face. I whirled around, searching for something, anything, that I could see, but found nothing. How did I protect against this? How did I defend against something that was everywhere, permeating the very air around me? And then it was in my lungs, choking me, suffocating me. I wheezed, gasping for air as tears sprang to my eyes and I fell.

Lark's arms were around me before I hit the mat. I couldn't see him but I could feel him and that was enough. I summoned that magic within me, that power that responded to him, but that I would teach to answer me as well. I collected it all within me and then pushed it out, pushed it against that smoke that surrounded us. My lungs cleared first and then my eyes. I could see him now, his face hovering inches over me as he held me aloft.

There was so much adoration in his eyes, so much longing, so much that we had never said. And it filled me with something so potent that I couldn't have stopped the magic exploding out of me if I had wanted to. In a second, the smoke was gone, replaced by clean, crisp air that was even brighter than it had been before. Lark breathed it in, inhaling my magic, inhaling me, and smiled.

"You did it," he whispered in wonder. "You're incredible, Ren. You know that?"

I couldn't help myself. He was so close and I felt so happy. With the magic coursing through my veins, touching on that connection, our connection, I wanted to show him how I felt about him. I wanted to take away any doubt in either of our minds that whatever this was between us wasn't meant to be.

So I leaned forward and pressed my lips to his.

The magic around us intensified, my wind blowing his mist about. They danced together, tangled and entwined, as he kissed me back, pulling me closer and holding me tightly against him. His lips worked against my own, devouring me, my very soul, with that single kiss. And I felt it coursing through him as well. This absolution, this answer, this completion. We were together and so we were whole. It was like coming home, like finding the calm amidst the storm, like peace and passion all at once. It was everything. And it was so powerful that it pulled me completely, entirely under and I never wanted to resurface again.

"Seems like we're interrupting," a familiar voice said then.

It was the only thing that could have pulled me away. I pushed back, my head swiveling to the center of the room where Rook and Cass were standing, both of them with raised brows and smiles on their lips. Lark was smiling too, broader than I'd ever seen, as he cleared his throat and helped me to my feet.

"I was just starting to think I was intruding myself," Gemini said, that tone of hers always bordering on scolding, as she crossed her arms and tilted her head in our direction.

"I used physical magic," I blurted and they burst out into a chorus of congratulations as Lark raised a thumb to wipe the lip gloss from his lips, still smiling.

Cass ran forward to hug me while Rook thumped Lark on the back, grinning like a fool and legitimately believing I hadn't seen. Lark shook him off with an unconvincing shake of his head.

"That's fantastic, Ren, really," Rook told me with a smile. "But if you think we're not going to talk about that lip locking we walked in on a second ago, you've lost your damn mind."

Everyone laughed as my cheeks flushed pink and Lark met my gaze, still smirking as though he genuinely couldn't wipe the look from his face.

"I wondered when you two would arrive," Gemini huffed into the joviality. "Never far from this one, are you? I suppose you're going to tell me where you were?"

The chuckling stopped at once as Rook, Lark, Cass, and I all exchanged a glance. Cass broke the silence and answered her first.

"You might want to sit down for this one, Aunt Gem."

Chapter Thirty-Three
A Lack of Control

"You're telling me that the five of you went to Hellscape alone to bargain with Medusa for information regarding the princess of the Court of Peace and Pride and found a rift through the divide into the mortal realm," Gemini repeated, dumbfounded, as she stared around at all of us where we were gathered upon the furniture that Lark had summoned back once the others had returned.

"Technically, we already knew about the rifts from when we helped Ren with hers," Rook intervened.

"Again, not my rift," I grumbled.

"Do you know what this means?" Gemini asked, turning to her niece and nephew.

"That the heir to the Peace Court, who doesn't much care for me—" Lark began.

"I wonder why," Cass muttered under her breath.

"And whose daughter is currently staying in my apartment after a failed rescue or abduction attempt, not quite sure about that, from the Court of Friends is tearing hole after hole into the Divide from the confines of Hellscape, risking the exposure of our existence to the mortals as we speak?"

"Why would she do that?" Cass asked.

"Ariadne is obsessed with mortals," Gemini explained, her tone growing grim. "Specifically, controlling them. If she has amplified her power enough to tear through the Divide, imagine what she might do to their minds. She could control legions of them, all mindlessly marching to their death to win her war, to do her bidding. Millions of minions succumbing to her every desire, suffering the same fate as your father."

Gemini's gaze flicked to me and I felt bile rising in my throat.

"She wouldn't do that," Cass said in a horrified whisper but I could tell that she hadn't even convinced herself. "Why would she do that?"

"It's not for me to answer for madness," Gemini replied with a shrug. "But I know she's always longed for the day where she could rule over the mortals. I thought the position of ambassador would satisfy her but it's clear to me now that this was a threat I should have taken far more seriously."

"How can we stop her?" Lark asked, his eyes dark, his tone unforgiving.

Gemini looked at me again.

"No," Lark growled.

"Ariadne has gone too far, Canis," Gemini snapped, the use of his given name from the lips of someone he trusted making him flinch. "Seren might be the only person left alive who could talk some sense into her. We should try. Even if it doesn't work, we should try. Think of the countless lives we could save."

"She has a point," I told him, reaching over and laying a hand on his. "If I could stop her—"

"Absolutely not," he said, his voice rough. "I won't allow it."

"Lark," Cass chided gently.

"You know how this goes, Canis," Gemini said slowly, letting the meaning of her words sink in. "When Fae begin to consider the possibility of mortal subservience, when they seek a way to enslave humanity—"

"This isn't like that," Lark argued but I saw his shoulders slump, his eyes dart from her to me and back again. "The Immortal War ended two thousand years ago."

"You don't have to tell me, boy. I remember. I was there."

I glanced between them, at their narrowed gaze and, though it likely wasn't the time, my academic side got the best of me and I had to ask.

"The Immortal War?" I inquired.

Lark and Gemini held each other's gaze in challenge and, when it became clear that neither one of them was going to answer, Cass sighed and accepted the role of my educator once more.

"Two thousand years ago, we lived among the mortals. All of us together, entwined. But then some Fae started to believe that equality wasn't the right way to coexist, that our magic and our immortality made us superior to humanity. They fashioned themselves as gods and ruled over human subjects that they enslaved over generations. The Fae who disagreed decided on a route of separation. Though they preferred the idea of living amongst humans, they recognized the mortals would be safer without them, without the threat of enslavement to surface again later. So they fought the Immortal War, the first civil war of our kind, a war of ideology. Brother against brother, sister against sister, parents against children. You chose your side and you were willing to die for it. In the end, the separatists won. They executed the slavers, hunted down the beasts threatening the mortals' existence, and erected the Divide. They made Hellscape later, a prison in a hollowed out volcano in the middle of the lands forever dead from the fighting."

"Even now, two thousand years later, it would be foolish to believe there are not slavers among us," Gemini added, narrowing her gaze in her nephew's direction. "Alban was on the right side of the Immortal War but Ariadne is not her father."

"You were there?" I asked, amazed. "You fought in the Immortal War?"

"Gemini, our father, and Alban Dawnpaw are the only ones still alive from that time," Cass told me and my lips parted in awe.

"I don't intend to see another come to pass," she snapped, her stare fixed upon Lark.

"Why isn't Alban stopping her?" I asked, looking between them.

"A good question," Gemini acknowledged with a raised brow.

"We can't know until we get there," Lark replied, standing suddenly from his spot on the couch.

"You can't possibly still mean to go through with this foolish plan," Gemini hissed.

"It's better than sending Ren in to die or lose her mind, or worse."

I raised a hand to my mouth. Cass patted my knee reassuringly.

"Seems like the same thing from where I'm sitting," Gemini snapped, standing with him and following him as he paced into the kitchen. "How do you intend to cross her borders without her knowledge?"

"No magic," he said, holding up his hands. "She can only trace me through magic and, believe me, I've had enough practice avoiding it."

"She hasn't," Gemini argued, pointing to Cass and then pointing at me. "She's a magic cannon. She has absolutely no control over herself. Taking her into enemy territory will be like firing a flare."

"I don't intend to take her."

I dropped my hand to my side, wide eyes darting up to him but he stood with his back to me, every muscle tensed. Even Gemini faltered at that, some of the fight going out of her at the revelation she wasn't expecting.

"You would leave her here?" Gemini asked, stunned.

"She will be with a trusted family member," Lark replied, turning cold eyes on her. "A beloved aunt."

"You would dare—"

"Keep her safe until we return. That's all I ask."

Gemini's words fell away. Her mouth remained open, working but failing to find the words she wished to say.

"For the love you bear me," Lark said, gazing intently into Gemini's eyes to make her see how fervently he cared about my safety, "for all that we have ever done in the name of good, protect her until I return, Aunt Gem."

How could anyone deny him that?

She didn't. She just closed her mouth and gave one curt nod and suddenly everyone was moving at once. It seemed that having a plan spurred them into action and they were big believers in the mantra that there was no time like the present. Rook was already strapping weapons to himself. Cass was watching it all, wide eyed, staring at her aunt in awe. I wondered if she had ever seen Gemini Morningstar back down before. It wasn't a sight that I would forget anytime soon.

Lark waved a hand over himself and his black tee shirt disappeared, replaced by that signature black, embellished tunic. I stood from my spot and strode toward him. Gemini stepped away as I passed, rightfully assuming this was a moment with him that I would rather have alone.

"You're leaving," I said, my tone more accusatory than I had intended as I reached him. "Now?"

"Every moment we wait it becomes harder to locate the gorgon," he explained, reaching out to take my hands. I stared down at the contact, still having not gotten used to that yet. "Believe me when I say that right now leaving you is the absolute last thing I want to be doing. But you're safer here."

He left the rest unsaid. That they were all safer with me here as well. Gemini was right. My lack of control over my magic meant that if I loosed even an ounce of it in the Peace Court's territory, it would be like a homing beacon to our location.

"I'll get better," I promised. "I'll learn how to control it."

"I know," he told me with a sad smile, raising a hand against my face in a gentle caress. "Why do you think I'm leaving you with the best trainer in the entire realm?"

I smiled.

"Don't tell her I said that," he added with a wink, reaching up and brushing a strand of hair from my face. "Besides, I made you a promise that you wouldn't have to face this, face her, until you were ready. And I'll do everything in my power to make sure you don't have to set foot on the Peace Court's lands until that day."

I leaned forward, onto my tiptoes, and pressed my lips against his.

A moment later, his arms were around me, pulling me into him. I put everything I had into that kiss, leaving my mark upon him, begging him to come home. And the kiss he gave me in return felt like a promise that he would.

"Alright, seriously," Rook interrupted, slapping Lark on the back so hard that he broke away from me. "We really have to talk about this when we get back."

He gestured between us and we smiled back at him.

"Are you ready?" Rook asked and I peered behind him to see Cass already waiting by the door. Lark gave a curt nod and Rook strode off to join her.

"Don't let her kick your ass too bad while I'm gone," Lark told me with a wink.

I laughed, landing a playful punch on his arm as he pushed away from the counter and headed toward the door with the others.

"Don't worry," I called back. "Nobody kicks my ass quite like you, Fae."

He grinned before wrenching open the door and ducking through it. Rook followed right behind him. Cass hesitated a moment longer, giving me a sad smile and a small little wave before she went. My brow furrowed at the sight. It was unlike Cass to be so nervous when heading out on one of her brother's missions.

"You want to go with them next time?" Gemini asked from over my shoulder, drawing my attention back to her. "Get into position."

Then she waved her hand and the furniture disappeared.

Chapter Thirty-Four
A Court of Chaos

I fought like hell for three days.

Gemini was using my frustration at having been left out of this adventure to convince me to train even harder for the next one. But really, I was only training so hard because it was something to do that kept my mind off of what might or might not be happening in an undisclosed location within the Court of Peace and Pride. It wasn't that I didn't trust Lark or that I lacked faith in him and the others to free the gorgon and return with him. I had just learned far more about my mother in the last few days than I ever expected to and that knowledge made her presence seem as though it was looming over us always.

I feared her. Truly feared her. So much so that I thought, perhaps, I was feeling fear for the first time. And if I stopped moving for too long, gave myself too much time that wasn't dedicated to training or eating or sleeping, then I might succumb to that fear. I might let that fear pull me under and I might never emerge again.

So I fought. I fought Gemini, I fought her magic, I fought myself and my own thoughts. I fought whatever barrier seemed to keep my power away from me. I fought every little feeling that flitted through my connection with Lark as much as I craved them. They were few and far between but each one let me know he was alive. And I thought maybe he knew that, that he was sending me those little jolts of emotion to comfort me, to reassure me that everything was alright. But I didn't know that for certain. All I knew was that he was alive, because I could feel him, because I did not feel the loss of him. But I hadn't the slightest idea where he was or what state he was in. He could have been bruised and bloodied and locked in a dungeon of the palace of the Russet Throne itself.

I lost focus and Gemini used that moment to strike, lifting her hands and lashing out at me with that smoke. It blew into my face, filling my lungs, freezing them. I gasped and fell to my knees, wheezing.

"Fight it," she hissed, but I couldn't.

I just choked, tears streaming down my face, and she removed it a moment later. She let me fall flat on the floor, gulping down air.

"If you're losing focus, perhaps we should stop for the evening," she muttered, striding away from me to fetch her cup of tea on the counter.

"Where are they?" I gasped, still fighting to catch my breath.

"Who, dear?" she asked. "And breathe first. I have no interest in speaking with a fish flopping around like that."

"Them," I hissed. "Where do you think they are by now?"

"Ah, yes. Who else? Well, by my estimation, they've likely crossed the border. I don't know where your little gorgon friend might be, though, so that presents a number of problems with any further estimation."

My breathing evened and I stood, bracing myself with a hand against my abdomen, assisting myself with breathing.

Gemini had explained to me how long it might take until they returned once they'd left. Using no magic meant no shadow stepping, not even near the border. So they would have to shadow step miles out and walk in on foot. Then they would have to find Lycurgus, extricate him from whatever situation he was in, and hoof it all the way back here, undetected, with a gorgon in tow. It felt like an impossible feat and yet I knew that if anyone could do it, it was Lark. Nevertheless, that glance that Cass had given me before she'd left had haunted me ever since. It felt like the goodbye of a friend who wasn't sure she would ever see you again. It gave me goosebumps just to think about it.

I was on edge. I was jumpy. So by the fifth night, when Gemini proposed we take a stroll through town, I jumped at the chance to get out of that apartment, to let my bruises heal a little before she created more of them.

We wore cloaks with hoods that fell over our faces and we walked through the market, not daring to even speak to one another in the more crowded areas where we could be overheard. I didn't ask her about the group's progress again. I had found, on the fourth day, that my constant questioning of her knowledge of the Peace Court's terrain was grating on her already frayed nerves and I didn't have any desire to turn away the only company I had.

"Did you help put up the Divide?" I asked as we turned a corner where some shops lay out of the way of the larger marketplace. I chose the question partly to make conversation and partly because I was curious if the process of creating the Divide might be helpful to know in the process of destroying it.

"No," Gemini answered with a shake of her head as we paused outside of a leather shop for her to examine a pair of black gloves. "I was away dealing with the creation of the courts and the political assignments. But Perseus did. And Alban. My brother claimed it nearly killed him to create it but he would have gladly died to do so."

"The courts were created after the Immortal War?" I asked, curiosity peaked by the mentioned tidbit of history from this strange world.

"We had to find some way to divide the power of our new realm. There had been three leaders before. Though they hadn't ruled over land, just subjects who chose to follow them. After the war, the Court of Light and Life's King then kept his northern city, the only place untouched by the horrors of the war. He had claimed it was a necessary refuge for any Fae that did not wish to fight in the conflict and even kept the laws of refuge in place afterwards to back up his claim. But I knew he was just a coward. Remaining neutral when everyone else went off to fight for what was right wasn't noble. It was weak."

I nodded, thinking about the time we spent in the Court of Light and Life after having been given refuge status ourselves. I was grateful for it then and I was sure any Fae who did not wish to be a part of the fighting in the Immortal War would have been just as grateful for it as I was. So I couldn't necessarily say I agreed with Gemini's assessment of the former King of the Court of Life being a coward. His successor was cunning, though. I knew that already from my limited interaction with her. If she was so important, if her court was so strong, that helped to explain why Lark was so intent on getting on her good side during our visit. Even if thinking about it again, even now, made my jaw clench.

"Each of the six lower courts were appointed based on our categorization of gifts and the six generals who led our battalions in the war," Gemini continued. "Alban and Perseus split their own lands apart to create the six lower courts and their lords, to reward the highly gifted Fae that fought loyally with them and to give Fae who might not identify with the inclinations of the Peace Court or the Bone Court somewhere to go, some freedom to find for themselves. And, of course, my brother got Hellscape. Not that he wanted it. But he accepted the responsibility anyway. Oh, how he must have raged when Casseiopia told him that Taurus had lost the key to a gorgon."

Gemini sounded exasperated at the idea but I could see her smiling under her hood. I couldn't help but grin myself. I could imagine how he might have reacted and was only grateful that I hadn't been there to see it.

"When did the King—" I started to ask but never got the chance.

A loud booming sound erupted from somewhere above us, followed by intermittent screams that grew louder as the crowd surged away from the crowded marketplace and into alleys like the one we occupied. I looked over at Gemini to find her looking over her shoulder at the market behind us from which the chaos had originated.

"Come," she said simply and strode right through the fleeing Fae, hurtling forward in the opposite direction, toward the mayhem.

I followed, feeling for my magic as I moved, reaching for it, gathering it as best I could. But it flickered and faltered every time someone bumped into me. I nearly lost my footing once as a girl, screaming in terror, ran right into me. Gemini reached out and steadied me without even turning my way and we moved onward into the crowd.

Those who had not run were gathered along the street, staring up in shock and awe as an otherworldly light danced across their faces. I looked up to see what they were all staring at and froze.

At first, I thought we had doubled back too far, crossed too many alleys, and found ourselves in front of that arched, swirling portal to the mortal world that this Court of Wanderers was known for. But then I realized this one was different. It was larger and unframed and it wasn't an inky mass of black. It was like the one we had seen in Hellscape, like a window. And these Fae, lined up along the street, were staring into it. But this time, the mortals on the other side were staring back.

I gasped when I saw Wyn Kendrick, front and center, pale faced and slack jawed as he stared into this portal to another dimension and saw a horde of ethereal bodies draped in various shades of orange. And the Fae stared back, whispering to one another, amazed.

"You have to close it," I hissed, turning toward Gemini only to find that she was gone. "No, no, no, no."

Was it too late? Was the immortal plane exposed? Was two thousand years of separation over in an instant because of my mother, because of what she was doing to the Divide, because of the magic she was playing with?

I felt a fury rise within me then, brighter and hotter than anything I had ever felt before. I felt a whisper from Lark as well, a faint tugging as if telling me to calm down, reminding me to watch my temper, a warning. I ignored it. I poured sixty years of abandonment issues into that rage, stoked it, let it grow bigger and bigger. My mother was trying to bring down the Divide. She was tearing holes in the fabric between the planes. She had controlled my father for years, used him for breeding without his consent, to have me. She had stolen Perseus' power, turned Lark's people against him, and let a minotaur loose in the mortal plane.

I pushed through the onlookers until I stood in front of the portal and then I let all of that rage building up within me consume me. I saw Wyn's eyes widen a fraction in recognition the moment before it happened. I gripped my fists tightly, clenching them so that my nails cut into my palms, leaned forward, and screamed. I felt the magic flow from me, drain through my fury, my fear, my regret, and spill into that rift. I kept screaming because it was working, because it was healing. Slowly but surely, the edges were moving inward, knitting together along the seams. And Wyn and his people were backing away, raising their hands in front of their faces to shield themselves from the blistering wind filtering through to their side.

When it was done, when the rift blinked from existence and the sky was whole again, I fell to my knees, eyes drooping with exhaustion from what I had done. I thought I understood what Perseus had said about creating the Divide now. I could have died from that and I probably would have if necessary. But that was one rift, one small hole. I couldn't imagine what it had been like to create the whole Divide.

I collapsed.

"Move," someone was screaming. It took me a moment to recognize Gemini's voice in the haze of my exhaustion. "Get out of my way."

People obeyed. She was kneeling in front of me a moment later.

"We need to go," she hissed into my ear.

"Where were you?" I muttered, unable to rise but allowing her to lift me, hoist me onto my feet.

"I thought she was here. I thought she must be nearby to create such a thing so I went looking. I didn't know you would, you could—what did you do, Seren?"

"Get me out of here."

"I will. I am but we can't go back to the apartment. They're staring at us, all of them. They've never seen that kind of power before, the power of a royal Fae. They'll want to know who you are. They might follow—"

"Can you shadow step us away?"

"Of course. But where—"

"The Court of Peace and Pride," I mumbled, already dropping off into a fitful sleep. "It's time I had that talk with my mother."

Chapter Thirty-Five

A Daughter's Last Stand

Lark would be furious. I should make sure I tell him that this was all my idea and not hers at all. I heard it all from Gemini the next morning when I awoke in a warm inn somewhere I didn't recognize.

"It's not that I'm afraid of my nephew," she was clarifying while fussing over her unwieldy hair at a nearby vanity table, "but, well, maybe I am just a little."

She whirled around to face me.

"Are you even listening?" she snapped.

"Where are we?" I asked, rising slowly from the bed and padding over to the window to peer down on rich, fertile farmland as far as the eye could see.

It was early morning, if the workers in the field were any indication. All of them weathered from a life spent in manual labor, straw hats atop their heads and soft shirts beneath their long brown jumpers. Brown.

A lump settled itself in my throat and I turned, slowly, back to face Gemini.

"Where are we?" I repeated myself, my tone firmer than it had been before.

"You said you wanted to speak to your mother," Gemini answered with a shrug. "I couldn't tell if you were serious or delirious. So I brought you here. It's an inn right on the border of your mother's court. If you truly wish to see her, you can simply step outside and be on your way and how would I stop you? If you've changed your mind, we can have a nice breakfast and head back to that infernal apartment. The choice is yours."

She shrugged again, as if the matter truly were of no consequence to her. I stared at her for a moment, trying to sense the trick.

"That's it?" I asked. "But Lark—"

"Lark will rage for centuries if something happens to you and likely, it will start a war rather than prevent one, but, as we seem to be on the path to war already..."

She trailed off with another shrug that showed her belief that I truly couldn't possibly make things any worse than they already were.

"Out of curiosity," she spoke into the silence that fell when I lost myself in thought, "what happened back there?"

I blinked at her.

"One moment, a portal to the mortal realm rips open in the center of a busy market. The next, it's closed and you're muttering some nonsense about your mother before collapsing," she said.

"I—I closed it. I don't know how but—"

"That's powerful magic, girl. Two days ago, you couldn't craft a simple shield to defend yourself," she reminded me and I winced. "Tell me what you were feeling."

"What I was feeling?"

"When you closed it, what emotions?"

"Hate," I spat, remembering. "Rage, Fear."

"Powerful emotions, indeed. Did you feel him?"

My gaze shot up to hers.

"Your power is greater when he is around," she told me. "His is weaker when you're not."

"It is?"

"Infinitesimally. Lark is a very powerful Fae who chooses to use that power sparingly and cleverly so any reduction of his power isn't all that noticeable if you don't know where to look."

My lips parted and I turned away in thought.

"If you tell him I called him powerful, I'll call you a liar," she added.

"You said before that there was a chance that I could stop all this if I went to her," I reminded her, still thinking.

"I think it's possible that all this tearing into the mortal realm is an effort to find you," Gemini answered slowly. "They stopped entirely during the time you were being held at the Bone Court, a time in which she knew where you were. They resumed again when you disappeared and, most recently, she tore one right into the Court of Wanderers, right into the very marketplace where we were. You don't think it odd, girl, that these things always seem to pop up either to draw you out or right near where you are?"

"Hellscape," I murmured, eyes widening in realization as I put it all together. The rifts from before I met Lark were all over the mortal world but I went to them every time. I hadn't known they'd stopped while I was at the Bone Court but now that I did, it put the following ones into more perspective. The rift that tore into Hellscape while we were there, when

I saw Wyn on the other side. The rift that tore into the marketplace of the Court of Wanderers. I closed my eyes, wondering how I hadn't seen it before. "She isn't going to stop."

Gemini didn't answer so I knew I was right.

"She's tearing the world apart to find me," I breathed in awe.

"She is," Gemini nodded her agreement this time. "But it's entirely possible Lark would tear it apart to get you back."

He wouldn't. I knew it and she did, too. He would want to and Gemini was right. He would rage for centuries if something happened to me. But Lark wouldn't break the world for anything. Not when everything he had ever done, not when every move he ever made, was to save it.

"I can stop this," I said, mind racing at the implications of all that I had learned. "All I have to do is go to her and it all stops. The rifts, the risks of exposure, the destruction of the Divide. It stops."

"Maybe. Maybe not."

"If I don't go, she keeps at this and then eventually this realm is exposed to the mortal realm once and for all. More beasts might get through, more people might die. A war might start."

"And if you do go, you may never leave again."

One life, my life, for the lives of many, for the salvation of the Divide. She might try to control me, keep me under her spell like she did to my father, but I am better equipped to deal with that than he ever was. She was powerful, supremely so, but I had magic too, magic from her, and I could use it. I might be alright. I might survive, and someday, I might escape.

Maybe this was my fate. Maybe Lark only saved me all those years ago so that I could save him, save all of them, now. He had been exiled, he had been sentenced to death, to save me. He had given everything to do the right thing. So I could too.

"You said she fancied herself your friend," I said then, looking at Gemini with determination. "Could you take me to her?"

Gemini's lips slanted into a frown.

"The last time I saw her I was complicit in her newborn daughter's kidnapping," Gemini recalled. "I can't imagine she will be pleased to see me."

"Even if you're bringing me back to her?"

Gemini raised a brow, watching me closely.

"You're going to do this?" she asked.

"Tell him I'm sorry," I said, steeling myself because I had to. "Tell him I had to."

"I will."

She reached for my hand and I took a deep breath. I sent out a feeling, huge and raw and real. I'd never told Lark how I felt, not truly, but maybe an outpouring of the love I held in my heart could reach him wherever he was in this court. I felt that tug a moment later. A question. I pushed it aside and focused on my task. Reaching for Gemini, I felt his panic when I didn't respond, just before I grasped her hand and the world squeezed shut around us.

Chapter Thirty-Six
A Mother's Welcome

My feet found the hard, russet marble ground below them moments later. I only stumbled slightly as Gemini and I materialized before a grand bronze throne. Steps made of the same russet marble with rivulets of bronze and copper woven within them flowed downward to where we stood before it. The walls were made of the same material, all the way to the hard, mahogany ceiling and the shining copper chandelier. The light was dim, like a candle guttering out. No one was here. No one had been waiting for us, preparing for this room to be occupied.

"What—" I started but was interrupted by a sudden feminine voice calling out from beyond the mahogany doors at our backs.

"I know you aren't so stupid as to shadow step right into my throne room, Gemini Morningstar," the voice sang as the doors flew open and a woman with blonde hair and a flowing chocolate gown strode inside. She flicked a wrist and the copper fixtures on the wall as well as the matching chandelier above us flamed to life, lighting the entire room.

Her eyes settled on Gemini for a moment before flicking to me. She froze, her hand still held aloft from the gesture she had made to light the room. Her lips parted as her eyes widened.

"Seren," she breathed.

"Mother," I replied, disgust roiling in my gut as I addressed her.

She rushed forward, the train of her gown flowing out behind her, and embraced me. I froze, every muscle tense as she squeezed me tightly. Her heavy necklace pressed into my collarbone and I winced.

"You're here," she said in wonder, pulling away but still holding onto my shoulders, shaking me as if to prove to herself that I was real. "You're alive."

I nodded because I didn't know what else to say to this woman I had never known but who called herself my mother, who claimed some maternal hold on me.

"Your father will be so happy to see you," she told me and I froze, my fake smile faltering.

"My father?" I asked, stunned. "I thought he was dead."

Her grin turned wicked at that.

"And I thought you were dead," she mused. "Seems the Morningstars have a penchant for faking deaths."

She raised one arched brow to Gemini, letting her judgmental gaze flick over her from head to toe. My heart pounded against my chest at her words. A penchant for faking deaths? Did she know about Lark, that he was still alive, that they had never executed him? How could she?

"We do what we must to escape those who would do us harm," Gemini professed through gritted teeth, her gaze narrowed to a glare.

"And that's me, I suppose?" my mother asked with a roll of her eyes as she strode past us and ascended the steps to the throne. She collapsed lazily atop it, propping her feet up on one arm and leaning her back against the other as she draped one arm lazily off the side and looked at us. "I always forget what they think of me in the Bone Court. Am I the mother who went crazy after losing her daughter and started seeking vengeance? Or am I some crazed, narcissistic autocrat trying to take over the realm? Remind me, dear Gemini, for I can never keep track."

It caught me off guard, how callously she discussed all the perceptions of her that I had been exposed to for the last few months.

"All of that and more," Gemini hissed.

"And today?" my mother asked, raising a brow. "What must I be today for you to finally return my precious child to me after nearly sixty years?"

"The woman who keeps tearing the world apart to find me," I said.

My mother turned to me, a smile growing on her lips.

"Fierce, like her mother," she observed with a grin.

I just gritted my teeth and did not answer.

"Where is Alban?" Gemini asked, narrowing her gaze at the woman sitting carelessly upon a throne that wasn't hers.

"My father is indisposed at the moment," my mother answered, not even looking at Gemini anymore. Her gaze, instead, was fixed on her nails as she inspected them one after another. After a moment, her gaze slid back to me. "But he will be so pleased to finally meet his beloved granddaughter."

She shifted slightly and I noticed it then, the soft glow emanating from her necklace. No, not a necklace. An amulet. I stopped breathing.

"As much as I'm looking forward to so many reunions," she started, her gaze darkening as she rose slightly in the throne, peering down at us again, "we have business to take care of first."

She waved a hand and Gemini fell to her knees. I gasped and reached for her but then I was spinning away, floating upwards and toward my mother. The floor beside her bubbled and then rose, that russet marble material liquefying and shaping itself into a chair. She placed me firmly in it and turned back to Gemini who was struggling against some invisible bonds I couldn't see.

"Such a strange thing, the mind," Ariadne mused, sucking on her teeth as she watched Gemini's struggle. "You don't even have to be bound. You just have to think you are. Paralysis by thought. Neat, huh?"

"Let me go, Ariadne," Gemini hissed. "I returned the girl. I brought her to you."

"And I will keep that in mind as I mete out all necessary punishments."

Punishments? My gaze snapped up to my mother's as she raised a hand and called out.

"Bring them in."

Horror filled me as I turned to the doors on the opposite side of the room to find Rook being led inside by half a dozen guards in bronze armor. He was shackled with chains of some material that I didn't recognize but could feel as it ate away at my power even from this distance. I couldn't imagine what it was doing to him against his skin. Behind him came Cass, her hair half unbound, her eyes dreary and full of sorrow. Then it was Lark's turn. Over a dozen soldiers surrounded him, yanking painfully on his chains as they walked. After all of them came a gorgon, Lycurgus, I hazarded a guess.

"No," I gasped before I could stop myself.

I tried to rise but my seat grew manacles around my wrists and locked me into place. I met Lark's gaze and felt a weak attempt at reassurance. My heart fell when I realized that this was why it had been so difficult and so rare to feel him while he had been away. It wasn't the distance between us. It was those chains restricting his use of magic. My breath hitched. How long had they been captured?

"I assumed you would come for them eventually," my mother said, rolling her eyes in my direction. "I just didn't think it would take so long.

I had to rip that hole open into the Court of Wanderers just to get your attention."

"I—I didn't know you had them," I confessed.

"No?" she asked and seemed genuinely surprised. "Well then, out of curiosity, what are you doing here?"

"I came to convince you to stop the rifts and because…" I trailed off, my gaze flicking down to the amulet hanging over her breast.

"Ah, they put you up to this then, did they? Traded you to get their precious father back his power? Well, you're barking up the wrong tree, dear. This amulet doesn't hold their father's power. It holds mine's."

My jaw slackened.

"You—you stole your own father's magic," I repeated because I couldn't believe it. "My grandfather. You—"

"I tried to reason with him," she told me with a dramatic sigh. "But the man hardly ever listens to me anymore. Thinks I've lost my mind with maternal grief."

"Now, why would he think that?" A familiar voice drawled from before us.

Ariadne's gaze snapped to Lark where he knelt beside his aunt, sister, and best friend. She flicked a wrist and he grunted but remained upright, though his arms and legs were shaking with that effort alone.

"Stop!" I cried. "Please."

My mother's eyes flicked between us for a moment.

"Oh," she said, her tone holding a note of interest. "That's new."

I looked to her, desperately.

"Let them go," I begged. "Please, just let them go. I'll stay. I swear it. I'll stay with you."

"Ren, don't—" Lark started but my mother flicked her wrist again and he growled in pain.

"Please," I gasped. "Please don't hurt him. I'll do anything."

Tears were running freely down my face now as I pulled against the marble manacles around my wrist. It wasn't my best negotiation strategy, I would admit, but I wasn't in the right state of mind to haggle. I could feel Lark's pain through the bond and I could feel him pushing away from it, trying to maintain that brave face for me, for all of us.

"Anything?" she asked, raising a brow.

Lark's pain stopped. I could feel the moment it cleared. He hung his head, taking deep, controlled breaths. Cass watched him, her eyes wide with terror. Rook was pulling against his bonds, snarling. Gemini just closed her eyes and waited.

"Richard," my mother said and a door off to the side opened up.

A man with honey blonde hair and keen green eyes stepped into the chamber and my heart bottomed out. Because I knew, at very first glance, that this man was my father and that meant I knew what he had endured at the hands of this woman. All the abuse, decades of mind controlled subservience and trickery. Decades.

"How?" Lark growled, eyes wide as he beheld my father who was not a day over thirty.

Ariadne's grin was fiendish.

"I have a few new tricks up my sleeve, Canis," she answered, standing from her throne with a flourish. "Come to me, husband."

Husband.

Ariadne backed toward me a step, taking my manacled hand in hers and reaching out the other toward him. He crossed the room in a few long strides, taking her hand and peering over her shoulder at where I sat, chained. I thought he must be under her control, that nothing else could compel him to stay here, with her, to marry her. But then his eyes met mine and they were so full of sorrow and such a deep, visceral regret that I couldn't imagine any of those feelings were of her making.

"Look at us," Ariadne said, beaming as she gripped our hands. "A family, whole, finally."

"Where is grandfather?" I asked.

"Resting," she told me. "Comfortably. How sweet of you to worry over him, child."

She caressed my cheek and I fought the urge to bite those pale white fingers.

"What have you done, Ariadne?" Gemini asked, her voice low as she stared right at my father, the mortal who seemed frozen in time beside her.

"Oh, this?" Ariadne asked, waving a hand over him as though it was nothing of consequence. "I made a deal with Sophierial and she handed over this little ancient recipe her court has been holding onto for millennia. They call it the Elixir of Eternity. A bit dramatic if you ask me. But it works. One sip and you live forever, just like us. Only without the magic. Sorry dear."

She glanced over her shoulder at me and I understood two things at once. One, that she did not know I could use magic and that might be an advantage if I played my cards right. Two, that she intended for me to drink the elixir myself. My eyes widened as I looked at my father at her side. His jaw clenched but he didn't say a word.

"He—you made him immortal?" I asked, stunned.

"I did. And I intend to make you immortal too, dear," she answered with a smile that I thought might be an attempt at maternal nurturing. "Just one sip and we can be together forever. Well, it's a bit more complicated than that, I suppose. Sophierial did warn me it wouldn't work if the drinker was not willing and your dear dad here nearly died quite a few times before he emerged, made anew. But you're half immortal already so I can't imagine it would be as hard for you."

"No."

She paused, blinking in confusion.

"No?" she asked. "What do you mean no?"

"No, I won't take it," I replied, shaking my head.

"I'm offering you eternal life."

"And I'm denying it. I enjoy being mortal. I like that part of me that's tied to them, to him."

I nodded in my father's direction and saw his gaze soften somewhat.

"They raised me," I told her. "They were there for me when you weren't. You didn't even start looking for me for fifty years."

"He told me you were dead!" she shouted, pointing at Lark.

"I want to die someday," I told her and she paled. "Old and gray and surrounded by people who loved me, knowing I lived a life that made a difference, a life that mattered. Because time matters, mother, when you don't have an endless supply of it. Every moment counts. Every relationship touches your soul. I won't abandon my mortality and I won't become a pawn in whatever game you're playing here."

She stared at me for a moment, stunned, and I felt a swell of pride from deep within me, where I had locked that fragment of Lark away so that she could not find it. My father was looking at me in a way that gave me strength. Lark was flooding my soul with pride. Because of them, I stood my ground. Because of them, I held my head high and told her no.

But then Ariadne flicked her wrist and Lark went skidding forward on his knees, still bound in chains. My eyes widened and shot to where he came to a stop at the foot of the stairs.

"Mortals," Ariadne hissed as she descended those steps until she reached him. "So small minded. So wrapped up within their own brief lives they're incapable of seeing their potential, of seeing the bigger picture."

She raised a hand, flexing her fingers, as she came to a stop beside him.

"I'll give you one more chance," she ground out through gritted teeth. "Say you'll take the Elixir."

My eyes widened in my panic, shooting from her to Lark where he knelt at her side. His jaw was set, that dark, intense gaze upon me as he shook his head slowly.

"Don't," he muttered in warning and then the hall filled with the crack of bone and Lark's thunderous cry of agony.

Chapter Thirty-Seven
A Vow Above A Bond

My heart cleaved in two at the sound. Tears streamed down my cheeks, an unending river of sorrow, as I listened to my soul bonded Fae cry out in pain.

Cass was crying as well, her head lowered so that we could not see her tears but her body shaking with them. Rook alternated between trying to break free of his restraints and muttering curses toward my mother. Gemini just watched, eyes hard and jaw clenched in rage. How was this happening? How had it all gone so wrong?

"You can stop this," Ariadne told me, shouting to be heard over Lark's screams as another crunch of bone filled my ears. "Agree to take the Elixir and I will stop."

"Ren," Lark muttered, weaker this time, as he slumped forward. "Don't."

Ariadne whirled on him, landing a savage blow with her fist to his stomach. He doubled over, coughing blood onto that polished russet marble. I looked at my father. He shook his head so slightly that I almost missed it. Panic gripped me as Ariadne squeezed her fist again and Lark cried out in pain, though there had been no audible bone breaking this time. It was almost worse, not knowing what she was doing to him, but knowing how bad it must be.

Still, amidst all that pain, he sent a feeling my way. A bit of encouragement, a bit of strength he needed far more than I did at the moment but he gave it to me anyway. My lips quivered at the gift, at the depth of his feeling for me.

Another crack of bone, this time louder. The sound reverberated through the cavernous throne room, vibrating in my ribs, clenching around my heart. Silent tears trickled freely down my cheeks. I pulled against my manacles and then collapsed back into my makeshift chair. She was going to kill him. She was going to kill him right here and now, in front of me, in front of his family. I almost caved when she snapped her fingers again and he writhed wretchedly, this time too tortured to even cry out, but then Ariadne released him, snatching her fingers away and letting him fall to the floor.

"Lark!" I cried.

But I could feel him, like a caress against my soul. He was alive. He was breathing. And he even turned his face slowly so that I could see him. I hated the hurt in his expression, the pain there that was all my fault.

"Fine then," my mother snapped, turning and strolling down the line of my friends. "She will do."

She gripped Cass by the shoulder and dragged her forward.

"No!" Rook screamed.

He snarled, pulling feverishly against his bonds. Lark's eyes widened then, for the first time, in terror as my mother raised her fist, intent clear in her eyes.

"Can't finish the job?" Lark wheezed, coughing another spot of blood onto the polished marble as he raised his head with some effort, blood streaming down over his eyes. "You mean all of this wasn't to get your revenge on me? For what I did to you? For what I took from you?"

My mother's lip curled into a snarl as she dropped Cass right in front of where I sat shackled on the dais. My eyes flicked from Cass to Lark. I knew what he was doing. I wished he would stop.

"This is between us, Ariadne," Lark told her, rising somewhat, spitting blood at her feet. "It always has been. Let the others go. I'm the one you want."

"Oh, yes," my mother snarled, spinning around and glaring at Lark. "I will kill you. I will tear you limb from limb and flay you until you beg for the sweet mercy of death. But first, you're going to watch me take the ones that you love. First, you're going to know what it means to lose someone precious to you."

Ariadne curved her fingers and a gleaming blade appeared in her hand. She lowered it slowly to Cass, lifting it against her perfect, porcelain cheek, until a drop of blood fell from the prick onto the shining dagger. Ariadne smiled, baring all of her teeth, as she turned to the thrashing Rook, toward Lark who was making every effort to rise despite his legs and one arm which were splayed at unnatural angles, obviously broken.

My mother lowered that dagger, pointed it straight at Cass' heart, dangerous eyes glinting in the light of that bronze chandelier. Cass heaved a shaky breath and waited, not daring to move. Rook howled in rage, in agony, pulling viciously against his bonds, swinging wildly. Lark's mist coiled around his waist, up his broken arm, slithering across the floor. Ariadne stared at them, surprised, for a moment before making a slicing gesture with her hand. They blew away in the breeze like smoke on a pile of ash.

"Enough of this," Ariadne spat and reared back with the knife poised to strike.

"I'll take it," I said.

Everything froze. My mother stilled entirely, turning slowly to face me. My father closed his eyes and gave that same minuscule shake of his head. Rook gaped at me. Cass' lips quivered. Gemini was glaring at me. And Lark, that man it had taken me far too long to realize I was falling in love with, he crawled slowly forward, leaving a trail of blood behind him, one word whispered on his cracked lips.

"No."

"Swear it," Ariadne spat. "Make a vow."

My gaze flicked to Lark and then back to hers.

"You'll let them go?" I asked. "All of them. You'll let them leave in peace and you won't hurt any of them again."

"If you'll drink the Elixir," she nodded in promise. "If you'll stay. I will vow it. We will make this bond with magic so that it may not be undone."

"Ren, please," Lark rasped from the floor.

"I will," I vowed and that was it.

I felt the weight of my promise seal me within it and knew that Ariadne had used her magic to seal the bond. I didn't know what that magic was, didn't recognize it. But it felt old and ancient, like the final nail in my proverbial coffin. All hope of escaping vanished from my heart and from my mind as she rose back up those steps to take her throne once more, smiling down at her captives, victorious.

"Get the goblet, Richard," she ordered and my father hesitated, meeting my gaze once before hastening off to do her bidding.

"Let me say goodbye," I said then, pulling at my manacles as I looked out at my friends.

"Fine," she replied, rolling her eyes, and raised a finger.

My manacles vanished and I rushed forward, falling onto my knees in front of Lark. I lifted his head until his gaze met mine, ignoring his blood staining my gray pants beneath him.

"I'm so sorry," I told him through my tears.

"Don't do this, Ren," he begged me and I felt his sorrow overwhelming me, suffocating me. Desperate, he was so desperate.

"Just go. Just live. Please. Promise me."

"I can't. Not without you."

"Lark, promise me."

"I promise."

I leaned in and kissed him, tasting his blood on my lips, my tears wetting his skin. I let his longing fill me, let my love grow and grow until it was a balloon sitting on my chest, daring me to pop it. Then I pulled away and moved to Cass. She was shaking when I embraced her.

"Thank you," I whispered into her dark hair. "For being the only friend I ever truly had. I won't ever forget the kindness you've shown me."

"Don't let her control you," she answered, her voice shaky. "You fight that bitch every step of the way."

"I will," I promised with a sad smile, collecting that friendship and storing it in my soul beside Lark's love, and let go.

I moved to Rook, standing before him.

"Keep him safe," I told him, wiping away tears that wouldn't stop coming. "Don't let him come back here."

He nodded once, tearing up himself. I felt his defensive nature, his disappointment at being unable to save Lark, to save me, his gratefulness that I had stepped in in his place and found a way to save him. That undying gratitude, I found a place for it inside me as well and that balloon of love and light from my friends grew even bigger. Then I moved to Gemini. She was surprised when I embraced her and even more surprised at what I muttered into her ear.

"Find my grandfather," I said. "Get him out of here."

And then I stepped away from her and closed my eyes. Reaching within myself, I found that balloon.

And I popped it.

The sound of shattered glass filled the room as the manacles on each of my friend's wrists burst into a million pieces. And up there, on that dais, my mother's victorious grin turned to an expression of outraged shock as she realized that not only were all of her prisoners free but that amulet against her chest had shattered as well and from it flowed a glowing blue magic that drifted upwards and disappeared from her.

"No!" she cried, enraged as she reached for it, shot out for it, and missed.

I collapsed onto the floor just as Gemini blinked from existence. Rook ran toward me as Cass went to Lark. Rook gripped my wrist and I knew what he was doing even as he failed. He glanced down at the contact with confusion.

"I can't leave," I muttered through my post magical haze. "I'm bound to her now. Go. Please. Both of you get out of here. Now."

They exchanged a glance just as Lark screamed my name.

"Ren!" he shouted, reaching for me.

But Rook met Cass' gaze and she understood without being told. She grit her teeth and grabbed her brother and they disappeared with one final, guttural cry from him.

"No!"

"We will come back, Ren," Rook promised, his gaze boring into me. "We will find a way."

"Seize him!" Ariadne screamed furiously, and her soldiers stepped forward.

"Go," I whispered but he was already gone and my mother's howls of rage followed me into unconsciousness.

Epilogue

I gripped the russet marble beneath my fingers and listened to the sounds of forks scraping against plates with my jaw clenched and my head held high.

My mother had crafted the same sort of manacled chair for me in the dining room as she had in the throne room. So now I was shackled at the end of the table, my mother and father on either side, eating in complete silence, keeping their eyes focused on their plates and nothing more. My father, for his part, glanced up at me once or twice throughout the duration of the silent meal as if he could hardly believe I was actually here. He was worried about me. I could feel the concxern emanating from the very core of his soul. A true paternal fear.

The only thing radiating from my mother was anger.

I did not say a word. Just kept my gaze focused on the opposite wall, gritting my teeth and spearing out silently with my magic against my manacles. But to no avail. So they forced me to take part in this ludicrous facade of a family dinner, this unholy exhibition of relative connection.

"Eat or not, as you wish," Ariadne snapped halfway through the course of her own dinner. "But you will drink."

Her eyes snapped to mine and narrowed.

I couldn't help but allow my gaze to flick to that menacing goblet sitting just a few inches from my plate. It was filled with a strange, clear liquid. Almost like water but more viscous. I knew it wasn't water. Nor was it any sort of spirit or mortal beverage. It was the Elixir. The one that my mother had undoubtedly started a war with the Bone Court just to get me to drink. My lip curled in disgust as I whipped my head back to face her.

"And how, precisely, am I supposed to eat or drink while shackled to this ridiculous chair?" I barked back.

"You have your magic," she sneered. "You made that plain enough in the throne room, didn't you? Since you're so capable, you should have no trouble."

I frowned, glaring at her as she turned back to her food. Did she know? Was she aware of just how little control I had over my magic? That explosion in the throne room had been the result of a volatile outward burst. I knew how to blow it up. I didn't know how to aim it. So the idea of wrapping that unpredictable force around something as small as a fork and bringing bits of meat and bread to my lips was control like I had never known. I suspected she knew that and was testing me. Would I rather starve than admit to her I had no control over my magic? I thought, perhaps, I might.

"Why do this?" I asked after another moment of silence. "Why go to all this trouble? Why make us immortal at all?"

"You're my family," she replied simply, her soft voice so at odds with her usual bitterness.

"No," I replied, making sure my glare was as cold as I could make it. "I'm not."

Ariadne was on her feet in an instant. Her chair scraped against the marble below, letting out an earsplitting groan in the otherwise silent hall. She stomped toward me, heels clicking against that same hard stone, and reached for the goblet.

My father tensed, knuckles turning white where he held his fork above his plate.

"Where is my father?" Ariadne murmured, her voice low, dangerous.

"I don't know," I answered for the tenth time. She had asked me every hour on the hour since the moment he disappeared and I had given no other answer but this.

"You know where they would have taken him. Tell me."

"I'd rather die."

"And here I am, making sure you live," she mused, shrugging her shoulder. In one quick motion, her hand shot out and gripped my chin. She pried my jaw open, squeezing so hard I knew I would bruise. She leaned forward with a wicked grin and whispered, "Forever."

The moment the elixir touched my tongue, I felt the change. It began on the tip of my tongue, numbing, slithering. It wasn't just a draught. It was a living thing. Poking, prodding, searching. I looked to my father to find that his eyes were closed now as he faced away from me, his head bowed low to his plate.

"If you survive," she whispered, leaning in close to me as the elixir snaked down my throat, filling my esophagus with a liquid fire that plummeted straight down to my chest, "I will teach you how to control your magic and we can discuss this war you think is coming."

My eyes widened. She had read my thoughts. Throughout that terrible silent dinner, she had been listening to my innermost thoughts. I opened my mouth to respond but only an icy breath escaped. Her lip curled into a smirk of delight as she hefted herself off of the edge of the table and stood upright. She clapped her hands together once, whipping her head toward the soldiers that stood at attention near the doors.

"Fetch the healer," she commanded. "My daughter will need her. Richard, come."

With that, she strolled from the dining room, hips sashaying in that long, sparkling brown dress, blonde hair flowing behind her. My father watched her go, rising to obey her command.

I felt the burning sensation spreading out against my ribs, pushing against them, burning through my lungs, my stomach, my heart. I tried to gasp, but could no longer open my lips. It was as if someone had glued them shut. In a blind panic, I kicked out. My feet connected with the table and my chair went toppling backwards. My vision spotted when my head connected with the hard marble floor. One soldier lurched forward to help, but was held back by another's hand upon his arm. I kicked and flailed, eyes bulging, my breath a thin whistle through my nose.

"Fight it," my father was muttering. He was beside me now, kneeling on the floor next to me. "You have to fight the initial pain. You can breathe. You can. Just calm down. Just breathe."

My legs stilled. As did my arms except for a bit of twitching. I focused on that shrinking access to air and breathed heavily inward, mouth still firmly wired shut.

"Through your nose, that's it," my father was saying.

I was breathing now. It was a shaky wheeze but it was air and I was thankful for every morsel. I swiveled so that my wide eyes were on my father, taking in the mournful expression, the pitying gaze.

"It's going to hurt," he told me bluntly. "But you will have a choice."

My brows furrowed even as I fought another flare of that icy burn, screaming through my closed mouth as I writhed forward on the floor. My father pressed down with a hand, holding me still as I caught my breath again. The pain was agonizing. My body was going into shock, my consciousness blinking in and out.

"You have to want to survive, Seren," he said, his voice firm, willing me to hear him, to understand. "That's the only way to fight it."

My closed lips quivered, a tear sliding down my cheek as my heart became encased in that icy blaze. I screamed again, falling into sobs this time. My vision blurred around the edges.

"I will understand whatever choice you make," he whispered, much softer than anything he had said before.

Then he was standing, striding out of that dining room and leaving me to whatever fate this elixir had in store. I wept silently, my lips stuck together, my chest a fiery inferno. Then I heard a crack and thought I might have split open right there in the middle of the dining room. I heard the gasp of a trained soldier as I fell prey to the utter darkness of unconsciousness.

About the Author

My name is A. N. Horton. I am a two-time award-winning author living in Nashville, TN with my husband, children, and moderately chunky Corgi. When I'm not writing, I'm reading, baking more cookies than my family can eat, and plotting crimes against my characters. I'm best known for crafting characters that steal my readers' hearts as much as they shatter them. I am a cross-genre writer focused mainly on fantasy and romance.

Award-Winning Author of the Divinaxy Saga.
Aspiring Writer. Avid Reader. Lover of Literature.
See my LinkTree for all things social and creative!
https://linktr.ee/ANHorton
http://authoranhorton.com/

Also by A. N. Horton

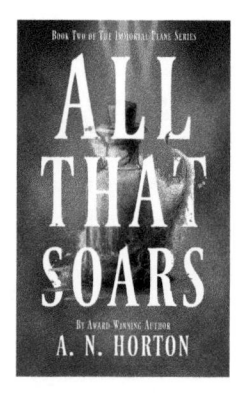

All That Soars — Book Two of The Immortal Plane Trilogy
Ren Belling made a vow to save her friends.
Now she's stuck in her mother's hostile court, expected to play the role of Ariadne Dawnpaw's beautiful heir, the girl worth tearing the Divide apart to find. But the elixir demands a cost that she isn't willing to pay and she bends until she nearly breaks.
Refusing a crown that is hers by birthright and a court that might have been home in another life, Ren feels utterly alone. Until she finds companionship from an unlikely source. She isn't willing to trust again, not yet. But her heart is more willing to give itself away than she logically wants to admit.

Backed into corners again and again by her own mother's scheming, Ren lashes out in any way she can. And when that desperation sends her spiraling, she reaches out with the only thing that remains.
Faith.
Buy All That Soars

All That Ends — Book Three of The Immortal Plane Trilogy
War has arrived.

With cryptic gods and ancient beasts in play, no one is safe.

It turns out freeing the god of time has consequences and Ren Belling is dealing with them. But fighting a war to guard the Divide and protect the mortal plane from her mother takes precedence. As court politics shift, Ren finds herself unsure of who she can trust. Sometimes, being on the same side of a battlefield doesn't mean you're allies.

As she learns her world is much more affected by the forgotten deities than she thought, Ren comes face to face with a power that no one has ever held; a power that should have remained buried.

Despite her best efforts to save her people, Ren has to admit that the more she learns of the Immortal Plane, the more she realizes...

Secrets can kill.

Buy All That Ends

Want to know what court you would belong to? Take the official quiz here.

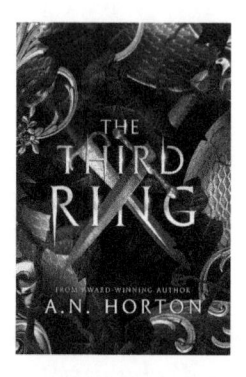

The Third Ring — Book One of The Sanctum Series
Ten Trials. Two Oaths. One Chance.

To Adrian, the gods were never anything to be worshipped, just tolerated. But in the walled city of Sanctuary, whether through the religious fervor of the elite or the quaking fear of the poor, the Geist have always been served. And now it's Adrian's turn.

Born into power and raised for greatness, Dante stands for everything Adrian has come to despise, but he may be her only hope of survival. When the two of them are bonded against their will and forced to compete together in the Trials, the god's ancient gauntlet of physical brutality and psychological torture, they have no choice but to set aside old prejudices and work together.

Navigating religious zealots, a patriarch intent on breeding the pair for power, and the increasingly obvious cruelty of the gods, Adrian must come to terms with the fact that, whether Culled or Championed, we all serve the gods in the end. And, for her, betrayal has always been waiting just around the corner.

Buy The Third Ring

www.ingramcontent.com/pod-product-compliance
Ingram Content Group UK Ltd.
Pitfield, Milton Keynes, MK11 3LW, UK
UKHW040656100325
4920UKWH00026B/94